"I was thinking...you've got problems, I've got problems. We both need cheering up. So, I think I've got the solution. Let's have an affair."

Kyle was so close now that Barbara could feel his breath brush across her cheek. A featherlike touch of his tongue on her lips shook a shudder from her.

"I am going to take all of your clothes off," Kyle said softly.

"Why?"

"Because I want to," he replied.

"Do you always get what you want?" she asked.

"I always try."

It wasn't fair...she had been married before and thought she knew about sensual love, but nothing had ever happened to her like this....

Twice in a Lifetime

REBECCA FLANDERS

Harlequin Books

TORONTO • NEW YORK • LOS ANGELES • LONDON
AMSTERDAM • PARIS • SYDNEY • HAMBURG
STOCKHOLM • ATHENS • TOKYO • MILAN

Published January 1983

Second printing March 1983

ISBN 373-16000-3

Printed in Canada

Dear Reader,

It is our pleasure to bring you a new experience in reading that goes beyond category writing. The settings of **Harlequin American Romances** give a sense of place and culture that is uniquely American, and the characters are warm and believable. The stories are of "today" and have been chosen to give variety within the vast scope of romance fiction.

Rebecca Flanders is a native of Georgia and has been writing since she was a little girl. Her first novel was published in 1979 in hardcover. From the hills of Maine to the tranquility of Oregon, *Twice in a Lifetime* captures the American spirit.

From the early days of Harlequin, our primary concern has been to bring you novels of the highest quality. Harlequin American Romances are no exception. Enjoy!

Vivian Stephens

Vivian Stephens
Editorial Director

Chapter One

Barbara sat in the crowded airport lounge, waiting for her flight to be called, and fingered the letter of invitation from her sister somewhat uncertainly. Barbara was twenty-six years old, self-sufficient, and mature, and she had been managing her own life since the first day she had left home for the independence of the state university. But, sitting alone amid the bustle and confusion of excited travelers, she felt somewhat like a lost and frightened child. She had felt that way a lot since Daniel had died.

She had been widowed a little over a year, and she knew her sister, via long-distance conferences with their mother, was worried about her. Perhaps with good cause, Barbara had to admit uneasily, for although most of the time Barbara managed to convince herself she was getting along just fine, there were still feelings of bitterness and periods of black depression she did not seem to be able to control. Of course it was a tragedy to be widowed so young, and everyone commiserated, everyone claimed to understand what she was going through. The real tragedy was that no one understood. No one could understand what it was to lose the one and only love of her life, not just a husband, but a lover and a friend.... Most people would go their entire lives without ever finding what she and Daniel had shared, and to have their life together severed so abruptly and so cruelly was more than unfair, it was incomprehensible....

She felt the anger and the depression beginning to steal over her again, and she took herself firmly in hand, glancing again at the lines of her sister's hand-writing as though for reassurance.

Michael and I have talked it over and we both agree—nothing will do except that you come stay with us for the summer. The sun will put some color back into your cheeks and the sea air does wonders for the appetite (I should know—I've gained five pounds in the past month!) and you really need a change of scenery. Now, don't give me any excuses about your petty little job—jobs like that are a dime a dozen, and that's another thing I want to talk to you about—you're much too talented to be wasting your life as a clerk!—or about being unable to afford it. We've taken care of all of that. I just ramble around this big house all by myself most of the time while Michael is working on his book, and you can't imagine how much I'm looking forward to having someone to talk to! Michael is looking forward to my having someone to talk to too so he can finally get some work done! So, you see, we simply won't take no for an answer. Consider it an early birthday present—and know that we do love you, Babs dear.

Your overbearing (and insistent) older sister,

Kate

Kate had signed her name with a flourish that took up a quarter of a page of delicately scented, powder-blue stationery, and Barbara smiled affectionately as she folded the letter back into its envelope. Despite all her misgivings about this trip, she found herself looking forward to seeing her vibrant blond-haired, blue-eyed sister again.

She still was not quite certain what she was doing here, sitting alone in the Cincinnati airport awaiting a flight for Maine. She had been so careful this past year to keep her life stable, organized, and carefully insulated. She made no impulsive decisions. She went to work, she came home to a cheap efficiency apartment, sometimes she had dinner with friends, more often she ate alone. She called her mother in nearby Glendale once a week and told her she was doing fine.

But when Kate's letter had come, something had changed. As she held the tempting airline ticket in her hand, Cincinnati had seemed dirty, her little job boring, her apartment cramped. And the coast of Maine was unimaginably appealing. Before she knew it, she was calling Kate, and they had talked and laughed for almost half an hour, just like old times. And suddenly she was here, and her flight was being called.

A moment of panic overtook her as she watched the crowd begin to move toward the boarding gate. She should never have told Kate she would come. Being with Kate and Michael for three months—so happy, so successful in their big house by the sea, so blissfully in love—was not what she needed to help her get over the memory of Daniel and the few short years they had shared together living on love and dreams. Nor did she need anyone tiptoeing around her, the way her parents had done, casting her covert glances brimming with sympathy when they thought she was not looking. Or Kate's overenthusiastic methods of cheering her up.... No, all she wanted to do was to be left alone and nurse her grief in her own way, by herself.

She wanted her own little apartment and her dull

little job and familiar places and faces. She didn't
need complications.

The last boarding call was being announced. It was
now or never. She took hold of herself firmly, shook
away the last of her indecision, and gathered up her
things.

She had almost hesitated too long. She had to run,
and she was the last to board. The other passengers
looked around at her curiously as the stewardess directed her to her seat, and as she always did in a
crowd, she felt conspicuous. She smoothed back an
imaginary strand of hair toward its severe ponytail,
pulled her light summer coat around her more securely, fumbled with the strap of her oversized purse, and
murmured soft apologies as her carryon luggage
bumped the knees of other passengers. She hated to
travel alone.

She anxiously scanned the cabin for empty seats
and found none. She had to go slowly down the aisle,
looking for her number, and after an interminable
time she found it. 17-A. She had a window seat. That
was good. But the man in the aisle seat had both legs
stretched across the narrow space, and as she hesitated politely, he showed no sign of rising to make
room for her to pass.

After a moment she said deliberately, without
looking at him, "Excuse me. Can I get by, please?"

"Well," he drawled in reply, "I would imagine
that's up to you. What do you think?"

She stared at him, indignant and annoyed. And she
was surprised at what she saw.

Somehow it seemed unfair that rude, self-absorbed,
and irritating people should be so contrarily good-
looking. He should have been short and bald and
paunchy. He was, in fact, tall and lanky and tanned a

golden brown. His fawn-colored hair fell toward his forehead on either side of the part and just above his collar, and was sun-streaked with silver-blond. He needed a shave, but that did nothing to detract from the firm, square shape of his face and features that were almost too perfect to be true. When he smiled, she knew, there would be a dimple just left of his chin. He might have been in his early thirties, but he dressed much younger: his skintight jeans were faded and patched, and he wore a sloppy plaid lumberjack shirt under which was a black T-shirt with "Porquois Pas?" written on it in tacky silver letters. His lips twitched with the suggestion of a smile, and his bottle-green eyes looked up at her with lazy humor.

"It took two flight attendants and a navigator to get me in this seat," he said, "and I'm afraid it's going to take more than a pretty face to get me out again. You'll have to climb over."

He gestured vaguely toward his feet and she noticed in chagrin that one leg of his jeans was slit up the side to reveal a white cast; there was a crutch under the seat. She was embarrassed for the uncomplimentary things she had thought about him, but she was also in a hurry, because just then a voice came over the intercom. "Ladies and gentlemen, will you please take your seats and fasten your seat belts."

Maneuvering the bulky overnight bag and her purse, she stepped quickly over him toward her seat, and she knew that if ever clumsiness were to strike her it would be then. It did. She tripped and lost her balance; she saw him grimace and duck his head to avoid her swinging bag. She gasped apologies as his hands came up firmly to take her waist and guide her securely to her seat.

"Did I hurt you?" she inquired anxiously, sinking to her seat and still struggling with the luggage.

He winced and bent to rub his ankle. "No," he replied. "That was my good foot."

He straightened up and had to duck again quickly to avoid being hit by her overnight bag, which she was unsuccessfully trying to force into a storage compartment. He cried, "Hey, watch it! Give me that." He took the bag from her. "Lady, you're a menace."

She said stiffly, "Sorry."

He shoved her bag under the seat and glanced up. "Any more concealed weapons? Are you quite settled?"

She fastened her seat belt and turned deliberately to stare out the window.

When they were airborne, he unfastened his seat belt, turned to her, and draped his arm comfortably across the back of her seat. He studied her for a long time, in the uninhibited, unhurried manner of a man who has a deep and natural appreciation for women of every type, and she tried not to blush. She tried to ignore him. "So. What's a nice girl like you doing in a place like this?"

She scowled irritably and wiggled closer to the window, casting a disparaging look at the informal arrangement of his arm. She wanted to retort, "Is that the best you can do?" but thought it was better not to encourage him.

"Business trip," he pursued, "or pleasure?" When she made no reply, he continued, "No, don't tell me, let me guess. For you, business only. You hate to fly and you don't look like you've had a day's pleasure in your life. Now, what kind of business?" he mused, then answered himself with a joyful snap of his fingers. "I know. You're a librarian, of course, and you're on your way to collect a rare, out-of-print book, which you will guard with your life until it's safely behind its glass case.''

She said quickly, ''Will you please leave me alone?''

''Oh, don't worry,'' he assured her, eyes twinkling. ''I have a weakness for librarians. Especially very stern ones with golden-red hair—which is much too pretty, by the way, to be pulled back and hidden like that. Your scalp must be screaming for relief.''

At first her eyes widened with astonishment and insult, then darkened to a murky violet with anger. ''I am going to change my seat,'' she warned him tightly.

''Good luck,'' he replied and leaned back, removing his arm from across her seat.

For a time an uneasy silence reigned, and she turned again to the window, seething and uncomfortable. There was a low cloud cover, so there wasn't much to see.

And then he said mildly, ''It's a three-hour flight. I didn't bring anything to read and one piece of sky looks pretty much like another. Worse yet, we're going to be forced to have lunch together and there's nothing more barbaric, so I'm told, than a meal without conversation. So we may as well talk.''

Now she turned to him. ''I don't talk to strange men,'' she told him coldly. ''Especially rude, conceited ones with corny come-ons who dress like refugees from the sixties and look old enough to know better.''

Now his eyes widened. ''Come on, lady,'' he said softly, ''give me a break.'' But beneath the mock insult in his eyes was patient humor, and this only irritated her more.

''Furthermore,'' she continued, enjoying her vicious little stabs, "I think it's in unspeakably poor taste, not to mention stupid, to try to pick up a girl on an airplane. It shows a definite lack of class."

He appeared to consider this thoughtfully. "You're right," he decided after a moment. "It is stupid. After all, if I succeeded in picking you up, where would I take you?"

She realized suddenly that she had walked right into his trap, and the mild, sparkling humor in his eyes told her that he was enjoying the victory thoroughly. He had wanted her to talk to him, hadn't he? And he had baited her until she had. She turned quickly back to the window, seething.

After a moment he said softly, "Aha. You're married. That could explain your rotten disposition as well as anything else. What're you doing, then, going home to Mother?"

Still, after all this time, it hurt. But it was getting better. This time wasn't bad at all because the hurt was swallowed up in anger. She said shortly, "I'm not married."

"Then why are you wearing a wedding ring? That is a wedding ring, isn't it?" He made to reach for her hand, but she jerked it away quickly and held it clasped protectively in the other, touching the broad gold band lightly, as though for reassurance.

She swallowed hard on outrage and pain, wishing this irritating character would simply leave her alone. "My husband...is dead. I'm—" She could not say that word, conjuring up visions of wrinkled old ladies in black mourning dresses. "I'm not married."

He inquired, in a slightly different tone, "Accident?"

"Leukemia," she replied briefly, and that was all she intended to say.

She waited for him to utter the insincere and uncomfortable "I'm sorry" that everyone, even the remotest stranger, felt compelled to offer. She was surprised and unwillingly impressed and somehow grateful that he did not. It took a lot of self-control, she knew, and perhaps a special kind of person, not to resort to meaningless platitudes in a situation like that.

He only said gently, "Widows wear their rings on their right hands."

Whatever softness she felt for him all but vanished. She unclasped her hands and jerked her head toward the window again. "Thank you," she returned sarcastically, "for that lesson in etiquette."

He was silent during the half hour that remained before lunch was served, and she wondered what he was thinking. He was probably wondering how he had stumbled into such an awkward situation. He was probably wondering what, if anything, to say to her now. People became so uncomfortable when they knew, always afraid of saying the wrong thing. A widow of twenty-six was somewhat of a freak in this day and age, and everyone she met reminded her of it. He was probably feeling sorry for her and trying to think of some clever way to change the subject and wishing he had not been so quick to hit on her. *Well, she thought bitterly, maybe he won't be so quick next time.*

Lunch was served, and she ate silently and deliberately, forcing herself to eat though she was not hungry because she could feel him watching her. He had made no move to pick up his knife and fork, and his meal was getting cold. She pretended not to notice.

And then he said mournfully, "Uh, I don't know how to tell you this..."

She glanced up.

"I'm left-handed," he confessed. "Unless we want another accident, which our—er—rather tenuous relationship really can't afford right now, we can't both eat at the same time."

She struggled with a smile and won. "Well," she demanded severely, "what do you want me to do about it?"

"If you'll just wait a minute," he suggested, "while I cut my meat, and then we could take alternate bites—"

She felt a helpless giggle seeping to the surface and she touched her napkin to her lips to hide it, shaking her head. "Go ahead." She pushed her tray away. "I'm finished."

"You haven't eaten anything," he protested.

"It's not very good, and I'm not very hungry."

He took up his knife and fork, and she sat back. After a moment he glanced at her askance. "By the way," he commented blandly, "you didn't fool me. I saw that smile."

She looked at him and this time let the tight, dry little smile come. "You think you're very charming, don't you?"

He shrugged as he lifted his fork. "So I've been told."

"How did you break your leg?"

"I fell off a mountain."

"And you called *me* clumsy," she murmured under her breath, and he grinned.

"I didn't call you that," he reminded her. "I only thought it."

He turned his attention to his meal, and she relaxed a little as their destination grew closer.

To her relief, he announced his intention to take a

short nap after the trays were removed—to which she replied it was no concern of hers. But it seemed he had barely closed his eyes before the captain was announcing that they were circling Portland airport and they were touching down. She began to gather up her belongings, excitement building.

"Careful," he drawled as she stood, glancing up at her cautiously. "Remember you've got an injured man on your hands."

She said, rather awkwardly, "I'm sorry I stepped on your foot before."

"It was only the beginning of a very memorable journey," he assured her, eyes sparkling. Then, "You don't like me much, do you?"

She glanced down at him and responded evenly, "No. Not much."

She stepped over him carefully and efficiently and was safely in the aisle when he said, "It's a good thing I wasn't successful, then."

She glanced back curiously. "At what?"

"Picking you up." He grinned and she moved quickly away.

She scanned the crowd at the departure gate anxiously and had no trouble at all spotting the slender, graceful form of her sister, waving joyfully over the heads of others. All doubt was gone and Barbara moved quickly through the crowd and into the waiting arms of Kate.

They embraced tightly and breathlessly for a long time, laughing, starting and not finishing sentences of welcome, hugging again. Then Kate pushed her away and said, "Now, really, let me look at you! Oh, Babs, you're so thin—and so pale! How could you let yourself get into this shape? Well, we'll fix that in no time at all and— Oh, baby, it's so good to have you here!"

She hugged her again and Barbara surrendered helplessly, laughing and glad for the familiar domineering presence of her sister. Then, with her arm about her shoulders, Kate said, "I have so much to tell you, but the first thing is we're going to have another houseguest while you're here. It never rains but it pours!"

Barbara looked at her hesitantly. She had counted upon being among family for this vacation. "I hope it won't be too much trouble for you. . . ." she ventured.

Kate laughed. "Are you kidding? We'll love it. Besides, it's just Michael's brother. We're used to him popping in and out as he pleases. He has a set of keys to the guest house and hardly ever bothers to warn us when he's coming—which is one reason I didn't tell you before. I just found out myself this morning."

Barbara frowned thoughtfully. "Michael's brother? I don't believe I've ever met him."

"No, he wasn't at the wedding," she replied absently, scanning the crowd. "As a matter of fact it's difficult to say where he is at any given moment. He travels all over the world."

"I might have heard Michael mention him," commented Barbara, although she was not certain whether she had or not. They lived so far apart, got together only on rare family occasions, and it was sad how little they knew about each other's lives.

"Oh, I'm sure you have. Kyle is a favorite subject with Michael's family—not always complimentary, either. And he's still as unpredictable as ever." She turned to Barbara with a sigh. "He was supposed to be on this flight, which I thought worked out amazingly well, too good to be true, as a matter of fact, and apparently it was, because I don't—"

There was a call from behind them, and Kate cried happily, "There he is!"

But Barbara knew with a dread certainty before she turned to see the limping, crutch-supported gait, before she caught the mad twinkle in those green eyes, before he drew Kate to him and exclaimed, "Hello, beautiful!"

And by the time Kate, blushing and scolding, drew him forward, Barbara was hollow and sick with embarrassment and dread. "Kyle," she said, "this is my sister, Barbara Ellis. Babs, meet Michael's renegade brother, Kyle Waters."

Chapter Two

"Well, this is what I call a happy coincidence, don't you?" Kyle said, his eyes still dancing wickedly. He turned to Kate. "We've already met on the plane."

"Well, how about that!" exclaimed Kate. "I'm glad you were able to make this flight, Kyle, it certainly saved me a lot of trouble."

"I had to change planes twice and had an hour layover in Cincinnati," he confessed, with a grin at Barbara, "but it was worth it."

Barbara avoided his eyes. "Shall we get our luggage?" she suggested.

It took some time for them to get settled in Kate's little Datsun station wagon for the fifteen-mile drive from Portland to Kate and Michael's house. Kyle had to sit in the front seat with Kate to accommodate his leg; Barbara was relegated to the backseat with the luggage and she tried not to resent it. She tried not to resent that fact that her sister seemed to have forgotten all about her from the moment she fell victim to Kyle's overpowering personality, and she tried not to think that he was spoiling her vacation.

"So," said Kate, when they were under way, "aside from the obvious, how was South America?"

"I try never to judge a country from the inside of a hospital room," he replied, and Kate made a sympathetic sound.

"I take it that your expedition was not a success."

"Not at all," he denied, grinning. "I bagged two nurses and a blond Peace Corps volunteer."

Kate laughed merrily, obviously completely captured by his charm, and Barbara put in, "What is it exactly that you do, Kyle?"

He glanced at her. "I'm a professional playboy," he answered, and then turned back to Kate. "By the way, do you suppose you could manage to put me up in the house this time? I haven't quite got the hang of steps yet and the guest house, if I recall, has exactly seventeen."

"No problem," Kate assured him. "I've already had the downstairs guest room made up for Babs, but she won't mind taking an upstairs room, will you, honey?"

Barbara gave a weak smile to her sister's inquiring look in the rearview mirror. She thought, *He's taken my seat in the car, my sister's attention, and now my room. What will he take next?* And she was immediately ashamed of the childish thought.

Kate inquired, "How much longer will you be in a cast?"

"With luck, not more than a couple of weeks. But I was going stir-crazy at home, so I thought I'd come out here and talk Michael into helping me with my book."

Barbara made one more attempt to be polite, mostly to make up for the resentful thoughts she had been having about him. "Oh, are you a writer too?"

He laughed. "Me? Lord, no. I've never written two cohesive sentences in my life. That's why I need Mike. He got all the talent in the family," he confided to her with a twinkle. "I got all the looks."

"Now, you just leave Michael alone about your book," Kate warned him with mock sternness. "He's got all he can handle with his own work. And I can see right now I've got my work cut out for me this summer too. First, to get Babs fattened up and rosy-cheeked—'' she smiled into the mirror at Barbara ''—and you—'' she shot a glance at Kyle ''—look like you've been dragged through places nice girls don't even know about.''

''Which proves you're not a nice girl,'' he teased her.

''Can't you afford a razor?'' she shot back imperviously. ''And where did you come up with that outfit—army surplus? As for your hair—''

''It took me six weeks to grow it this length,'' he protested with a vain toss of his head. ''I think it's rather magnificent. And for your information, I'm in the process of growing a beard.''

''Ha!'' scoffed Kate, and Barbara let the cheerful, bantering voices fade as she stared sightlessly out the window.

Barbara felt depression sinking down on her and she tried to fight it, even though she knew it was useless. It always came upon her unexpectedly like this, usually when she was around happy people, and once it started, there was no controlling it. She wished she hadn't come. When she heard Kate sigh contentedly, ''There's nothing in the world as wonderful as families, and I can't tell you how glad I am to have mine with me this summer!'' she was lost. She felt tears begin to sting her eyes and then roll helplessly down her cheeks.

The worst of it was, she couldn't explain it. She had no reason to be sitting in the backseat of the car crying like a lost child, but she couldn't help it. It made her angry and embarrassed and the more she tried to control it, the worse it got. She hoped against

Twice in a Lifetime 23

desperate hope that Kate did not notice, and she
edged closer to the window, out of range of the mirror, and tried to hide her face with her hand.

"What's Michael working on now?"

"Oddly enough," Kate replied, "a novel about
South American Indians. And since you've just returned from there, maybe you could help him out for
a change."

Kyle laughed. "And since when have I ever been
known to be useful to anyone with anything?" Then
he glanced over his shoulder, as though to include
Barbara in the conversation, and Barbara wanted to
sink through the upholstery.

There she was, completely out of control, crying
like an idiot over absolutely nothing, her face red and
wet. What would he think of that? What would he
say? It was the worst thing that could have possibly
happened, and there was nothing she could do about
it except duck her head and fumble ineffectually
through her purse for a tissue, waiting for him to say
those fatal words, "Why Barbara, what's wrong?"

But he didn't. He simply looked at her quietly for a
moment, then turned easily back to Kate. "Besides,"
he continued, as though nothing at all had interrupted his train of thought, "you know Mike gets his
biggest kicks out of researching his own material.
Why don't you two hop a freight down there?"

"We thought about it," Kate answered, and Barbara experienced a sense of bleak and confused relief.

When she looked up again, a little more in control
now, his arm was resting casually across the back of
the seat as he engaged Kate in continuing conversation, and in his hand was a folded handkerchief. Barbara took it in mute gratitude. In a moment the tears

dried up as quickly and unexpectedly as they had
come, and by the time they pulled up in front of
Kate's big white house, she had made enough repairs
to her face that no one, not having seen, would have
guessed anything was amiss.

The front door opened and a large red setter burst
out, bounding across the yard and barking joyfully.
Michael followed at a more leisurely pace, his hand
uplifted in greeting.

"Down, Jojo!" Kyle said sternly as he opened his
door, and then countered the command, laughing as
he allowed the dog to wiggle onto his lap.

"So," Michael called to him, "all those wild
women finally caught up with you! Broke your leg,
did they?"

"Watch it, my friend," returned Kyle, pushing ineffectually at the affectionate Jojo, "or I'll be telling
Kate some stories about *your* past you wouldn't care
to have repeated!"

Michael opened Barbara's door and bent to kiss
her cheek as she got out. "Welcome home, Barbara." He smiled fondly.

She laughed, looking around her with an eagerness
that totally vanquished her former misgivings.
"Don't tempt me! I could very easily call a place like
this home for a long, long time!"

"Just take a deep breath of that sea air," Kate advised her, and she did, relishing it. "Makes you feel
better already, doesn't it?"

"Yes," she agreed happily. "It does."

Michael went around to Kyle's door. "Need some
help?"

"Just call off your attack dog," replied Kyle.
"It'll be all downhill from there."

"Okay, then, you're on your own."

He opened the back to begin removing the luggage, and Kate caught Jojo's collar, scolding him. "I'm going to take him around back," she called over her shoulder, running a little to keep up with her pet, who had already caught scent of some new excitement. "You both know your way to the front door!"

Barbara went around to help Michael with some of the smaller pieces of luggage, but he insisted, "No, you go on in the house and freshen up. I'll come back for the rest later."

"Just my overnight bag, then."

She stretched inside for it, and he went up the walk ahead of her, calling back, "Kate made a great cake this morning. We're having it on the terrace."

"Be right there," she returned, and she came around the car just as Kyle was steadying himself on his crutch, breathing an exaggerated sigh of relief.

"Well," he said, "the worst part is over." Then he grinned at her. "This answers my question, anyway."

She looked at him, embarrassed and awkward as she remembered the scene he had witnessed in the car and the strangely sensitive part he had played in it. But she said lightly, following his lead, "What question?"

"Where to take you after I've picked you up." He offered his arm to her. "Care to help a cripple up the walk?"

She hesitated, lowered her eyes briefly, and then pushed his handkerchief into his hand. She said with as much composure as she could manage, "Thank you. . . for what you did before. For not telling Kate, I mean. She worries and— It's hard to explain. . . ."

She ventured an uncomfortable glance at him and was surprised to find only placid understanding in his eyes. "No problem," he said mildly, tucking the handkerchief into his back pocket. "You just didn't look like you needed the hassle."

They went slowly up the walk, Barbara matching her pace to his, and he did not speak of it again.

Kate ushered her upstairs immediately, inviting the men to entertain themselves for a while, and Barbara unpacked her overnight bag while Kate made up the bed, chattering all the while. "The bath is right across the hall," she told her, "and you'll have it all to yourself because Michael and I have a full bath in our bedroom and there's one adjoining the guest room downstairs." She glanced up. "I hope you don't mind his being here, but there was really nothing we could do about it. No one ever says no to Kyle." She laughed. "Mostly because he never gives them a chance to. Besides," she decided, "it will be good for you to be with people outside the family for a while."

"I'm with plenty of people outside the family," Barbara replied patiently. "Every day. How long is he staying?"

She shrugged. "With Kyle, who knows? A few days or a few months. However the spirit moves. Now." She fluffed the last pillow and straightened up, facing her. "House rules. Breakfast is at nine, lunch is every man for himself, and dinner is around seven. And I hope you brought some more comfortable clothes to wear, because no one wears stockings around here and we do *not* dress for dinner."

Barbara laughed. "Unless your hamburger casserole has improved since last time, it's no wonder!"

"Also..." She walked over and deliberately removed the clasp that held back Barbara's hair. "The first thing you do upon entering my house is to let your hair down." She smiled appreciatively. "You look more comfortable already."

Barbara groaned. "I should have known what I was letting myself in for!"

"Now, change into something more casual, for goodness' sake!" Kate rummaged through the un- packed articles in Barbara's bag and came up with a pair of light blue slacks and a matching sweater. "This will do, I suppose. Tomorrow we're going shopping."

"I don't think I can take this for three months," Barbara teased.

Kate smiled and sat on the edge of the bed while Barbara changed. "The important thing," she told her, "is to relax. Do whatever you feel like for a while. Just let go. What you need," she said decisive- ly, "is a new romance."

Barbara scowled at her. "Don't be ridiculous."

"I mean it," Kate assured her quite seriously. "Tell me the truth. Have you seen anyone else since Daniel died?"

Barbara quickly pulled the short-sleeved sweater over her head, muffling her voice and hiding her face. "No, of course not." The very idea was almost blas- phemous, but how could she expect her sister to understand that? No one had ever loved like she had loved Daniel, and the thought of replacing him—even momentarily—was both treacherous and absurd.

"Don't you see what I mean?" returned Kate mildly. "Why 'of course not'?"

"Because I'm not interested," Barbara returned sharply, giving her hair a few deft strokes with the brush. "And the day you start trying to fix me up with somebody is the day I pack my bags for home. I mean it, Kate."

Kate retreated tactfully, coming over to pat her sister's arm gently. "I wasn't suggesting that you get serious about anyone," she said. "I know that will be a long time coming. Just open up a little. Have some fun. Okay?"

Again Barbara felt a brief surge of anger that anyone would dare suggest that life should go on just as if nothing had happened, just as if she could really have a life without Daniel. Kate didn't know. Kate couldn't know what it was to lose so cruelly, to know that love would come only once, and to have that love snatched away without warning or reason and with such ultimate finality.... But then she hoped Kate would never know that pain. She regretted her snappy tone and her impatience with her large-hearted sister, and she managed a smile. "Michael said something about a cake," she suggested.

The house was situated on a small promontory overlooking the Atlantic on the back side. The terrace stretched into a velvet lawn decorated with bright beds of azaleas and climbing camilla bushes, with a wooded rock garden to one side. A set of red-wood steps led down the cliff to the private beach, and in the distance the white-capped blue of the ocean sparkled in the sunshine. A mild sea breeze blew continuously, and Barbara sighed, admiring the view through the patio doors, "It's just beautiful. You're so lucky!"

Kate laughed and handed her a tray, which bore a pitcher of lemon tea and four glasses. "You wouldn't think so if you had to keep this place clean and in working order."

"Why don't you get some help?"

"Because I love every minute of it," replied Kate. The men were already on the terrace, leaning on the rail, laughing and talking as they took in the view. Barbara found it hard to believe that the two could be brothers. Michael was shorter, somewhat heavier, and his coloring was much darker. She remembered what Kyle had said about looks versus talent, and she grudgingly agreed. It seemed a shame, though, that the outer man did not reflect the inner self.

They sat around a hexagonal redwood table while Kate cut her spice cake into overly generous slices and Barbara poured the tea. As usual, the conversation was dominated by Kyle, talking about his travels in half fiction, half fact, and keeping everyone in stitches trying to figure out which was which. Barbara began to relax, almost against her will, and thought the unexpected turn of events might not work out so badly after all. For all Kyle's arrogance and self-absorption, his charm was not easy to resist.

Michael said, "So, you've finally decided to write that book you've always talked about. Or is this just another bluff?"

"Worse than that," Kyle replied sadly. "I've got a contract on it. Say, Kate, I don't suppose I could talk you into another piece of cake, could I? It's been so long since I had home cooking, I'll probably eat you out of house and home."

Kate happily cut another slice of cake while Michael pretended to be impressed with his brother's announcement. "A bona fide contract?" he mocked. "With a deadline and everything?"

"Which I have no hope of meeting," replied Kyle, "unless I find a ghostwriter, and quick. Are you beginning to take the hint?"

"Barbara's the one you need to talk to about that," Kate said suddenly, and Barbara winced, trying to signal her sister with her eyes to drop the subject. Kate deliberately ignored her. "She has a degree in journalism, which is doing her absolutely no good right now, and she used to edit a small magazine back home. Of course she's not involved with anything like that now."

Kyle looked at her with interest. "Is that right? What do you do now?"

She remembered the flippant reply when she had asked him about his job, and she answered flatly, "I'm a stripper at the Blue Light Club in Cincinnati."

"Oh," he replied without a flicker of expression. "You're the one." And he turned back to his cake.

Through her laughter Kate informed him, "Barbara doesn't do anything right now—unlike my husband, who is very, very busy. So I suggest the two of you work something out between you."

Kyle replied with a twinkling glance in Barbara's direction, "Now *that* sounds like a proposition worth pursuing. What do you say, Miss Ellis, shall we work something out between us?"

Barbara ignored him by staring out over the ocean and bringing her glass to her lips.

Michael picked up the thread of the conversation. "Well, I'm not very busy today. Today, in fact, I'm taking a holiday, and to celebrate, we're taking you two out to dinner tonight—the restaurant of your choice. What do you think?"

"Sounds great," replied Kyle. "But now, if you'll excuse me. . ." He got to his feet rather clumsily, supporting himself on the back of the chair. "I've been sitting on one plane or another for almost six hours today and I think I'd like to take a walk." He hesitated. "Barbara, would you like to come with me?"

She replied politely, "No, thank you," and sipped again from her glass.

After a moment he shrugged and whistled for Jojo. The dog came loping up gladly, and he limped off, a concerned and attentive Jojo at his heels.

After a moment Michael said mildly, "Kyle takes a little getting used to. I hope you won't let him scare you off."

She laughed lightly. "It will take more than that to get rid of me, now that I'm here. As a matter of fact, you might have to force me to leave at gunpoint when the summer is over."

He smiled. "I don't know whether Kate mentioned it or not, but the invitation is open-ended. We want you to stay for as long as you like."

She waved the idea away, touched. "Nonsense! Nobody wants in-laws hanging around indefinitely."

"We do," he assured her seriously. "You're not getting over this thing like you should, Barbara, and we want to do everything we can to help. What else are families for?"

Quickly she blinked back another threat of tears and stood. "Listen," she said brightly, "what I would really like to do right now is take a nap. Does anybody mind?"

"Of course not," Kate assured her quickly. "You look exhausted."

"Well, a little," she admitted. "And about dinner—would it hurt your feelings very much if I begged off? The rest of you go, though, and have a good time, but I would just like to stay at home tonight and get settled in, you know?"

"Sure thing," Michael smiled. "It's your vacation."

She did not really expect to sleep. She had just

wanted to be alone for a while, to gather her energy
and try to act like a cheerful guest. But she must have
been more tired than she had thought, because when
Kate woke her up, it was six o'clock. "We're going to
take you up on your offer and go to dinner without
you," she told her, smiling. "It's so rarely that
Michael takes a day off I'm taking advantage of it!
There are sandwich fixings in the fridge, and ice
cream in the freezer, and oh, just about anything you
would want. We won't be late."

Barbara stretched and got out of bed, feeling refreshed and relaxed. She wandered down to the kitch-
en but was not really hungry. The sea air tempted her,
and the golden sunset danced off the whitecaps just
visible from the kitchen window. With a sudden enthusiasm she decided to go for a walk on the beach.

She kicked off her shoes at the stairs and was just
beginning to descend when she heard a voice behind
her. "Wait up a minute! Where are you going?"

She turned and was surprised to see Kyle limping
toward her. "To the beach," she replied. "I thought
you went with Michael and Kate."

He smiled as he drew up. "I decided to stay behind
and keep you company instead."

She turned with an air of deliberate indifference.
"I don't need any company, thank you."

"Well, since it looks like we both had a walk in
mind, I don't see any reason why we shouldn't do it
together."

She shrugged and started down the stairs, but
stopped when he spoke again.

"Those stairs look treacherous," he said, "and if I
get sand in this cast there'll be hell to pay. How about
walking along the cliff instead? That way we can
talk."

She said carelessly, "I'd rather walk on the beach."

"Suit yourself."

But something made her look back in a moment, and she saw him beginning to descend the stairs, cautiously gripping the rail with one hand while he maneuvered the crutch with the other. "You're going to fall!" she cried.

"And probably break my neck," he agreed. "How would you like to have that one on your conscience?"

"Oh, for goodness' sake!"

She came back up the stairs in exasperation and slipped on her shoes. "All right," she said impatiently. "I'll walk with you. What do you want to talk about?"

"I want," he declared, swinging into place beside her, "to negotiate the terms of a truce."

She glanced at him uncomfortably. "I don't know what you're talking about."

"For Mike and Katie's sake," he added, a little more seriously. "They're not dumb, you know. Sooner or later they're going to get the feeling they're caught in the cross fire."

She laughed, a little falsely. "Really, I can't imagine what gave you the idea that there's any need for a truce."

"First of all," he continued, perfectly serious now, "I would like to apologize for my behavior on the plane. I wish I could say I don't usually come on to girls like that, but unfortunately it wouldn't be true. It's one of my many bad habits—a sign of insecurity, they tell me."

She laughed. "You? Insecure?"

"Yes, me."

He seemed blandly sincere, and Barbara could appreciate honesty. After a moment she said, "Well, I guess I'm sorry too. I was pretty rude. I seem to have a tendency to snap at people." She began to twist absently her wedding band on her finger. "I wasn't always that way."

He said quietly, "Bitter?"

She hesitated. "Yes," she answered after a moment. "I suppose so. It doesn't seem fair."

"It must have been rough on you," he agreed kindly. "Was he ill long?"

"Three months," she answered flatly and tried to push from her mind the memory of that bleak hospital room, watching day and night the only man she had ever loved waste away before her eyes.

"No children, I assume."

This would have been the year they had promised themselves they would start a family, whether they could afford it or not. Daniel had loved children and, dreamer that he was, had wanted to start a family as soon as they were married. It was Barbara who was the practical one and persuaded him to wait at least three years, to give him a chance to get settled in his career. "But not one second longer," he had made her promise, and even now she could see his slightly crooked grin filtering through the twilight as they reached the agreement she now regretted so bitterly. Kyle could not know what a sharp stab of pain that simple phrase "no children" sent through her, how much of her grief had been concentrated on that one added emptiness. Daniel was gone, and his death seemed more final because there was nothing left of the love they had shared.

She said with brittle brightness, "No, thank goodness."

The look on his face in the deepening twilight was surprised, and something else she could not quite discern—disappointment? "You don't like children?" he inquired.

She tried to push aside the memory of those nights they had lain in one another's arms. "Three boys and four girls," Daniel had said, and she had countered with, "Four boys and three girls, and all of them will be musical prodigies." "And all of them will look just like you," he had interjected and they had laughed and dreamed and never doubted that their dreams would come true. She pushed those torturous memories aside forcefully and brought herself back to the present.

"Oh, sure," she replied in that same false tone. "As long as they're someone else's. Motherhood is not for me, I'm afraid." It was a patent lie, born of self-defense, but it helped ease the pain of a double loss. There was no point in yearning for what she would never have: a home, a husband, dozens of children, and love filling every corner of her life—all the things she had envisioned for the future with Daniel. It was so much easier to pretend she had never wanted those things at all.

He fell silent, and she quickly changed the subject. "What is your book about?"

"Oh," he replied vaguely, "my work. Pretty dull stuff."

"Your work?" she prompted. "Which is?"

He replied flippantly, "I'm a hit man for the Organization."

"Sounds like a best-seller."

"If I live to tell it."

She gave him a bemused glance of silent laughter, but he offered no further elaboration. She supposed many girls would find that hint of mystery part of his overall charm—and she also supposed that he knew it. She had to admit she was almost enjoying his game, for he was an expert in the art of light flirtation.

They had reached a small overhang, resplendent in wild blackberries and flowering shrubs, and he gestured to the wrought-iron bench nestled near the edge for sightseers. "Mind if we rest here for a minute?"

She shook her head and wandered closer to the edge, catching her breath at the magnificent prism of colors shed by the last dying rays of the sun upon the water. He lowered himself stiffly to the bench and she saw him wince as he stretched his leg out before him.

She came back over to him. "Does your leg hurt?"

"Just a twinge, now and then," he admitted and tucked the crutch under the bench. "What really bothers me is my arm, from leaning on that piece of wood all day. The whole thing is a pain, if you want to know the truth. I never realized before how much I took for granted a simple thing like walking. Getting dressed in the morning—" he laughed "—now, there's a comedy! Getting in a cab, eating in a restaurant, taking a shower—a hundred things that normal people don't even think about. And," he added with a gleam of mischief, "you wouldn't believe what it does to my love life."

"I can imagine," she murmured.

"Another thing that's really getting to be a bore," he confessed, "is having to look up to people when I'm talking to them. It's what you might call a pain in the neck."

She laughed and sat beside him. "Better?"

"Much." He smiled at her. "Did you know you're very pretty?"

She blushed and pushed back her hair with both hands. It was thin and naturally curly, and the sea air had a tendency to make it friz. The wind was blowing it in a dozen gentle directions at once. "I'm a mess," she said.

"Don't do that," he said, touching her hand lightly. "I like it like that."

She gave a small uncomfortable laugh and moved her hand away from his.

He continued to smile, his eyes a very deep green, searching and examining her face with an intensity that made her feel awkward; she had to look away. "You have a very interesting face," he said. "You can read a lot on a person's face."

She glanced at him, wanting to get up and walk away, wanting to change the subject, but somehow intrigued by the natural fascination of the boy-girl game she had not played in too long. "Is that right?" she murmured.

"It is indeed. Your mouth tells me that you are a very sober little creature, you take life very seriously. Your pointed little chin says you usually get what you want. Your eyes—"

"Are two bottomless pools brimming with passion," she supplied dryly. "I've heard this before."

His own eyes twinkled. "But your pert, slightly upturned nose belongs to a person of wit and innate humor. And this line, here—" lightly he touched the bridge of her nose, sobering somewhat "—is a 'want' line. It tells me you've wanted too much and gotten too little out of life, and you'll have to be careful because you can't afford to let it get any deeper."

She was embarrassed and uncomfortable but would

not let him see. She turned the tables on him. "Well, I think I've got the hang of it now. Let's see what I can tell about you."

He did not flinch from her gaze, but returned it steadily, his eyes warm with humor. She pursed her lips in mock thoughtfulness. "I would say merely that you are a very frivolous and carefree person, who takes nothing seriously, wants for nothing, and spends ninety percent of his time laughing."

"How can you tell that?" he demanded.

"Elementary, my dear Watson," she retorted. "Those millions of little laugh lines around your eyes."

He laughed. "A very shallow assessment!"

"But isn't it true?"

He sobered slightly and shifted his gaze. "Oh, I don't know. Not entirely. You never heard of the sad clown—laughing on the outside and crying on the inside?"

"Yes," she admitted. "But I don't think the description applies. What have you got to cry about?"

"Everyone has something to cry about," he returned lightly. "Anyway, I try not to let it get me down, so I suppose in a way you're right. Whenever things start getting heavy, I just take a trip to Maine and soak up some of Mike and Katie's happiness for a while. A miracle cure for all ills."

She half thought he was serious, and that both surprised and disturbed her. She had been prepared to take Michael's free-wheeling brother at a face value—a flirt, a clown, a happy-go-lucky jet-setter—and there was no room in her assessment of him for the deeper side of his nature. She did not want to be drawn into shared intimacies, so she changed the subject. "Where did you learn so much about faces, anyway?"

He bent to retrieve his crutch. "Oh, it's a hobby of mine. I'll tell you about it someday. Right now I'd rather go raid Katie's refrigerator. Are you with me?"

They walked carefully back to the house in the shadowy twilight, and after a while he said, "Does it bother you to talk about your husband? What he was like, how you met, all of that?"

Usually a door would have automatically slammed shut on a question like that. She was surprised at how easily she kept it open this time. Maybe it was time, after all, to start letting go. . . .

She shrugged. "There's not much to tell." Only a million and one things, beautiful things, loving things, which would never live again outside her memory. "He was a musician-songwriter. We met through the magazine I was working on. He was very talented, very gentle, very loving—but not very successful."

"That's odd," he commented. "That you and your sister should both be attracted to the creative, artistic type."

She shook her head. "That's like the man who was classified as a dog-lover, and he replied, 'I don't love dogs at all. I love *a* dog.' "

He nodded, "I see what you mean."

"Personally, I don't care much for the artistic type as a whole. I'm too pragmatic, and I generally try to avoid dreamers. And I don't think creative people should *ever* marry."

"Why is that?"

"Because they're already married to their art. There aren't too many people who can keep two wives happy. Daniel," she added softly, "was one of them."

There was no sound for a while except the crackle of their footsteps on the path, and then Kyle said suddenly, "I've been married."

She looked up at him in surprise—surprise because she wouldn't have guessed it, and surprise because she couldn't understand why he was telling her. But she thought this fact might shed some light on his earlier statement about crying on the inside. She said softly, "You loved her?"

"I thought I did," he answered. "I guess what I really loved was the idea of being married. You know, house with white picket fence, wife in the kitchen when you got home from work, the whole bit. And she, apparently, was just in love with my checkbook."

She ventured hesitantly, "So what happened?"

"She found a guy with a bigger checkbook. We've been divorced almost two years."

She did not know what to say. They had reached the house, and he turned to her, leaning on the crutch. "I just thought I should tell you," he said, no sign of mirth in his eyes now at all. "Some women are really turned off by divorced men."

That statement, more than anything else, flustered her. She reached quickly to open the back door. "It's no concern of mine at all," she replied coolly.

"I figured you would say that," he answered dryly and followed her inside the house.

He opened the refrigerator and peered inside. "Well, look at this. Half a ham, roast beef, pickles, cheese.... Katie knew I was coming, all right." He began to remove platters, balancing them in his free hand, and Barbara came quickly to assist.

"Let me do that," she said. "You go sit down."

"I have got," he replied in mock seriousness, "to learn to do these things for myself. You put on some coffee. Or better yet, see what kind of wine Mike has hidden in that top cabinet over there."

She made a studied search through the cabinet while he made the short trip between the refrigerator and the breakfast nook several times. "Rosé?" she suggested, pulling out a bottle.

"Perfect."

She found plates and utensils, and his muffled voice came from inside the refrigerator; "Eureka! Cheesecake." He deposited it on the table with a flourish and admitted, "I sure am glad we decided to stay and dine at home tonight. You couldn't get a feast like this at a restaurant at twice the price."

She laughed and put on water for the coffee.

He lowered himself to a chair and she could feel him watching her as she brought the glasses and began her search for napkins. Then he said suddenly, "Does anyone ever call you Bobbie?"

She found the napkins, and came over to the table, shaking her head. "Why would anyone want to?"

"Well," he said thoughtfully, "you look like a Bobbie to me, and that's what I'm going to call you."

She retorted, "Do I get a choice in this?"

He grinned, "You can always refuse to answer when I call you."

She sat down and responded pertly, "I might just do that."

He poured the wine while she began making the sandwiches, tasted it with the exaggerated air of a connoisseur, and then lifted his glass to her. "A toast," he declared.

She wiped her hands on a napkin and took up her own glass.

"To the truce." He smiled and touched his glass to hers.

She accepted the toast, and they sipped from their glasses. He swallowed quickly and set his glass on the table, snapping his fingers. "I *knew* there was something missing!" he announced, and hobbled off toward the dining room. "Back in a minute."

He returned with an elaborate candelabrum that had been part of a formal centerpiece on the dining room table. "What's wine without candlelight?"

She laughed, choking a little on her wine. "You're just a little bit crazy, you know that? Kate will kill you if you ruin her centerpiece!"

He took a pack of matches from the drawer and lit two of the candles, then turned off the light on his way back to the table. *"Voilà,"* he said with a flourish. "Atmosphere!"

"And Kate's going to have a lopsided centerpiece," she commented dryly.

"Forget Kate." He took up his glass again. "To Bobbie."

"Whoever she is," returned Barbara.

He kept up a comfortable banter of conversation as they ate, and Barbara began to relax under the influence of the wine and the soft light. His occasional teasing come-ons were lighthearted and corny; he was flirtatious and unpredictable and definitely not her type, but his company was cheering. And it had been so long since she had had fun, even so mild a type as this, that the experience was a little heady.

Then he said with an unexpected serious turn, "I don't want to bug you by bringing this up all the time, but Mike mentioned this afternoon that it's pretty close to a year on the dot since your husband died. There is such a thing as anniversary crisis, you know."

She tried not to let that reminder bring her down. It was easier to be objective than she had supposed. "I know. That's what everyone keeps telling me. I suppose that has something to do with my crying jags."

He nodded. "It might be easier for you if you set your mind on finding a new project right now. You know, a new job, a new house, a boyfriend...."

She glanced at him slyly. "Funny, that's exactly what Kate said. And I suppose you know just the man."

He grinned. "I might." Then, "No, I'm serious. After my little house with the white picket fence went on the market, I found the best therapy was to get into something else right away. So I built a cabin in the woods, which was something I'd always wanted to do—you know, a kind of refuge in the mountains—and started a new life for myself up there. It helped."

She said gently, "She must have hurt you very much."

"No," he replied thoughtfully, looking into his glass of wine. "Losing her didn't hurt so much. I guess I had been prepared for that from the day we got back from our honeymoon. What hurt was—" An absent, painfully introspective expression crossed his face in the flickering light, and he broke off. He took a sip of wine and added in a more normal tone, "Anyway, the cabin-in-the-woods idea didn't work out too well after all, I guess, or else what would I be doing here? I don't suppose I'm the one to be giving advice."

"Why not?" she pursued, interested. "Why didn't it work out?"

He shrugged. "Too lonely. What it really needs is more than one person living in it."

"Well," she replied flippantly, "you shouldn't have too much trouble furnishing *that*. You're the guy that can charm the birds out of the trees, after all."

He leaned his head on his fist, smiling, studying her. "I'm pretty choosy about my company. And birds are not exactly what I had in mind."

Conversation flagged. The way he kept studying her, gently, musingly, searching the very depths of her eyes and every line on her face, was more intimate than a caress. She tried to avoid that look and found she could not. The candlelight and the wine and the tender, thoughtful expression in his eyes were combining to stir memories of emotion in her that were so long buried they were almost alien. Then he said softly, "What would you say if I asked if I could kiss you?"

For a breathless moment she could not answer. She felt a heat come to her cheeks; her pulses speeded unexpectedly. And then she managed in a whisper, "I—I'd say no."

"I see." His smile did not fade; his eyes remained steady. "I'll remember not to ask you, then."

And then the front door opened and Kate's voice called, "Where is everyone?"

Barbara got up quickly to answer, and Kyle calmly began to cut another slice of cheesecake. The moment was spoiled, and Barbara was not certain whether she was glad or sorry.

Chapter Three

Barbara was awake at sunup the next morning, refreshed and full of energy. She could not remember when she had felt so well. Perhaps Kate's prescription was working already—or perhaps it was simply that she was beginning to take her sister's advice, to open up and have some fun.

She left the house quietly and took Jojo for a run on the beach, thinking about last evening with Kyle. It was a relief to be with someone who didn't tiptoe around her feelings, someone who took her no more seriously than he took himself, but who could switch moods from lighthearted nonsense to more sober conversation with as much ease as a well-tuned car changed gears. Being around him was easy, which was unusual because she did not make casual friends. She was relaxed in his presence—except for those few times when he embarrassed her with romantic overtures, and even that, knowing it was all in the spirit of fun, was strangely enjoyable.

She threw pieces of driftwood into the tide for Jojo to retrieve. She cuffed up her jeans and splashed through the icy water herself, loving the sting of salt spray on her cheeks and the warm sun on her shoulders. Jojo became more playful, trying to trip her by jumping and barking and running in circles around her; she distracted him with another piece of driftwood and ran, laughing, for the safety of the steps.

Kyle was sitting at the top of the stairs, his hands

propped on the crutch, looking strangely reflective. He smiled vaguely when he saw her.

"My," she gasped as she approached, whipping her hair out of her eyes. "You look terribly thoughtful for this hour of the morning."

"That's probably because," he returned, "I was thinking."

"What were you thinking about?"

"Oh," he answered absently, "I've got my troubles, like everyone else."

"There are a lot worse troubles," she retorted, "than having a broken leg."

"That's for sure," he agreed soberly, and just then Jojo came bouncing up the stairs, shaking himself and leaping joyfully on Kyle. "Hey, watch yourself, you big sloppy beast!" he cried, pushing him away good-humoredly. "When I want a bath, I'll let you know. Now go on." He gave him a firm shove, followed by an affectionate slap on the flank. "Go find somebody else to play with."

Obediently Jojo trotted off, and Kyle turned back to her. "Now, where was I," he mused, "before I was so rudely interrupted...."

"Thinking about your troubles," she reminded him.

"Ah, yes," he recalled seriously. "I was thinking...you've got problems, I've got problems. We both need cheering up. So I think I've got a solution. Let's have an affair."

She stared at him in a moment of shock before she caught the gleam of humor in his eyes. Then she was able to return in kind, "You've been talking to my sister again. That's her magical cure for all ills."

"A very wise woman, your sister," he agreed, perfectly deadpan. "Of course I wasn't suggesting we rush into anything."

"Of course not."

"Take a couple of weeks to get this cast off my leg and to sort of get the feel of the idea.... I'm quite a good lover," he assured her, "when I'm not hampered by a ton of plaster."

She inquired without blinking, "Are you, now?"

"It will give us both something to look forward to. What do you think?"

She pretended thoughtfulness. "I think," she decided at last, "that you are about as subtle as a billboard. I think I would prefer someone with more finesse. I think," she added as she stood, "I will do my shopping elsewhere."

He broke down into laughter as she started to walk away, and she was glad he dropped the game first because she was having difficulty restraining her own mirth. "Okay, okay," he called after her. "I promise I'll work on 'subtle' and 'finesse.' Meanwhile you're not just going to leave me here, are you?"

She turned back, her eyes dancing. "I should, you know."

"But you won't," he replied confidently. "Your heart is too soft. Come on, give me a hand."

She came back to him, inquiring dubiously, "How did you get down there, then, if you can't get up by yourself?"

"Sitting is always easier than standing," he replied. "Here, just let me lean on you till I get the crutch...."

She bent down and grasped his arm as he got slowly to his feet, maneuvering the crutch into place with difficulty. And then suddenly he swayed against her unsteadily, lost his balance, and the crutch went clat-

tering down the stairs. She cried out and clutched
him to her, trying to balance him with her weight.
And before she knew what was happening, he no
longer seemed to need her support, his arms came
about her firmly, and he bent his head and kissed her
gently on the lips.

It was a very brief kiss; she was too shocked to respond one way or the other, and when he lifted his
face, she was staring at him in dazed confusion.

"And you said I had no subtlety." He smiled.

"You," she gasped, trying to wrench away, "you
tricked me!"

"I have one or two up my sleeve," he responded,
and just as she was about to angrily step away, he
caught her to him again, guiding her face to his with
a firm, swift, graceful motion.

His lips explored hers tentatively at first, tasting,
searching, testing for resistance. But there was none.
She was shocked and helpless as the ashes of emotions she had thought long dead blazed to life with a
frightening intensity. The feel of his lean, hard body
pressed against hers sent a tingle of liquid heat puls-
ing through her veins; his hands, pressed against her
back and warm against her neck beneath her hair,
made her limbs weak and watery; the rising insistence
of his lips against hers caused silver dots of dizziness
to explode behind her closed eyes. She had to pull
away, fighting for control, frightened by what she
did not understand. "Please," she whispered, twisting her face away. "Don't."

He released a long breath against her cheek and
kept his eyes closed for a moment, as though he too
were fighting for control. She was too weak to move
away and he made no move to release her. Then he
looked at her, and she could see the effort it took for

him to get the familiar mask of casual humor in place over a deeper emotion. "That was nice," he said softly, his eyes searching her face. "Let's do it again."

She managed, "Let's not," and tried to pull away.

He held her for a moment and inquired gently, "What I felt from you just now—was that just instinct?"

She swallowed hard, struggling through a haze of confusion, afraid of the opening of a door she could not enter. With a great effort she found the right answer, forced nonchalance into her tone. "That's all it ever is, isn't it? Boy-meets-girl, boy-kisses-girl.... It's as old as Adam and Eve. No big deal." Then she added quickly "I—I'll go get your crutch."

"I'd rather lean on you."

She tossed over her shoulder, "Lean on the rail!" as she went hurriedly down the stairs.

When she returned it to him, a little breathless from the exercise, he caught her hand and made to draw her to him again. "Once more with feeling?" he suggested.

She pulled away. "Come on, cut it out. Kate and Michael will see."

"They're still in bed," he informed her, and his eyes glinted mischievously. "We could take a leaf from their book."

She relaxed now into the familiar banter. "I'm not interested in clumsy lovers," she retorted and started for the house.

In a moment he called, "Bobbie."

She half-turned, only her tightly clasped hands betraying her anxiety over a near escape from something she could not yet define.

"You okay?" he inquired softly.

That was almost her undoing. She caught her breath, glancing down at her hands, searching for composure, reaching for a flippant reply. None seemed to serve, and at last she answered only, "Yes, I think so." She glanced up at him and managed a weak smile. "Just don't try it again, okay?"

He shook his head. "I can't promise that."

She turned and went quickly back into the house, trying not to run.

Inside she gripped the kitchen counter and angrily fought back the stinging tears. It was just a silly little kiss, that was all. It happened to thousands of men and women every day. Then why should she feel as though it had suddenly changed the world?

The best antidote for the depression and the anxiety of confusion she felt creeping in on her was to get busy, and quickly. Kate came down twenty minutes later to find her frying bacon and making pancakes.

"Oh." Kate smiled through a yawn. "I thought I was dreaming. That smells delicious."

Kyle came in from the back at the same time. "What?" he demanded. "She can cook too?"

"Coffee's on," she told them. "Place your orders, folks."

"I'll start with a dozen," Kyle replied, taking mugs down from the cabinet.

"I'd love it," Kate replied with a little moan and came to help Kyle with the coffee. "But I'm watching my weight."

Michael came down with more compliments on the breakfast smells, and when they were finished, he declared, "If you keep on like this, we'll be so spoiled we won't be *able* to let you go at the end of the summer."

"I love to cook," Barbara admitted. "But I hardly

ever get a chance to. It's no fun cooking for one.''

"Well, then," commented Kyle, "what you need is a roommate. Did I mention I was in the market for one?''

Barbara ignored him, and Michael warned mildly, "All right, little brother, no soliciting on the premises." He relished the last sip of coffee and stood. "Well, I'm off to the old typewriter. And I suggest," he added to Kyle, "that you do the same. What do you ladies have planned this morning?"

"We're going on a shopping spree," Kate replied, her eyes twinkling. "We're going to spend every cent you have and a few you don't."

Michael groaned, "Have mercy." Then, to Kyle, more sternly, "Get to work, old fellow. Discipline is a writer's first tool."

"I'd rather go shopping," Kyle protested.

"You," Kate told him severely, "are not invited. Get to work.''

He gave an exaggerated sigh of martyrdom and got to his feet. "Slave driver," he shot back to her.

In the car Kate commented, "Kyle is nice, isn't he?''

Barbara glanced at her sister for a deeper suggestion behind those words, but Kate's expression was bland. "I suppose so," she admitted. "A little strange."

She chuckled. "Oh, he just likes to have fun. Although since the divorce—" She glanced at Barbara. "You knew about that?"

Barbara nodded.

"Sometimes now he seems like he's trying a little too hard to have fun. You know, moody. I think it really shook him, more than he likes to admit. Although I could have told him that would be the way it would end the minute I laid eyes on her. She's the type," she added, "who would have made a terrific concubine if she had been born a century earlier. We still hear about her now and then, living it up on the Mediterranean or gambling away Kyle's money in Vegas—with a new man every three months." She shook her head sadly. "It's a shame he had to get mixed up with someone like that. He was so trusting."

"Trusting," suggested Barbara, "but not trustworthy?"

"He's a nice man," reiterated Kate evenly, but this time there was a note of warning to her voice. "But he does have a reputation with women. It's his way of getting over her, I guess. I wouldn't take him too seriously."

"Oh, I have no intention of taking anyone seriously," replied Barbara. "That's the last thing I need right now." Then she glanced at her sister slyly. "You saw us on the beach this morning, didn't you?"

Kate hesitated, looked abashed, and then nodded.

"Well," replied Barbara lightly, "a girl can have a little fun, can't she?"

"I want you to have fun," insisted Kate. "As long as you know what you're getting into."

Barbara smiled. "Thanks for caring, Kate."

And Kate returned her smile, a little embarrassed. "But you're a big girl now."

"Right." Barbara answered.

Kate's biggest weakness was in her extravagant shopping sprees, but what disturbed Barbara was that, except for a few minor cosmetics purchases, all the selections Kate made were for her sister. She chose pretty voile sundresses, fresh seersucker culottes, and tank tops trimmed with lace, and she insisted that Barbara have a new swimsuit. Over Barbara's protests she explained, "Don't be silly. You know I love these darling little things but I would look ridiculous in them. It was Michael's idea," she added, "so don't think about the money. Consider it our birthday present."

Barbara was touched, but she felt compelled to object. "You've already given me my birthday present. This trip—and two months early, I might add."

"And a party," added Kate suddenly. "And for that you'll need a new dress." At Barbara's surprised look of objection she laughed and explained, "All right, the party has been planned for a long time—we give at least one big party every summer—but since it happens to be on the day of your birthday, we can celebrate that as well, can't we? Now, let's find something really dazzling. . . ."

They spent an enjoyable afternoon searching for the perfect dress and found it at last in the form of a lavender printed crepe with a floating petal skirt accented by a knotted gold rope at the waist, with a deep ruffled neckline and billowing transparent sleeves.

"Not many girls can wear that style," Kate said enviously. "But on you it looks gorgeous."

Barbara could not help agreeing. She stayed away from the traditional greens and peaches most redheads wore, and lavender was really her color. It turned her fair skin to porcelain and brought out the violet depths of her eyes, and she was more pleased than she admitted over her selection. It had been too long since she had known the fun of buying a new dress just for the frivolity of it.

But when Kate brought out her credit card to pay

for their purchases, Barbara sternly overrode her. "It's not that I don't appreciate the thought," she told her, taking out her wallet, "but I'm not exactly destitute, you know. You and Michael have done enough."

Naturally Kate objected, but Barbara was firm. Barbara paid for her own purchases and even had enough left over to impulsively buy a pair of matching lavender shoes.

They had a long, chatty lunch in a little restaurant overlooking the town square, and Barbara could not remember having spent a more enjoyable day. She was tentatively amazed at the change that had come over her since arriving here a mere twenty-four hours ago. Could Kate have been right—that all she needed was a change of scenery? Or could it be her new-found enthusiasm for life was derived from something else—a lanky, green-eyed stranger who would be sharing her roof for the duration of her vacation?

Impatiently she tried to dismiss that possibility, but thoughts of Kyle would not easily retreat to the background where they belonged. He was not the type of man who would fade easily into the background of anyone's thoughts. There was so much she would have liked to know about him, and she waited for Kate to bring up the subject of her brother-in-law, but she never did. Barbara wondered, for example, how he had broken his leg. She had assumed it had been while skiing, but in South America? And what kind of work did he do that enabled him to travel so blithely all over the world, and that he apparently did well enough to be asked to write a book on the subject? And what about his ill-fated marriage? There were dozens of questions she could have asked and was certain Kate would have given her frank, unbiased answers, but pride prevented her. After all, it was not as though she had any particular interest in him, only curiosity....

They did some late marketing for dinner, and by the time they arrived home they had to rush to unpack the groceries and get dinner started. Barbara did no more than dump her packages on her bed before hurrying downstairs to help Kate.

"The house is awfully quiet," she commented as she came in to the kitchen. "Where is everyone?"

"I heard the typewriter going in Michael's study," answered Kate, stretching to place a package of macaroni on a top shelf. "As for his illustrious brother..." She nodded over her shoulder toward the window.

Barbara, taking four baking potatoes to the sink for scrubbing, glanced out. Kyle was lying on a lounge chair on the terrace, his eyes peacefully closed to the sun. He was wearing nothing but a pair of snug white shorts, and his perspiration-oiled body gleamed goldenly in contrast to their bright glare. His hands were linked behind his head, revealing a light mat of hair under his arms, and the muscles of his shoulders, even in that relaxed posture, were defined in intriguing sinewy lines. His chest was smooth and bare except for a small gold medallion, which winked with the reflection of the shimmering water below. His deep tan made the hairs on his legs appear almost golden, drawing attention to the well-muscled thighs and hard, firm shape of his calf. It was, Barbara thought in surprise, one of the most beautiful male bodies she had ever seen, and she continued to gaze at him as one would a fine work of art, helpless to the stirring of buried sensations only the sight of him aroused, until Kate's step behind her startled her into a furious flush and she turned back quickly to the sink.

Kate did not appear to notice anything out of the ordinary. She leaned forward and slid open the window, calling, "Is this what you've been doing all day, you worthless creature? You're supposed to be working!"

Barbara happened to glance up from her violent scrubbing of the potatoes just as his eyes opened a crack. The emerald-green slits seemed to hold her mesmerized, though he spoke to Kate. "Do not disturb," he drawled lazily. "Can't you see I'm creating?" He turned his face back to the sun and closed his eyes but added, "By the way, something happened while you were gone. Let me think what it was."

Kate released an impatient breath, waiting with her hand on the window latch, until he decided, "Oh, yes. The exterminators. You've got termites."

Kate groaned and Barbara looked up from placing the potatoes in the oven. "Oh, Kate," she offered sympathetically. "That's too bad."

"I told you not to buy a house that was forty years old," volunteered Kyle lazily from the terrace.

"Does Michael know?" Kate asked.

"Umm-hmm. I think he made an appointment for a couple of weeks from now to get rid of the little darlings."

Kate opened her mouth to retort but just then the telephone rang. She crossed the room to answer it and Barbara busied herself by preparing the steaks for the broiler, deliberately avoiding looking out the window as she passed it. Why did Michael have to have a brother who was so extraordinarily good-looking, and why did he have to choose this time to visit, and why did he have to sunbathe half naked right under her nose?

In a moment Kate called, "Telephone, Sleeping Beauty. Long distance."

She handed him the receiver as he made his way slowly inside, and informed him, "Your attorney."

He grimaced as he took the receiver, balancing himself on the crutch, and Kate turned to Barbara. "I think I'd better go consult with the head of the household on this latest crisis. Can you handle things in here?"

Kyle said into the phone, "Stan. What's up?"

Barbara answered her sister, "Sure. What kind of vegetable do you want?"

"We'll have the frozen peas," she replied on her way out of the kitchen, and Kyle frowned as he tried to cover his ear with his hand while maintaining his balance. "I'll be back to help you with the salad."

"What's that?" Kyle was saying. "Oh, sure, I'm fine. I'm seeing a doctor here tomorrow. Say, you're too cheap to call long distance to inquire about my health. What's on your mind?"

Barbara bent over to place the steaks under the broiler, and she was suddenly aware of Kyle's eyes on her. When she straightened up, there was a lazy twinkle in his eyes, and he made a circle of his thumb and forefinger, indicating approval of the view he had just had. She scowled and went quickly to the refrigerator.

It was impossible not to overhear his conversation, and equally as impossible to ignore his eyes following her about Kate's airy blue and white kitchen. Their awareness of one another, alone for the first time since the episode on the beach that morning, was almost a physical thing. She moved stiffly and self-consciously, trying to look occupied and unaware of him, but she knew she was falling much short of her goal.

Kyle said, turning his attention momentarily back to the phone, "So get to the point. What did he say?"

There was a sharp silence, and then an explosion. "The hell he did!"

Barbara almost dropped the platter she had taken down from a shelf. The angry exclamation went against what little she knew of the mild, easygoing Kyle Waters, and she could not help venturing a glance at him.

He had half turned from her now, his wrathful attention focused on the blue plastic cover of the telephone, as though he might at any moment rip it off the wall. A dark flush had crept over his cheekbones and the knuckles of the hand that held the receiver to his ear stood out in a taut white line across his fist. "What kind of half-witted judge did you dig up?" he shouted. "Where does he come off—"

Uncomfortable, Barbara turned the water on full force to drown out the sound of his voice, but then realized that the noise would also serve to make it difficult for Kyle to hear the party on the other end. She wished she could slip unobtrusively out of the range of this angry and obviously very personal conversation, but Kyle was blocking the exit to the kitchen.

"No, you listen to me," he demanded in tight fury, his back now turned to Barbara. "You've screwed this whole thing to hell, and who's going to suffer for it? Not you, with your ten-thousand-dollar fee, and not even me. . . . Don't give me that, you son of a—"

Barbara was appalled. She did not want to be around when he finished that conversation and possibly turned the remainder of his wrath on the nearest available object. She made her way quietly over to the patio doors and slipped out.

For a while she heard nothing but the muted rushing of the tide and the gentle sighing of the breeze. She thought Kyle must have either found his temper or hung up on his caller. And then his voice floated through the kitchen window. "Now, get this straight. I don't want to hear any more about having exhausted all legal resources. Because the next thing I'm going to do is try a few that aren't so legal!"

She walked away from the window.

"I don't want another attorney, dammit! I want service from the one I've already paid for!"

Barbara sighed and sat on the rail, trying to focus her attention on the sea.

When next he spoke, his voice sounded a little calmer. "All right...all right, try that, then. What do I have to do?... Okay, I'll wait to hear from you.... Yes, I'll be here." And then, impatiently, "Until I notify you otherwise!" And the receiver was replaced with a force that jarred the bell.

She was in no hurry to go back inside. She would wait until he had time to leave, or until Kate returned and perhaps exerted a calming influence. She sat on the rail with the cool breeze ruffling her hair and relaxed in the beauty of the glowing pink and red azalea bushes that bordered the path before her.

She heard the patio doors slide open and Kyle swung his crutch over the sill, coming toward her at an easy, relaxed pace. Nothing in his face reflected the volcano of wrath she had just witnessed.

"Sorry if I embarrassed you in there," he offered

casually. "Sometimes you have to get rough with these guys to keep them in line."

"Well, I would say you've perfected that technique," she murmured, glancing at him.

He gave her an abashed grin as he propped the crutch on the rail and sat beside her. "I'm, er, involved in a slight litigation," he explained.

"Oh, really?" She pretended wide-eyed interest. "Paternity suit or breach of promise?"

His eyes sparkled. "I'll never tell."

He was sitting very close, so that their thighs almost touched. He exuded the warm scents of sun-baked perspiration and a faint musky odor of cologne, and she kept her eyes turned away from the sight of that lean brown chest that had had such a devastating effect on her earlier. She looked instead at his hands, which were linked casually about one knee. They were long and brown and slender, delicate hands, with even, blunt nails and soft, un-calloused tips. She wondered again what he did for a living to keep his hands in such condition. Probably nothing honest, she told herself derisively, and was assaulted suddenly by the memory of Daniel's hands, square and blunt, the fingers grooved and calloused by guitar strings. . . . To Barbara a man's hands were one of the most sensuous parts of his body, capable of displaying great power or giving enormous pleasure, and she quickly looked away, trying not to think about Kyle's hands.

He said lightly, "Notice anything different about me?"

"Yes," she responded automatically. "You're not wearing any clothes."

He gave a delighted roar of laughter, and she

flushed. That had not come out at all the way she intended.

"That's what I like," he managed in a moment. "A girl with perception."

She knew if she looked at him, his eyes would be mocking her rakishly, and she compressed her lips and started to move away, determined not to commit another blunder by opening her mouth to retort.

"I meant," he told her, catching her wrist as she stood, "to direct your attention to the upper part of my body, which is no more naked than it usually is— or at least not by much!"

She glanced at him through narrowed eyes and muttered unwillingly, "You cut your hair."

"And shaved. Do I still look like a refugee from the sixties?"

He looked anything but, although Barbara would not tell him so. The shaggy ends of his sun-streaked fawn hair were trimmed into a neater, more fashionable style that complemented him for the mature man he was. Brushed away from the forehead, it still insisted upon falling forward at the part in a manner favored by many young actors and imitated by up-and-coming junior executives, but she knew it was no affectation on his part. Everything about him was perfectly natural, from the style of his hair, which was the only possible frame for his firm, square face, to the faint five-o'clock shadow, which would be present no matter how closely he shaved, to the firm, athletic body burnished by the sun—what God had in mind, she thought unaccountably, when he created man.

Then, annoyed with herself for the thought, she said abruptly, "I have to check on dinner."

"Aren't you impressed?" he insisted, following her. The teasing light was still in his eyes. "That comment you made on the plane really hurt, you know. What a thing to say to a fellow who'd just escaped a jungle hospital!"

She looked him over once, critically. "You look very...neat," she told him finally. She turned to check on the steaks, kneeling this time instead of bending.

"Thank you for those crumbs, my lady," he replied airily. Then, "Can I help with dinner, or do you find the sight of an almost nude male body too distracting?"

She turned back to the oven with a great display of dignified nonchalance, which was just in time to hide her furious blush. He wandered off, chuckling, apparently convinced he was not going to get a rise out of her.

He changed into a more presentable pair of jeans and a short-sleeved cream-colored pullover for dinner, and he could not resist whispering to Barbara with a grin as she set his plate before him, "Better?" She frowned and made no reply, but she could not help noticing during dinner how well the light color of his shirt set off his tan arms.

When they were finished, Kyle volunteered, "I'll help Bobbie with the dishes, Kate. You and Mike go relax for a while."

Kate accepted his offer gratefully, and when they were alone, Barbara commented, "That was very gallant of you, I'm sure, but why didn't it occur to you to volunteer you and Michael to do the dishes? Kate and I cooked the meal, after all!"

"One," he replied, balancing a plate and a glass in one hand with difficulty as he made his way toward the swinging doors, "you're much better company than Mike, believe it or not. Two, Katie and Mike get little enough time to spend together as it is."

She took the dishes from him impatiently. "Go sit down before you break something. I'll do this."

"And three," he continued imperviously, holding the door for her as she pushed through, "Kate looked out on her feet. Didn't you notice?"

Barbara hesitated as she stacked the dishes in the sink. She honestly had not noticed anything about Kate—she had been too busy noticing everything about Kyle.

"I think the best way to do this," he suggested, "is for you to clear the table and let me rinse and load the dishwasher. It will avoid a lot of accidents in the long run."

"I really don't need any help," she insisted and went back through the swinging door.

"Don't you think I know that?" he answered mildly.

She was annoyed and impatient with the perverse attraction she was beginning to feel for Kyle. Was it because he had been the first man to kiss her since Daniel? Could she really be so shallow as to let a little thing like that set her emotions in a turmoil? Or was it simply that it had been so long—if ever—that she had been around such a vital, physically attractive man? Was it because—and this disturbed her most— he could make her laugh, when she had not felt like laughing in over a year?

In an uncomfortable state of confusion and irritability over these reflections, she demanded as she came back through swinging doors, "How long are you staying, anyway?"

His face relaxed into a sensuous half-smile. "Oh, I don't know. How long do you want me to stay?"

"It wouldn't bother me," she retorted, "if you left tonight!"

He sighed, "Fickle, thy name is woman! And to think, only this morning. . ."

She went back into the dining room to avoid the rest of his reminiscences.

When she returned with the last of the dishes, he suggested easily, "If it bothers you that much to have me around, you know how to get rid of me, don't you?"

"Pray tell!" She deposited the dishes under the stream of running water and he began to rinse and stack them efficiently in the dishwasher.

"All you have to do," he suggested, glancing at her with a twinkle, "is tell Katie that I've been hitting on her little sister, and she'll have me packed and out of here so fast it will make your head spin."

Barbara paused, regarding him coolly, although a smile was playing with her lips. "Kate already knows," she informed him.

He looked up in mild surprise. "Is that right? What did she say?"

"What could she say?" replied Barbara. "She obviously thinks you hold the secret to tomorrow, and I'm a little too old to be posted with a chaperone."

Kyle laughed. "Dear Katie! What a girl!"

"She did, however," Barbara added slyly, "mention that you have a certain reputation with women."

"A good one, I hope," he interjected.

"That depends on your point of view," she answered dryly.

He closed the dishwasher and locked it. "What else did she say?"

"She seems to think," ventured Barbara hesitantly, "that you might still be in love with your wife."

Now he was startled. He stared at her. "What a strange thing for her to say!" She did not think he was lying. "Katie knows better than that!" He peered at her curiously. "Are you sure you didn't misunderstand?"

She dropped her eyes. "Perhaps I did," she admitted and hurried back to the dining room to gather up the place mats.

She scolded herself inwardly for bringing up a subject that was none of her business. What did she care what Kyle's relationship with his ex-wife was? And Kate had not said that he still loved her, only that he had been upset by the divorce. Then why had she felt compelled to catch his reaction when she suggested that he might still be in love with the woman?

When she came back into the kitchen, it was empty. The dishwasher was running noisily, the counters had been sponged clean, and the patio doors were open, a slight breeze billowing the sheer curtains. She could see Kyle's silhouette in the moonlight on the terrace.

"Come out here for a minute, Bobbie," he called.

She hesitated, then folded the place mats into their drawer and went outside.

The night was dark and still, the only sound that of the gentle whisper of the surf below them. A crescent moon wandered lazily in and out of smoky royal-blue clouds, and the air was rich with the scent of clematis. She took a deep, luxurious breath and went to stand beside him, lifting her face to the cool night air.

"Beautiful, isn't it?" he said softly.

She nodded in silent agreement.

"Do you know the saying 'If I had two lives, I would spend one at home and the other traveling abroad'? Well, if I had two lives, I guess I would spend one on the seashore and one in the mountains."

She leaned on the rail, watching the foamy white-caps of the restless sea. "Seems like you already do."

"Have two lives?"

"Spend half your time in the mountains and half here on the coast."

He gave a small laugh. "Wish I could!"

"I believe a person can do anything he wants—if he wants to badly enough. So what's your excuse?"

"A very simple one," he replied. "Alimony."

She winced. She had unintentionally brought up the subject of his ex-wife again, and for some reason the prospect of discussing her seemed particularly distasteful standing here in the moonlight with him while the music of the surf sang in her ears and the gentle garden scents worked their subtle aphrodisiac magic on her senses.

As though reading her thoughts, he offered matter-of-factly, "I'm not still in love with Rose-anne, by the way. I think I may have mentioned to you that I'm not sure I ever was. I don't hate her," he added in a moment, "but I certainly don't love her. I just wanted to get that cleared up."

"It doesn't matter to me in the least," she responded, keeping her gaze determinedly fixed on the repetitively disintegrating whitecaps.

His tone was faintly mocking. "I know it doesn't." Then he changed the subject. "And what about you? Are you doing exactly what you want to do?"

She sighed dreamily, soaking in the view and the

gentle night air and the provocative floral scents. "Right now I am."

She knew that sounded like an invitation, and even though she had not meant it that way, she did not try to shrug away from the gentle caress of his hand on her shoulder. He said softly, "I'm glad to hear that."

The feel of his strong fingers through the light material of her blouse sent a light shiver of excitement down her spine, completely uncontrollable. He inquired, "Cold?"

She knew that to tell him she was not would be an admission of what his casual touch had done to her, so she said nothing and let him drape his arm around her shoulders and draw her a little closer, ostensibly for warmth. Then he said, "What I meant was, your work. Is that what you want to do?"

What she wanted to do was to relax completely in the crook of his arm, rest her head against his hair, let the warmth of his body flow through her and surround her. But she tried to put that thought out of her mind. Kyle's casual embrace was no more than a gesture of friendship to Kate's little sister, an action as natural to an open, unaffected man like him as breathing. She must learn not to forget that and to stop being so disturbed in his presence.

She answered noncommittally, "It's okay, I guess. I'm actually what you might call temporarily unemployed at the moment, but I was working in a record shop in Cincinnati before. It passed the hours."

"Doesn't sound very challenging."

"It wasn't."

"You were an editor on a music magazine before?"

She glanced at him. "How did you know that?"

"I asked Kate after she mentioned it at tea the other day."

She turned back to look out over the sea. That all seemed so far away. "Yes, I was."

"Why did you quit?"

She lifted her shoulders slightly. The movement caused a new awareness of the strong, warm protection of Kyle's arm. "I took a leave of absence when Daniel became ill. Afterward there just didn't seem much point in going back."

"Painful memories?"

"Maybe."

"And maybe," he suggested thoughtfully, "taking a menial, unsatisfying job seemed like a good way to punish yourself for continuing to live after your husband had died."

She jerked away from him, staring at him in shock and anger. Anger, perhaps because he had come too close to the truth? "What are you?" she demanded. "A psychiatrist or something?"

"No," he returned gently. "Just a student of human nature. Did I hit a nerve?"

She turned away from him with a jerky movement, trying to focus blurry eyes on the distant seascape. "It's none of your business."

"I've decided to make you my business," he responded softly, very close behind her. "Which makes everything about your past, present, and future my concern."

He was so close now that she could feel his breath brush across her cheek. She made herself go stiff as his hands touched her shoulders, but it was difficult to maintain her anger and her resistance toward him when her pulse was pounding in her ears and her lungs seemed to have diminished their capacity by at least fifty percent. She managed stiffly, "And suppose I don't care to have you meddling in my past, present, or future?"

"You haven't any choice." Whether he moved or it was the relaxation of her own body that caused the contact she did not know, but now they were touching at all points, the length of her back fitting into the warm envelope of his embrace as though they were designed to do so, his arms linked about her waist, his chin resting lightly atop her head. "There isn't much I can do about your past tonight," he continued in a low sensuously mesmerizing tone, "and for the future you already know my prescription—a new life, a new job, a new house...a new love. For the present..." He turned her around gently and looked deep into her eyes, his face very close.

"Don't," she whispered.

He did not move, nor lessen his light, caressing embrace. He said softly, "Don't what?"

She felt like putty in his hands, imagining that if he released her she would melt into a pool of helplessness at his feet. She could not even turn her head, to put a safe distance between her face and the soft warmth of his lips she remembered so distinctly from the morning. She managed, "Don't do what you were going to do."

He insisted in a low half whisper, "And what was that?"

She dropped her eyes. "You were going to...kiss me."

Still he did not move, but when she glanced up, she imagined the trace of a faint, tender smile curving his lips. "What makes you think that just because I'm standing in the moonlight with the sound of the surf in the background and romance in the air and a soft, delectable girl in my arms that I'm thinking of kissing anyone?''

She tried to step miserably away. ''Just...don't.''

She knew that Kyle was not the type of man to ever force his attentions on any woman. Probably he had never had to. His arms made to release her, but one hand came up to gently cup her chin, raising her face so that she had to look at him. ''Do you have any idea,'' he inquired softly, ''how beautiful you look after you've been kissed? How soft and moist your lips are, how deep and starry your eyes get, how rosy your skin is? Do you have any idea—'' one finger traced a lazy, sensuous pattern around the lobe of her ear, and she shivered ''—how badly you need kissing tonight?''

He bent toward her, and her resistance melted. She longed again for the possessive warmth of his mouth on hers, for the feel of his fingers light and caressing on her back and her neck and her face, for the strength of his broad shoulders beneath her own hands.

But, to her surprise, all he did was drop a light kiss on her hair, and then he sighed heavily, his fingers lingering on her face. ''Damn this cast.''

In her confusion and, yes, disappointment, she said only the first thing that came to mind. ''Why?''

''Because,'' he explained huskily, ''it's keeping me from doing right now the thing that I want to do more than anything in the world.''

A wild pulse began to race in her throat; she searched his face expectantly and breathlessly and managed, ''What is that?''

She saw his eyes crinkle with a smile, and he touched the tip of her nose lightly. ''I want to walk with you on the beach, of course. What did you think I meant?''

It must have been obvious what she thought, even before she dropped her eyes, because he laughed. "Say good night, you little tease, before I start believing what your eyes say instead of what your mouth says. You're as transparent as glass, Bobbie."

She flared at him. "I am not a tease!"

"No," he agreed equitably, "you're just a little mixed up. But I can wait. I don't want you saying later that I took advantage of your momentary weakness, and this morning we agreed on a couple of weeks to think it over, didn't we?"

She stared at him, speechless and outraged. "Y-you," she stammered at last. "You're impossible!"

As she stalked past him she heard him laughing softly. "Good night, Bobbie," he called after her.

Chapter Four

For the first time in the week Barbara had been there, she had the day entirely to herself. Kate had gone out of her way to keep her younger sister occupied, taking her on sight-seeing tours along the coast or browsing the endless antique shops dotting the highway. They had gone on long walks on the beach and had engaged in marathon talking sessions that lasted well after midnight. Those heart-to-heart conversations had done more to bolster Barbara's spirits than anything else. They had a year of catching up to do, and for the first time Barbara was really able to share with someone her poignant memories of Daniel and her own deeply buried feelings about his loss, and it helped. She began to wish she had made this trip much sooner, for there was no substitute for the confidence between sisters.

Almost as though sensing Barbara's need for her sister's restorative company, Kyle made an effort to put himself in the background for a while. He made a great show of grumbling and complaining about having nothing better to do than work, before retreating to his room with his typewriter every day, but Barbara was really rather glad to have the breathing space. Kyle's company was invigorating, but it was also a little disturbing, and she needed the time to put a few things about her life in perspective without the additional confusion of outside intervention.

As a result of Kate's preoccupation, Michael announced that he was able to make real progress on his book and expected to have it wrapped up within a few days. And also as a result of the two sisters' self-involving reunion, the housework had fallen slightly behind, for Kate was always able to find something more exciting to do than chores now that she had a reason for taking a vacation. The house had an over-all neglected, slightly dusty look—"lived-in," Kate called it—and Barbara decided to use her free time in pursuit of a craft she really enjoyed: housekeeping.

She was not really certain where Michael and Kate had gone, but her sister had told her not to expect them back for lunch. In the morning she made the beds with fresh linen, dusted and vacuumed the up-stairs, and gathered up the laundry and took it down-stairs to the washing machine. As she went about the dusting and straightening downstairs, she could hear Kyle grumbling and swearing under his breath as he pecked at the typewriter with painful slowness, and she smiled to herself every time she passed the half-open door of his room. *What he really needs,* she thought, *is a good typist.*

On her last sweep of the front room before going to check the laundry, she decided to offer him a break. She knocked lightly on the door and as it swung open she inquired, "Do you want some lunch?"

He was sitting at the small desk, glowering at the paper that protruded from the manual typewriter before him. On the desk and floor surrounding him were crumpled balls of discarded paper—he had made no effort whatsoever to hit the trash can. His notes and reference books were similarly scattered in a random display from floor to desk, with sheets of carbon paper and paper clips only adding to the general disarray. His bed was unmade, closet doors and drawers were open, and clothes spilled in a tangled litter across the room. Glasses and coffee cups were perched on every unlikely surface from the window-sill to the floor beneath the bed.

He hardly glanced up when she spoke, so she stepped in, wrinkling her nose in distaste. "This place is a mess," she announced.

"So I'm not much of a housekeeper," he grumbled, jerking the paper out of the typewriter. "I always clean it up before I leave."

"If the rats don't beat you to it," she returned, bending to scoop some of the crumpled papers into the trash can. Automatically she began to gather up his clothes from the floor. "Do you want these washed?"

"I don't know," he replied absently, rolling a fresh sheet of paper into the typewriter. "Are they dirty?"

She looked at him in exasperation. "Now, how in the world would I know?" she demanded. "They're your clothes!"

He looked at her, as though for the first time noticing she was there. Slowly his brow cleared as he took in her jeaned figure covered by Kate's denim work apron and topped with a blue bandanna over her curls, and he commented, "Say, you look kind of cute—the picture of domesticity. Do you do windows?"

She made a face at him and turned to go.

"Bobbie, wait."

When she turned again, the preoccupied scowl was back on his face, and he was studying a sheaf of papers in his hand. "Put those things down," he commanded. "The laundry can wait. Take a look at this."

As she hesitated he thrust the papers toward her. She dumped the clothes on a nearby chair and came over to him slowly, a doubtful frown disturbing her face. One thing she had learned from the years of living with Daniel and associating with his friends was never criticize a creative effort, no matter how much the artist begged, not if you wanted to keep a friend. She began, "Kyle, I don't really want to—"

But he insisted. "Just look at it," he demanded shortly. "That's all I ask. Just look."

Cautiously she took the papers and scanned them with a growing dread in the pit of her stomach, ever aware of his glare boring into her. She deliberately played for time, although she knew the project was hopeless after glancing over the first page. Filled with typographical errors, strike-throughs, inconsistencies, grammatical errors, and unfinished sentences, it made no sense whatsoever. She swallowed hard, twice, before returning the pages to him hesitantly.

"Well?" he demanded, glowering.

"Well. . ." She avoided his eyes. But she couldn't lie about something that bad. What did he expect from her, after all? *He* had written that mess, not she! "It's pitiful," she announced, and then quickly wished she had made a better choice of words. She could only add, "I'm sorry," and she turned quickly to make her escape, knowing Kyle would never forgive her and hating herself for being so cruel and the necessity for it.

But he stopped her with an impatient, "No, I mean, what do you think?"

She stared at him. His brows were still drawn together ominously, his lips tight, but now his frustration was directed at her, and not at the papers. She felt her own impatience mount. Could he possibly be so thick-headed? What did he want from her? Michael would have told him exactly the same thing.

"I mean," he clarified with an angry tone to his voice, "can you fix it?"

Her eyes widened in astonishment. "Fix it?" she demanded. "I don't even know what it's about!"

He made a sharp gesture that threatened to spill the papers on the floor; she stepped forward quickly to rescue them. "It's about houses," he explained shortly. "That is, not houses specifically, but designs and structure, more or less."

"No wonder your manuscript doesn't make any sense," she told him dryly. "Apparently even you don't know what you're talking about."

He glared at her. "Will you sit down and let me explain this to you?"

The corners of her mouth turned down as she debated. Then she decided, "It's your problem, okay? Just leave me out of it." She had already gotten herself into enough trouble by offering an unflattering opinion—no matter that it was asked.

"Get off your high horse and listen for a minute," he retorted. "It so happens that I am offering you a job."

She gaped at him in astonishment, and then decided to make light of it. "As what?" she retorted. "Your mistress or your housekeeper?"

That caused the perpetual frown on his features to smooth out into more relaxed lines. "I mean a paying job," he specified.

"Well," she returned thoughtfully, "I understood housekeepers made pretty good wages."

"*My* housekeepers," he returned, a mischievous spark in his eyes, "like my mistresses, have always been more interested in the fringe benefits."

She gave him a superior smile. "Your fringe benefits don't interest me in the least. And neither does your job. So if you'll excuse me. . .''

"Bobbie, I'm serious." He reached out a hand to detain her, the bantering smile replaced by the familiar worried scowl. "This thing is driving me up a wall. I know what I want to say, but I just don't have the patience to put it into words. If you'll just stay and let me outline it for you, then you can decide whether you're interested or not."

But she already knew she was not interested in working for Kyle—or with him. She silently cursed her sister for ever suggesting it. She said, as she hesitated in the doorway, "I don't want a job, thanks. I'm on vacation."

"Oh," he retorted. "Kate didn't mention her sister was independently wealthy."

Now it was her turn to frown. "That's not the point and you know it. I just don't want *your* job."

"How can you say that when you don't even know what it is?" he demanded. He added, "Ten percent of my royalty on every copy sold, or a cash fee in advance roughly equivalent. Take your pick. You couldn't ask for a fairer deal."

She hesitated, biting her underlip. He was really serious, and he seemed a little desperate. Then she suggested dryly, "Plus a cut on the movie rights?"

He grinned. "Plus movie rights. Now will you sit down?"

With his foot he hooked the rung of a chair and drew it up near the desk. After a moment she sat down.

"You told me the book was about your work," she said. "But you never told me what your work was. So far the only thing I know for sure is that you're *not* a writer."

"I'm an architect."

She glanced at him in wry amusement. "From the way you were keeping it secret, I expected something much more glamorous. CIA or double agent at the very least. What kind of architect gets to travel all over the world breaking his leg in the line of duty?"

"A very good one," he retorted. "Actually my claim to fame is in my designs for energy-efficient structures. I've patented a few devices that can be incorporated into specially designed buildings to make them almost completely self-sufficient. I also do a lot with passive solar heating and cooling, and *that*'s how I broke my leg—supervising the construction of a house that was being built into a cliff."

"I'm impressed," she murmured.

He was emptying out drawers, piling on top of the desk thick manila folders from which glossy photographs and illegible handwritten notes spilled out. "It's not going to be that complicated," he went on. "The bulk of the book is going to be photographs and illustrations. The trick is writing a text simple enough so that the average home-builder can follow it but with all the technical data an engineer would need to understand the principles."

She glanced through some of the photographs. "Are all these your houses?"

"Umm-hmm." He was flipping through one of the folders, looking for something. "Ah, here it is." He held the photograph out to her. "Your basic cave-dwelling. Three of the walls are earth and rock six feet deep at the narrowest point. The year-round temperature is seventy-two degrees."

She looked at it, and she really was impressed. The facade was an angular stone-pillared structure that seemed to fade right into the landscape. He brought out some pictures of the inside, pointing out various

energy-saving techniques incorporated into the deco-
rating scheme. Although it was all very rustic and
charming, she had to point out, "There are no windows."

"That can be a problem," he admitted. "Some
people tend to go a little crazy in a building without
windows. Fortunately in this one we were able to cut
a skylight here. It brought the temperature up a few
degrees, but it was a moderate climate so it didn't
really matter that much. Now, my underground
house was a different story altogether."

He brought out another set of photographs, and
Barbara was completely caught up in his enthusiastic
explanation of his work. "We were able to keep the
temperature here a steady sixty-eight degrees by
working with underground air pockets, and, see, the
illusion of windows by using murals and special light-
ing."

"This is fantastic," she had to admit. "Do you do
anything else besides underground and cave houses?
I mean, anything with real windows?"

He laughed. "Take a look at this. It's the Arizona
Sun House. It was an experimental project for the
government. It's been standing five years now and
hasn't used one therm of artificial energy." It looked
like a fantasy from the twenty-first century resting on
the surface of some barren planet, all glass and
chrome and angles. "The solar collectors actually inspired the design," he explained. "It's as ugly as sin
and twice as expensive, but it works."

She glanced through the remaining photographs,
unable to restrain a murmur of admiration here and
there. At last she looked up. "The first thing you
have to do, of course," she volunteered, "is organize
all the material under chapter headings. You can't

begin to put it together until you know where you're going."

"Can you do it, Bobbie?" he asked. "Can you help me write the text?"

She hesitated. "Of course I *can*," she answered. "But—"

"I promise," he interrupted with a sober expression that was only marred by the twinkle in his eyes, "I won't chase you around the desk during working hours, if that's what you're worried about. It won't be easy to keep my lust under control, but right now I'm more interested in your brains."

She turned back in irritation to the photographs, hiding a blush. "Don't be ridiculous," she snapped.

"Then maybe," he suggested, "you're afraid you won't be able to keep your hands off me?"

"You're about to lose a collaborator," she warned.

He laughed. "Okay, I'll behave myself. Will you do it?"

She really was not certain it was such a good idea to spend so much time with Kyle, but she could hardly admit that the reasons he had suggested for her reluctance were no less than the exact truth. Finally she agreed grudgingly, "All right, I'll help you get started. But I don't want any money for it."

He looked genuinely perplexed. "But why not? I'm getting money for it."

She grew uncomfortable. "It just wouldn't be right. You're Kate's brother-in-law, after all, practically one of the family...."

"I certainly hope you don't look at me that way," he interrupted seriously.

"What way?"

"As part of the family."

She was disturbed and flustered by the earnest light in his deep green eyes, and she continued quickly, "Besides, it's not really work. I don't have anything better to do and— It just wouldn't be right, taking money from you."

"A labor of love?" he suggested, eyes twinkling.

She scowled, and stood up. "Get this mess cleaned up," she advised. "I'm going to fix lunch."

"Can we start this afternoon?" he suggested hopefully.

She felt a small satisfaction in returning, "No, I'm too busy. Maybe tomorrow. Lunch will be ready in half an hour."

But then she turned, taking up the original papers he had shown her and studying them thoughtfully for a moment. "Tell me something," she asked, finally, returning the papers to him. "Are you really this bad?"

He grinned. "I had to get your sympathy somehow, didn't I?"

She made a small sound of exasperation and stalked away.

She served Kyle lunch at his desk while he attempted to make order of his notes and photographs, and she went about her chores. As she worked, her mind kept wandering back to the agreement she had made with Kyle, and she wondered again if it was such a good idea. At least his work was interesting, and she thought she would enjoy helping him put it together into a book—if he kept his promise and kept to business only during business hours.

She was folding clean towels in the laundry room when Kate suddenly burst in, her color high and her eyes sparkling. She closed the door behind her and leaned on it, and Barbara demanded in amazement,

"What in the world happened to you? Did you just inherit a fortune?"

"Better!" Kate said softly, her face radiant. "Oh, Babs," she whispered, "I'm going to have a baby!"

Barbara was stunned for just a minute, and then she ran to Kate and embraced her. "A baby!" she cried. "Kate, I can't believe it! It's wonderful!" Then she pushed her a little away and demanded, "Are you sure? When—"

"Just today!" Kate responded, laughing. "That is, we've suspected for a little while now, but Michael went with me today and the doctor confirmed everything." She brought her hands suddenly to her face and her eyes were two sparkling jewels between splayed fingers. "Oh, I just can't believe it! January," she added. "It's due in January."

"I'm going to be an aunt," wondered Barbara.

Kate clasped Barbara's hands suddenly and drew her down beside her on the low bench that served as a folding table, spilling towels to the floor. "Babs," she said with an unexpected touch of sobriety, "the reason I didn't mention anything to you before—before I was sure, I mean—is because, well—" She dropped her eyes briefly. "I know that this was the year you and Daniel would have started your family, and...well, I just hope..."

She lifted her eyes worriedly, and Barbara dismissed it with an earnest "No, not at all! I'm just so happy for you! And for me," she added with a giggle. "I'm going to be an aunt!"

The two girls embraced again briefly, and Kate said, her eyes shining, "It's just that we were beginning to think it might never happen. I'm over thirty, you know," she admitted.

Barbara teased, "A little bit!" and Kate made a face at her.

"The other thing is," Kate added happily, "Michael has to be in New York next week, to meet with his editor about the new book, and he's asked me to go along. As a kind of second honeymoon—or the last vacation we'll ever be able to take alone together! We thought we'd take about three weeks, and from New York go...oh, I don't know where! Just wherever the fancy strikes."

"That sounds marvelous," agreed Barbara, and she hoped Kate did not notice it was not with unqualified enthusiasm. For of course if her host and hostess were leaving, Barbara's own vacation would have to come to an early end. And she was really enjoying herself here. She didn't want to leave. Besides, there was Kyle—and his book, of course.

Still, she volunteered cheerfully, "That's great. I think I'll spend the rest of the summer with Mom and Dad, you know how they're always begging—"

Kate looked horrified. "Oh, no, I didn't mean that *you* should leave! My goodness, we'll only be gone a few weeks, that's no reason for you to leave. I want you to stay!"

Barbara smiled. "Thanks, Kate, but that's really kind of silly. I came to see you, after all, and I've seen you and had a great time, but what's the point—"

"But I was counting on you to stay," insisted Kate. "Why, there's the party coming up—we'll be back in plenty of time for that! And Jojo," she added suddenly. "Who's going to take care of Jojo if you leave? He hates kennels. And we've already made an appointment with the exterminators. Really, Babs, I was counting on you."

"Kyle," Barbara reminded her patiently, "will be here to take care of all those things. And I really don't think—"

"Oh, Kyle." Kate waved the suggestion away. "He can't be counted on to stay. He's in the middle of this court thing, and he could get a call about one of his buildings that would take him away on less than a day's notice. . . . If you're worried about staying alone in the house with Kyle," she said suddenly, "that's no problem. He's moving into the guest house as soon as he gets the cast off. Babs, please stay."

Barbara thought about it. She really did want to stay, and Kate and Michael would only be gone a few weeks. And if Kyle really was moving, it wouldn't be as though they were actually living together under one roof . . . and she was still old-fashioned enough to think things like that were important. She agreed at last, "All right. I'd really like to," and Kate hugged her again.

She and Kyle did the dishes together again that night, while Michael and Kate took a romantic stroll along the beach. "That was a great dinner," Kyle complimented her as she brought the last of the dishes in. "Don't tell Katie, but you're a much better cook than she is."

Barbara laughed lightly. "I'll be sure not to!"

"Do you like Italian food?" he asked suddenly as she began to sponge off the counters.

"Sure."

"There's a wonderful restaurant out on the highway. I'll take you there just as soon as I get mobile again—to pay you back for all the meals you've fixed for me."

"That's not necessary at all," she assured him

airily. "I fixed the meals for all of us, and I didn't do it on the installment plan."

He made a dry face and replied, "Nonetheless, we have a date. The day the cast comes off."

She inquired, trying not to sound overly anxious, "Which is?"

"Thursday," he replied and grinned. "Yes, Katie has already told me that while they're away I'm consigned to the guest house to protect your reputation. Don't worry, I'll be the perfect gentleman. Although," he added with a twinkle, "you should know I never lock my door at night, and I'll leave a light burning in the window."

"And you should know," she retorted, "that I *always* lock my door at night."

"Forewarned is forearmed," he murmured. Then he added casually, "What did you think of Katie's news?"

She glanced at him. They had talked of nothing else all through dinner, and it seemed a strange question. "I think it's great, naturally. Don't you?"

"Of course I do," he answered obscurely. "I just wasn't sure you would."

She stared at him. "Why not?"

"From what you said the other night." He locked the dishwasher and it began to purr. "About not caring too much for the idea of motherhood."

She was surprised that he remembered that casual comment, but she elucidated, "I was talking about me, not Kate. She'll make a terrific mother."

Maybe there was a note of reserve in her voice, for he seized on it quickly. "But?" he prompted.

She felt her own defenses rising to the surface. Perhaps there was just the slightest bit of jealousy of Kate after all, for even though she was thrilled at her sister's happiness and at her own prospects of becoming an aunt, she could not help wishing it were she and Daniel who were making the announcement.... She shrugged, trying to push the sorrowful thoughts aside. "It's not going to be easy on them," she said practically. "They've been alone so long, just the two of them, they have their life all arranged the way they like it. Now, suddenly, a baby, and everything is turned topsy-turvy."

He responded, involved in carefully rinsing the stainless-steel sink, "Some people might think that's a small sacrifice to make."

"Sure," she agreed. "It's just going to be an adjustment, that's all. I just wonder how Kate is going to feel when she really sits down and thinks about how it's going to change her life."

"I doubt," responded Kyle, "that she'll feel any differently than she does now."

Barbara shrugged. "Maybe. I just don't think I could make that kind of adjustment all of a sudden."

He turned to look at her, and the expression in his eyes was unreadable. "And maybe," he said quietly, "your sister is a better woman than you are." And he turned and left the room.

Barbara simply stared after him in astonishment.

Chapter Five

Michael drove Kyle into town Thursday for his appointment with the orthopedist, and Kyle returned home a free man. The first thing he did when he entered the house was to find Barbara and swing her off her feet, exclaiming, "Look, Ma, no crutches!"

She squealed and laughed as he whirled her around, beating his shoulders with her fists. "You're a nut! Put me down!"

He grinned and held her for a moment against his chest, her feet dangling a few inches above the floor. He murmured seductively against her ear, "You know what this means, don't you?"

She squirmed away from him, flustered with amusement and embarrassment. With her feet now on solid ground, she planted her hands on her hips and looked up at him, her color high and her wispy curls disordered. But her eyes were sparkling as she demanded, "No, I don't. What does it mean?"

He winked and informed her, "The time for thinking about it is over. Now we'll see some action."

"You're impossible!" she retorted, but her color deepened as she turned back to the plants she had been watering when he came in.

All the excitement had attracted Kate, and Kyle proudly showed off his new status to her. "You have a limp," she pointed out critically.

"Not to worry," he responded cheerfully. "It'll work out in a day or so. Besides," he added with a meaningful look at Barbara, "I understand climbing stairs is very good for it. And speaking of which—" he turned back to Kate "—If you'll round up your husband to give me a hand with my luggage, I'll start making myself scarce around here this minute."

"But there's no rush," protested Kate.

"No." Again he glanced at Barbara, who pretended to be very absorbed with the plants. "I'm a man of my word, and I promised I would be back where I belong the minute the cast came off. Besides," he admitted, "I'm kind of anxious to have my old place back."

Laughing, Kate went off to find Michael, and Kyle turned to Barbara. "Care to keep me company while I pack?"

She glanced at him. "Not really." It would seem strange without Kyle in the house penetrating every corner with his craziness and his humor. She thought about the three weeks ahead when she would have the entire place to herself, and the prospect suddenly seemed very lonely.

As though reading her thoughts, he gave her a crooked smile and commented, "Remember, I'll just be across the driveway."

The automatic blush that rose to her face made her scowl and turn away, practically drowning Kate's dieffenbachia with a jerky motion.

"Come on," he insisted, the teasing gone out of his voice now as he replaced it with a tone usually reserved only for working sessions. "I want to show you something."

After a moment, reluctantly, she followed him.

A transformation had come over the room since the first day she had entered it and criticized the way it was kept. Although Kate's upcoming trip had kept

Barbara too busy with her sister to spare much time for working on the book, she had seen to it that his files and working area were kept organized. Today, as well, the bed was made, the closet and dresser neatened, and the general litter that usually characterized his living habits was cleaned away. "Nice," she commented.

"I told you," he replied, "I always clean it up before I leave." He walked over to the desk. "If it's all right with you, I'd like to leave all my notes and things here, and we can continue to work in this room."

"It doesn't make any difference to me," she pointed out. "It's Kate's house."

"Oh, we'll be finished with the whole thing before they get back. She won't mind."

She lifted an eyebrow. "We've hardly started it! Do you really expect to finish an entire book in three weeks?"

"I'm a slave driver," he told her blandly. Then he continued, "I suppose you know where everything is—you set up the filing system, after all—the manuscript is in this top drawer, carbon to the left. This way," he explained, "you can work on it, proofing and editing, in your spare time when I'm not here."

"Kyle," she apologized as he turned from the desk to the closet, "I'm sorry I haven't been able to spend too much time on it this week. But it's Kate's last week and I felt I should spend it with her."

"No problem," he replied over his shoulder. "We have three weeks coming up, all to ourselves, and we're going to make up for every minute we've lost so far."

She could not tell whether there was a second meaning to his words, and she excused herself quickly and left him to his packing.

The move was accomplished without incident, and late in the afternoon Kate sent Barbara up to the guest house with a supply of clean towels and bed linen. The guest house was actually a spacious apartment over the garage, a little behind the house and toward the side facing the sea, shaded by oaks and sugar maples, but Barbara had never been inside. She climbed the steps to find the door open and Kyle bending over an array of cartons scattered on the floor. She stepped inside, murmuring "My, this is nice."

He glanced up. "Thank you. I designed it myself."

She put the linens on a dresser and looked around. The southern wall was made entirely of glass, which was of course the most striking feature. In addition a generous skylight had been cut from the roof, so that the entire room was bathed in the dazzling afternoon sun. A compact, ultramodern kitchen area occupied one corner, separated from the rest of the room by a mahogany bar and closed off with shutter doors inset with yellow and orange stained glass. The stained glass pattern was repeated on the shutters over the bar, so that the entire little kitchen, featuring bronze miniappliances and a cheery yellow and white dining booth, could be enclosed when it was not in use. The color scheme of the rest of the room was russet and pumpkin, from the gaily patterned draperies that framed the glass south wall and matching curtains on the two other windows, to the long low sofa in an earthy pattern and its companion easy chair in a solid pumpkin velvet. There were splashes of peacock-blue, scarlet, and sunshine-yellow in the patterns, picked up by throw cushions and bright red and blue and yellow scatter rugs on the gleaming hardwood floor. The king-size brass bed was covered with a puffy russet comforter with a narrow row of orange piping along the hem and the edges of the pillow shams. Overall, the unlikely combination of colors was stunning and exciting, especially in combination with the dazzling amount of natural light the room got. She knew it was an unusual color scheme for a man's room, but also thought it perfectly suited this man's vibrant, unpredictable personality.

She asked, "Did you decorate it yourself?"

"To the last hook, nail, and cushion," he replied, carrying an armload of books from a carton to the empty set of shelves near the bed. "I made a deal with Michael—he let me design and build and furnish this place to my own taste and I promised to stay out of their hair when I was visiting."

She smiled, admiring the rich wood finish on the open doors of the enormous walk-in closet and peeking into a small brown-and-yellow-checked bathroom. "You must visit a lot to go to all this trouble—and expense."

He shrugged. "Now, that depends on whom you ask, I guess. I don't think I visit enough. Kate and Michael—" he grinned "—might have a different version."

"What's all this?" she asked, poking into one of the cartons.

"Just some stuff I store here. Part of the deal is that Michael gets to use the place for other guests when I'm not here, but it makes me feel more at home to have some familiar books and pictures around when I come back."

She laughed. "From the looks of it, you *are* at home."

He turned and there was a small pensive smile on his face. "Not really, of course," he answered. "But

I spend so much time in foreign hotels that it's nice to think about a place that *feels* like home.''

"But what about your cabin in the woods?''

He took some more books from a carton. "I told you, it's too empty.''

She helped him arrange the last of the books on a shelf, and then he uncrated a stereo system and set it on the bottom shelf. Sitting on the floor, he unearthed a stack of albums from a deep carton and declared, "What is your taste, my lady? Hard rock, pop, jazz, classical, country-western. . .?''

"What?'' she replied in mock amazement. "No soft, sweet, wine-and-candlelight numbers?''

"Music to seduce pretty redheads by,'' he returned and swept one from the bottom of the stack with a flourish. "No self-respecting playboy would be without it.''

She laughed. "I'm not a redhead!'' she told him and started to step away.

But he caught her around the knees, and she squealed and flung her arms out as he dragged her, laughing, to the floor, so that she was resting half on his lap, her shoulders supported by his raised knee as he bent over her with mock scrutiny. "No,'' he agreed, delicately separating the strands of her hair with his long, slender fingers. "You're not exactly a redhead. What are you?''

"I'm *going* to be in traction,'' she replied, wiggling against the uncomfortable arch of her back, "if you don't let me go.''

He caught her wrists against his chest as she started to push away, but lowered his knee to the floor so that her back was in a more comfortable position and her head was cradled in the crook of his leg. "Natural color," he pursued, still pretending to examine her hair, "or ready-made?"

"You!" In mock anger she flailed at him, and he wrestled her playfully for a moment, laughing, until at last he subdued her and she was caught more securely than before between his strong legs.

He held both of her wrists in one of his hands and pinned them to her chest, and he leaned over her, a challenging gleam in his eye as he demanded huskily, "Had enough?"

She was laughing between panting breaths, her small breasts rising and falling rapidly beneath the light checkered material of her shirt. Her face was flushed a delicate pink and her eyes were sparkling. She retorted, "I'll bet I get you on the next round!"

But there was not going to be a next round. As she watched him the mischief in his eyes faded and was replaced by a warmer, more subtle light and the laughter turned into a gentle smile. "You're nice," he said softly, and his eyes were moving over her face in a leisurely, appreciative manner. "You're fun to be around. I hope you're around a lot, Bobbie."

His hair fell forward as he bent over her, shadowing his forehead. Barbara was very aware of his hand, strong and warm, clasped about her wrists, and the weight of it against her chest. She felt her own features soften as she looked into the gentle green lights of his eyes and her breath was not coming any easier, although the laughter was gone. She knew, in this happy moment, in this bright and colorful room with the afternoon sun streaming over them, picking up lazy motes of dust in the air and turning the glossy wood floor beneath them into a rosy-yellow hue, as she was wrapped in his arms and cuddled against his lap and everything seemed so right and natural, that he was going to kiss her. And she knew that she wanted him to.

There was a short raucous buzz, seeming twice as loud because it was so unexpected and so inopportune, and Barbara jumped. Kyle closed his eyes and said softly, "Damn."

Barbara began to squirm away as though they had been caught in an illicit act. "What is it?" she demanded as the buzzer came again.

"Telephone." He released her reluctantly, then brought her clasped hands to his lips and kissed them with a slow smile. "Next time," he promised softly, and for a moment Barbara's eyes were trapped by the steady assurance in his, and she felt a small shiver run down her spine.

Then he stood. "I have an extension to the main house," he explained, skirting the bed to reach the telephone table on the other side of it. "There's an intercom button on the main phone in the downstairs hall, also a hold. So if I ever get a call, just put them on hold and buzz me up here. I'll pick it up."

"So," she retorted, still a little high-strung from the unfulfilled encounter and the excited wondering it had left behind, "now I'm hired on as your secretary too?"

He grinned as he sat on the edge of the bed. "On the other hand," he added, "if you just want to talk to me, all you have to do is push the button. It might get kind of lonely in that big house all by yourself."

"I'll manage," she replied with mild sarcasm, and the buzzer sounded again impatiently.

Kyle answered it. "Yeah?... Okay, got it. Thanks, Kate." He turned to her with a wink. "See? Nothing to it." Then he pressed the other button and spoke into the receiver. "Okay, Stan, what've you got?"

Stan? Wasn't that the name of his attorney? And from the look that slowly crossed Kyle's face Barbara was afraid this conversation was not going to turn out much better than the last one she had overheard. She lingered at the door, uncertain whether to stay and be witness to another embarrassing one-sided telephone conversation or to leave without telling him. If he started shouting, she decided, she would sneak out.

But it was a long time before he spoke again. When he did, it was only to say quietly, "Yeah, that's what I was afraid of.... Okay, do your best, then." And at last, heavily, "Yes. So am I." He replaced the receiver, but he did not turn around immediately.

When he did look at her, there was an absent, distracted look on his face. All the good humor had faded from his eyes. It seemed an effort for him to form even the tiny smile that came to his lips, and it was not the kind of smile that she liked. It was as though he were addressing a stranger, and after the intimacy that had passed between them only a moment ago, it made Barbara feel rather cold. "Say, Bobbie," he began, and his voice sounded strained with the effort to sound casual, "I don't want you to think I'm the kind of guy who breaks dates..."

"Dates?" she repeated, frowning a little in confusion. "Did we have a date?"

His laugh was false. "Now I don't feel guilty for breaking it. I was going to take you out to dinner, remember? But to tell you the truth—" he dropped his eyes briefly, gazing aimlessly about the room "—I'm a little tired. Too much, too soon, I guess. Can we make it tomorrow?"

Barbara hesitated. He did look a little white and drawn about the lips, but only a moment ago he had felt well enough to be romping with her on the floor.... And suddenly she understood. His "fatigue" had begun with the telephone call. She said, with an uncertain smile, "Sure thing. Tonight wouldn't have been good anyway. You still have a lot to do, and I had really forgotten about it."

He nodded. "Tell Katie not to expect me for dinner. I'm going to go out in a minute and get some groceries, and I think I'll just fix a sandwich here and turn in early."

"I'll tell her." She lingered. "Do you need any help—unpacking and all?"

He hesitated. For a moment, as she looked at him, she was sure he wanted her to stay. And then he shook his head. "No, thanks. I'll see you tomorrow, okay?"

She nodded, smiled again, and turned to go.

He said, "And, Bobbie..."

She turned.

"Thanks," he added quietly.

She was surprised. "For what?"

"For not asking," he said simply.

The moment between them was honest and pure, and she could not face it for more than a moment. It had been too long since anyone had looked at her like that. She went quickly down the steps.

Her thoughts were with Kyle that evening. She had dinner with Kate and Michael, and although they did nothing to make it so, she felt excluded from their very special happiness. She tried not to think that if things had been different it would have been she and Daniel cuddling on the sofa and sharing secret smiles and looking through baby catalogs.... She thought

instead of Kyle. From the living room window she
could see the lights in the guest house still burning,
despite the fact that he had said he was going to turn
in early. She imagined he was still brooding about the
phone call, for whatever his attorney had said to him
had upset him badly.

She could only assume that his case, whatever it
was, was not going well. She wished she knew what it
was about, but clearly she could not ask. She was just
sorry for whatever his trouble was and hoped it
would be over soon. She liked him so much better
when he was being playful and boyish and just a little
nutty. . . .

Liked him. She realized suddenly that she did like
Kyle, in a way she had not liked anyone in a long
time. His companionship was easy and natural and
she felt good when she was around him. Before now
she had not thought of it that way. She knew she was
attracted to him, but what woman wouldn't be? He
was so handsome it was almost sinful, and when he
held her in his arms, she went all watery—but that
was just chemistry, just as she had told him that day
on the beach, wasn't it? She had thought it was that
chemistry that was making her a little shy of him,
afraid her senses and her perfectly natural instincts
would lead her into something she was not quite certain she was ready for. But now she wondered if it
was not something more. Wasn't it just a little bit
dangerous to be so physically attracted to the first
friend she had made since Daniel's death? Wasn't she
just setting herself up for a big fall?

Kate and Michael went to bed early, but Barbara
stayed downstairs and watched television. As she was
turning off the lights and closing up the house after
the late news, she saw Kyle's silhouette crossing the

lawn toward the beach. For a moment she was moved by the impulse to join him. But no, he had wanted to be alone tonight, he had made that clear. And she was not certain that a romantic stroll along the beach was what she needed tonight, either. She went upstairs toward her own room, disturbed.

Kate and Michael had not gone to sleep, and their door was cracked just enough to allow their voices to float across to Barbara's room.

"You may not have noticed," Kate was saying in a dry tone, "but your brother is what is commonly known as a woman-slayer. He's much too good-looking for his own good—or that of any unfortunate woman who happens to cross his path."

Barbara's curiosity was piqued by that, and she did not close her own door immediately. Michael replied airily, "I understand anxious mamas lock their daughters away when he passes through town."

Barbara smothered a giggle as Kate retorted, "You know I'm serious! I'm just not at all sure about leaving them alone together for all that time."

Michael's sigh was exasperated. "Come on, honey, my brother is not an animal, and both of them are, I believe, what is termed 'consenting adults.' It's none of our business and totally out of our control."

"It's just that I'm so fond of both of them," worried Kate, "and they're both so vulnerable right now."

"They're fond of you too," returned Michael sternly, "and if you would like to keep it that way, take my advice and stay out of it. So what if they fall into a little summer romance? It could be the best thing in the world for Barbara right now, and it wouldn't hurt Kyle in the least to have a girl like her around for a change. Whatever happens, it's their affair—if you'll pardon my choice of words. The best thing you can do is avoid the subject of Kyle with Barbara and vice versa. Just pretend you don't notice a thing.''

Barbara closed the door quietly. It was a natural concern, she supposed, knowing her big sister's tendency to be overprotective, and Kyle had not been exactly subtle in his playful pursuit of her. It bothered her to think she was worrying Kate. She decided the best thing to do would be to keep her interest in Kyle to herself, as much as she would have liked to discuss him with Kate. And it wasn't as though she had a real interest in him, exactly. . .just curiosity. And, right now, a great deal of confusion.

The next afternoon Kyle drove Kate and Michael to the airport, but before she left, Kate had a string of last-minute instructions for Barbara. ''You know where the household money is,'' she reminded her, ''if you need anything. The freezer's stocked, and so is the refrigerator, and there's a roast right on top that needs to be used before we get back. The plumber, electrician, and handyman are all listed in that little book on the telephone table. If there's an emergency, just have Kyle write the check and we'll pay him back.''

''Hey, come on,'' Kyle protested, laughing.

''Remember, Jojo gets a can of Alpo in the morning and keep his bowls filled with fresh water and dry dog food.''

''I know how to take care of a dog,'' Barbara put in impatiently. ''You're going to miss your plane!''

Kate gave her pet a hug and ruffled his fur affectionately. ''And his dog biscuits are on the shelf in the laundry room—''

"*Laundry* room?" interrupted Barbara incredulously.

"He'll eat the whole box," explained Kate seriously, "if you don't hide them from him. Now, I'll call you—"

"No, she won't," corrected Michael, grasping his wife's hand and pulling her inside the car. "We're on vacation and you can't reach us anywhere, so if the house burns down, call the insurance agent and make do the best you can."

"The insurance agent's number is on the..." began Kate, calling out the window, but Kyle started the car and drove off with a wave.

Barbara went back into the house, laughing a little and shaking her head. Yes, Kate would make a wonderful mother. After all, she had been practicing on her baby sister for twenty-six years.

Kyle had told her to be ready for dinner when he got back, and she was glad they were going out tonight. She was not certain how she would feel the first night alone in a strange house. Although she tried to tell herself she was not afraid to stay by herself, it had taken her a long time—perhaps too long—to get used to the nights without Daniel, even after she had moved out of their familiar apartment into the little efficiency. At home she had always left the radio on low to compensate for the sound of Daniel's deep breathing next to her. When she had been here with Kate and Michael, just knowing someone was in the next room had helped, but she was not certain how she would react in this big empty house now that she was alone again.

But for a while at least, she had something to distract her. She washed her hair and spilled a generous portion of Kate's bubblebath into the tub before stepping in. When she had soaked herself to a rosy, perfumy glow, she wrapped herself in a fluffy bath towel and sat down at the dressing table to do her nails. *Why,* she thought as she admired the pale pearl-pink polish on her nails, *I'm acting just like I'm going out on a date!* And then she realized suddenly that was exactly what it was—her first date since Daniel had died. That made her a little nervous, for some reason.

After a while she saw Kyle drive up in Michael's car and watched him go up to his apartment, taking the steps easily and with grace. Even in the cast he had somehow managed to appear confident and sure-footed; in his natural state every line of his body spoke of vital masculinity.

She assumed Kyle would only take time to shower and change, so she dragged herself away from the window to dry her hair. She fashioned it into a small pompadour and let the curls trail in little tendrils about her forehead and cheeks, then applied a small amount of shadow and mascara to emphasize her eyes. She chose one of the voile sundresses Kate had picked out for her, a white one splashed with an open pattern of peach-colored flowers. The tiny straps held up a low bodice that was gathered in the center; it had a tight waist and a circle skirt. She wore white sandals with a small heel and, as an afterthought, took up a light shawl just as she heard the front door open. It might get chilly later on.

Kyle called up the stairs, "Bobbie, are you ready?"

She appeared at the top of the stairs, and he took in his breath appreciatively as she came down. "I'll say you are," he answered his own question softly. "You look gorgeous."

She laughed lightly, but she was no more immune to the compliment than any other woman would have been. "I've never been gorgeous in my life," she replied.

"Gorgeous," he told her, tucking her arm protectively through his, "is in the eye of the beholder."

She gave him a sidelong glance and knew that if the term ever applied, it did to him. He was wearing a champagne-colored shirt beneath his light beige sports jacket, open at the throat to reveal just a hint of deeply tanned collar-bone. His cocoa-brown slacks were fashionably well fitted, and there was a high shine on his brown leather boots. The colors highlighted, rather than subdued, the golden-brown and silver-yellow tones of his hair and his tan. Barbara remembered his bedraggled appearance and tacky attire that first day on the plane and thought in amusement how little could be learned about a person from first impressions. She had never known a man who had such a natural sense of color and design, and who could put together a wardrobe so perfect that it showed not the faintest trace of vanity or affectation. She knew she would be the envy of every woman they passed tonight, and she was not wrong. A woman could always spot the admiring glances given her escort by other women, but Kyle appeared not to notice.

Some devilish streak in her compelled her to point it out to him as they were seated. "Did you ever consider traveling with a bodyguard?" she suggested mischievously.

He glanced up from the menu in slight puzzlement. "Why?"

"Didn't you see the drooling look the waitress gave you?" she insisted. "And I wouldn't be at all surprised if the other women in the place didn't try to attack you before you leave.''

He glanced around in feigned interest. ''Is that right?'' Then he turned back to the menu and murmured, ''Must be my cologne.''

She giggled. But then she felt compelled to add, ''You must know a lot of girls around here.''

''A few,'' he admitted. ''Do you feel exotic tonight, or do you want to stay with the staples? The manicotti here is out of this world.''

''Manicotti,'' she answered, but she couldn't let the subject drop, although she no longer felt like teasing him. ''I suppose,'' she added, toying with the edge of her napkin, ''you'll be looking some of them up, now that you're back.''

He folded the menu. ''Who?''

''Your girl friends.''

His lips curved into a patient smile and he shook his head slightly. ''I don't have any girl friends. And even if I did, I would have forgotten all about them tonight. Tonight I'm with the only girl I want to be with and I've waited too long for it to waste time talking about others.'' Now his smile became more tender, as though he were discovering an interesting surprise in her eyes. ''You didn't tell me you were the jealous type.''

''I'm not,'' she replied immediately and snapped open her menu. ''Let's order.''

He laughed softly.

''Do you think you'll be staying with Kate and Michael after the summer is over,'' he asked as the manicotti was served, ''now that Katie's pregnant?''

She glanced at him. ''Why should that make any difference?''

He lifted his shoulders lightly and reached for his

wineglass. "I'm sure they'll ask you. Pregnant women get moody, and it will be good for Kate to have you around."

For some reason it embarrassed her a little to hear a man as masculine as Kyle refer to pregnancy and its various discomforts so casually, but she quickly told herself she was being silly. After all, they weren't living in the Victorian age, and his sister-in-law's pregnancy was probably not the first Kyle had encountered. She admitted, "I would like to see the baby, of course, and if I go back to Cincinnati, I don't know when I'll be able to afford the trip again. But I can't impose on them forever."

"Why would it be imposing?" he inquired. "They're family."

She smiled. It all sounded so simple when he said it. She thought that she and Kate were every bit as close as he and Michael were, so why should she feel as if she was imposing when she came for a short visit, while he was confident enough to build his house in their backyard? Perhaps it was simply that Kyle was used to taking with certainty and enthusiasm whatever life offered and she was too afraid of rejection to ask.

"Anyway," she said, "I don't see what difference it should make to you."

"That's obvious," he told her, smiling. "I'm here. It would be convenient if you were too."

"Convenient, is it?" she replied airily and threatened him with her wineglass playfully. Then she added, "But you won't be here forever."

"True," he admitted easily. "But I would like to know where to find you."

The words, though she did not take time to analyze whether or not they were sincere, caused a small thrill of pleasure to course through her, and she turned back quickly to her meal before he noticed it.

"Besides," he added, serious now. "I'm not sure it's the best thing for you to go back to Cincinnati."

She looked up at him in surprise. "Why not?"

He met her eyes evenly across the candlelit table. "That's where you and Daniel lived together, isn't it?"

She dropped her eyes in confusion. "Yes, but—"

"And every time you walk down the street you remember walking it with him," he continued in a quiet, unconstrained tone that went right to her heart. "You can't go into a movie theater without remembering a picture you saw with him. You can't go into a department store without remembering Christmas shopping together, or pass a restaurant where the two of you did not go or promise yourselves you'd go...." Tears were beginning to sting her eyes; she blinked them back rapidly. "You thought you had gotten rid of the painful memories," he continued gently, "when you gave away his clothes and moved out of the apartment you had shared with him, but it wasn't that easy, was it?"

She shook her head blindly, staring at the steaming dish before her, which only a moment ago had been so appetizing. Then she struggled to get hold of herself. "Other people," she managed, "lose husbands and they don't have to move out of the state to get over it. I don't think that's the answer."

"Not everyone," Kyle pointed out, "was as much in love as you obviously were."

She looked at him, and in her eyes was mute gratitude and wonder for his sensitivity. Had anyone understood quite so clearly? Had anyone ever been able to impart that understanding to her in such a gentle, matter-of-fact way, somehow touching the most painful parts of her without causing it to hurt?

"It may not be an answer," he added, and his eyes softened with an encouraging smile. "But it's a start. Think about it."

She would think about it. Maine was beautiful, and though she knew she could not go on living with Kate, it would be nice to be near her, especially when the baby came. Of course she would have to find a job and a place of her own.... She began to be excited at the prospect.

"I don't think I'm ready for dancing yet," he told her as he paid the check and they left the restaurant, "but we can go someplace and have a few drinks, if you'd like."

She laughed as they stepped out into the night air. She was right, it had turned a little chilly, but the effects of the wine and Kyle's arm about her shoulders more than compensated for it. "Thanks," she said, "but the wine at dinner was more than enough."

"Fine," he agreed as he helped her into the car. "We'll move right along to the second of the three things I promised I would do as soon as I could walk again."

She glanced up at him. "The second?" She remembered the promise of the Italian restaurant, but—

"Walking on the beach with you," he reminded her. "Remember?"

"Oh." But she was still confused. "What was the third?"

He leaned over her with a provocative gleam in his eye. "Now, you can't have forgotten *that*," he told her and touched her nose lightly.

It came back to her as he slid behind the wheel of

the car, and she was grateful the darkness hid the tingle of color that touched her cheeks. She remembered his saying, "Let's take a couple of weeks to think it over, let me get this cast off...." He really was incredible.

She took her shoes off and swung them in her free hand as they walked along the surf's edge, loving the feel of the cool sand beneath her stockinged toes. The other hand rested quite naturally inside Kyle's large warm one. The breeze blew her stray curls about her face, tickling her cheeks, and the close, hypnotic rush of the surf was sensuous and absorbing. The moonlight turned the sand to a shimmering silver and reflected soft jewels in the foam of the rolling sea. Far in the distance a muffled foghorn sounded, and Kyle pointed out to her the barely discernible silhouette of an oil tanker on the horizon.

"How can you be sure it's a tanker," she inquired curiously, "at this distance?"

"Some things," he told her dryly, "you never forget." He explained, "My first job was on one of those things. I was underage, of course, but I made up for that minor deficiency in ingenuity and determination. I don't think they ever caught on to me. I may have been just a kid, but I was doing a man's work for eighteen months."

She looked at him in growing fascination. "That sounds like every boy's dream—to run away to sea! I never knew anyone who actually did it. Tell me about it."

He shrugged lightly. "There's not much to tell. I was crazy and headstrong, and while Mike was writing his first best-selling novel, I was seeing the world on the back of an oil tanker and driving my parents to an early grave. I returned home at the end of my hitch chastened and world-wise, saw the error of my ways, and went on to finish college like a good boy. It was a stupid thing to do to my family and I worked like hell the next few years to make up for it.''

"And went on to become an eminently successful architect," she suggested. "Steady and levelheaded and everything your parents had always wanted you to be.''

"Right," he agreed with a grin.

"But," she went on, "you never got over your restlessness, your yearning to see the world.''

"Wrong," he corrected, laughing. "I got over it the minute I set foot on solid ground again. I think maybe I saw too much of the world too soon, and that's why my biggest fantasy now is to settle down in one place and never have to move again. Sometimes I think all the traveling I have to do now is my punishment for running away when I was a teen-ager.''

"You should have listened to your parents," she told him in an exaggerated pretense of wisdom.

"Impossible," he assured her. "I'd like to hope my children will be a little smarter, but they probably won't.''

She thought how much she had discovered about him since she had first taken him for an annoying playboy on the plane, and how differently he had turned out than from what she had imagined. He was funny and sweet, playful and wise, tender and compassionate—a man with the world at his feet who wanted no more than a quiet place to call his own with wife and children at the door. A few weeks ago she could never have envisioned Kyle Waters fixing a leaky faucet or assembling Christmas toys; now it was not quite so hard.

"Kate's baby will be lucky to have you for an

uncle,'' she told him suddenly, for no particular reason.

There was a startled appreciation in his eyes, and it embarrassed her because she did not know why she had said it. But then he eased the moment by musing out loud, ''You know, I've been thinking. . . when the baby comes, you and I will be his aunt and uncle. I wonder what that makes us to each other?''

''Brother and sister?'' she suggested lightly.

He stopped and turned to face her, and he looked at her for such a long time that she began to blush. ''I hope,'' he said at last, seriously, ''that you don't think of me as a brother.'' Then he kissed her.

She was lost from the first moment. She felt her arms go around him instinctively, almost for support against the dizzying sensations his lips and the restless roaming of his hands on the bare portions of her back sent shuddering through her. Her heart was thudding wildly against her rib cage and she knew she shouldn't be reacting like this; it was only a kiss and she shouldn't let it sweep her away, but her body was betraying her. She was trembling all over and she knew it was not just an ordinary kiss. It was the kiss of a man who expects to wake up in the morning and find this woman next to him, and the worst was, she wanted it too.

Soon his hands were no longer content with her back, they traveled downward to gently explore the curves of her hips—lightly, so that she could stop him if she chose—and then to her breast. Something tightened in her abdomen, and the rest of her body went weak, so that she could not even nod when he whispered against her ear, ''Okay?''

Her arms tightened convulsively about him, and she was afraid he had taken that to mean she wanted

him to stop, because his hands came up then to cup
her face. She waited breathlessly for his kiss, but
what happened next was not a kiss. It was more, it
was richer and deeper, as he gently encouraged her to
follow him into a world of sensuality she had never
experienced before.

The featherlight touch of his tongue on her lips
caused her to shudder. The trembling threatened to
choke off her breath as he traced the pattern over and
over again until her lips were tingling and parted
from his touch, then his tongue swept over her teeth
and gently explored the inside of her mouth, before
tracing a course along her jawline and to her ear. A
moan escaped her and she arched her neck backward
as her fingers tightened about his arms, knowing she
would surely fall if she did not hold on to him. It
wasn't fair. She had been married and she had
thought she knew all there was to know about sensual
love, but nothing had ever happened to her like this.
Daniel had never aroused her like this.

It was that thought that compounded her helplessness, and the next sound that was released from her
sounded like a sob. Daniel had been her first lover
and she had thought he would be her last, but she
wanted Kyle now and it wasn't right that she should
want him. It was just her foolish body, just the exper-
tise of a virile man like Kyle, and she could not betray
Daniel's memory under the demands of her senses.
His memory was all she had left.

Kyle drew her into his arms and tried to still her
shaking, murmuring something soft and comforting
against her hair, and she tried to keep from breaking
into sobs. She did not know when the moment had
changed from burning sensuality to tenderness and
comforting, but she was glad—and at the same time

perversely sorry. She was still burning with a hot flush and it seemed every nerve ending in her body cried out for him, but the confusion that was pounding in her head against the dam of tears was only combining to turn it all into a sensation of abject misery. Kyle had called her a tease—was that what he was thinking now? Or was he thinking that if he gave her a moment to calm herself she would yield to him again, and that this time it would not end with a kiss or a little light petting? She hoped that was not what he was thinking, because he would be right. Her will-power was gone and the morning would probably find her in his bed and hating herself.

He lifted her face with his finger and his smile was not teasing or accusatory, just gentle and genuine. "I'm sorry," he said softly. "That wasn't fair. I didn't mean to push you."

The emotion that surged through her was something like gratitude, only deeper—almost like love. She buried her face in his shirt and held him tighter.

"Some men," he said in a moment, stroking her back soothingly, "would find it flattering to hold a trembling woman in their arms." The light tone he had forced into his voice dropped as he lifted her face again. "But you're not trembling from passion," he told her seriously. "You're shivering like a trapped rabbit. Do I frighten you so much, Bobbie?"

She could only shake her head mutely. Her breath escaped her lips in chattering wisps, and there was helplessness in her eyes. *Not you,* she wanted to cry. *I'm not frightened of you. It's me! The things I can't control....*

Almost as though reading her mind, he brought her again into a strong, reassuring embrace, and then kissed her cheek lightly. "Come on," he said, slipping his arm about her waist. "Let's go inside. Some hot cocoa will hit the spot right now."

She glanced at him, trying to laugh. "H-hot cocoa?"

"At this time of night," he assured her, "it's the safest thing I can think of."

She busied herself heating the milk and getting the cups, spooning generous amounts of instant cocoa mix into each one. The reassuring movements and the bright lights of Kate's kitchen served to calm her, and she tried not to notice that Kyle's eyes were watching her steadily from his position at the breakfast nook. He never said a word.

She brought the two cups and sat down across from him, managing a weak smile. His eyes were very serious, as though he were studying a problem and considering various solutions. Then he said, "First of all, I want you to know there's no need to be afraid of me. I would never hurt you, Bobbie. You're too valuable to me for that."

She almost burned herself on the cup. She set it down hastily, casting about in her mind for some light reply, something that would bring the tone of the evening back to the innocuous level of Kate's kitchen and steaming cups of cocoa, and away from the passions of a moonlit beach they had just left behind. "Of course," she replied brightly, forcing herself. "You wouldn't dare hurt me. I'm Kate's sister and she would have your scalp."

"It's more than that," he replied with a small frown, "and you know it."

She felt something begin to tighten in her stomach as, at the same moment, her hand clenched convulsively around her cup. She brought the hot liquid to her lips, hoping it would have a soothing effect. It did not.

"Secondly," he added, and his eyes were steady, "you don't have to be ashamed of wanting me. It's not as though it's the first time for either of us. It's natural and it's good, so don't try to turn it into something ugly."

She dropped her eyes, helplessness churning inside her. This was ridiculous, that they should be sitting at Kate's table over cocoa, discussing their sexual problems. Sexual problems? she thought incoherently. Had they progressed far enough to have sexual problems? *When all else fails, talk....* Her thoughts were wild and vagrant and a little panicky.

"It would be different with me," he told her. "Maybe not better—I certainly hope not worse—but *different*. Bobbie, look at me."

Unable to refuse, she lifted her face in all its misery at his command.

"Your life is not over," he said gently. "You didn't burn yourself on your husband's funeral pyre like the Indian women do, but for all the good your life is doing you now, you may as well have. I'm not asking you to forget him, I'm just asking you to go on with your own life. And don't keep telling yourself there will never be another man for you, because, if you do, all you'll succeed in doing is driving happiness away."

She shook her head, dropping her eyes again. "You don't know...you don't understand how it was...you can't know how I feel."

"Maybe I can't," he agreed fairly. "But I can see right now you're miserable. I know that if you had let me make love to you a moment ago you would have hated yourself in the morning." She glanced up sharply, surprised by his perception. "And that now that you're safe for another night, you're not any happier," he finished frankly. "What do you want, Bobbie?"

"I—I'm not sure," she admitted dejectedly, staring into her cup. "I'm so confused."

"That's allowed, I suppose," he agreed after a moment. Then he stood and started toward the door, his cocoa untouched.

She watched him go, wanting to call him back but unable to do so. Then he turned of his own volition, his hand on the doorknob. "Will it make you feel better," he asked very seriously, "if I told you I wasn't planning on a one-night stand?"

"I—I'm not sure," she stammered, confused as much by the words as by the deep, steady light in his eyes.

He smiled, as though that were a perfectly satisfactory answer. "Good night, Bobbie," he said gently. "Sleep well."

Chapter Six

The house resounded with Kyle's absence. She took the cups to the sink and washed them automatically, and managed to use up a few more minutes of the long empty night that stretched ahead of her. She wished she could make her mind as quiet as the house, but it would not be still.

Kyle was right, of course. He was only saying in a different way what everyone had been telling her since Daniel's death—she had to start living again. It was simply that she had never considered the possibility of letting another man into her life.

She knew there would never be anyone else like Daniel. He was her first love. What they had shared had been wonderful, it had been magic, it was something that happened only once in a lifetime and then only if one was very, very lucky. She was not expecting it to come again. But what was the harm in sharing a small part of her life with someone else? Someone easygoing and undemanding, with no promises or expectations. Couldn't she open up, just a little bit, to someone like Kyle? She knew she wanted to.

And he knew it too. But he would not pressure her, and for that she was grateful. He had summed it up that first morning on the beach. "We both need cheering up. Let's have an affair." Easy, uncomplicated, open-ended. That was nothing to be afraid of. She should be able to handle that. It wasn't as though he was asking for a commitment from her.

She felt a little better about herself as she started up the stairs, but it still did not make the prospect of the long empty night ahead of her more appealing. She thought briefly how it would be to be in Kyle's bed right now, wrapped securely in his arms, suffused with the warm, overpowering presence of him. How different everything would be right now if only she had found her courage on the beach. . .if only he had not been so sensitive to what was restraining her.

After a moment's hesitation she went back down the stairs and called Jojo in. She knew Kate did not allow him to sleep in the house, but she hoped her sister would forgive her this one transgression made from the demands of loneliness. She removed her makeup and changed into a long nightgown, a full-cut frilly peach affair with a lace yoke and puffy lace sleeves. It was the sort of thing she would have worn for Kyle if he had been there, and she scolded herself for the silly reflection as she got into bed and turned off the light. Jojo flopped to the rug at the foot of the bed and released a heavy sigh, as though he knew exactly what was expected of him.

She lay in the dark for a long time, sleepy but unable to relax sufficiently to close her eyes. Jojo's soft snoring at the foot of the bed made her smile and it was comforting, but it did not take her mind off the vastness of the house or the emptiness of her own bed. She wished she and Kyle had not parted on such uncertain terms. She hoped he was not angry with her. She did not think he was the type who would tolerate being led to the brink of fulfillment and then pushed away too many more times, and what would she do when he asked her again? She knew what she wanted to do—or at least what part of her wanted to do—but she had learned she could not always control her reactions when it came right down to making a decision. Her emotions were still too much in a turmoil.

She suspected Kyle was accustomed to having his women on the first try. A man like him would not have had to learn the delicate art of courtship, women probably fell all over themselves trying to please him the moment he walked into the room. That reflection made her smile a little in the dark, remembering Michael's dry observation about his brother's dubious charms the other night. Most likely Kyle had fully expected to sleep with her tonight— and why not? She had given him no reason to think otherwise. All things considered, he had handled the entire episode with appreciable grace and aplomb— but for how long? He would soon grow impatient with her, and annoyed, and that could make for a very strained relationship. That made her frown a little. It would be bad enough because they were working together and could hardly avoid one another while they were both staying here, but the worst part was the prospect of losing his friendship. She did not want to do that.

The fair thing to do, of course, would be to tell him quite frankly that there could never be anything between them and he would be doing himself a favor by calling off the chase. But she did not want to do that, either. She moaned in frustration and confusion and turned over in bed, seeking a comfortable position.

The shrill of the telephone made her jump, and for a moment she was frozen in a paroxysm of terror. Late-night telephone calls had done that to her ever since Daniel's illness. Then she remembered Kate, everanxious Kate, who had probably sneaked away from Michael's watchful eye and just could not resist calling home, just to make sure everything was all right.

She let it ring again while she pressed a hand over her wildly thumping heart and tried to unknot her muscles, then picked it up and said a cautious "Hello?"

"Were you asleep?"

It was Kyle's voice. Relief and pleasure flooded her. "Kyle!" She switched on the lamp and, squinting at the clock, noticed it was just after midnight. They had left one another over two hours ago. "No, I wasn't. What are you doing, calling here this time of night? Where are you?"

"I'm just across the lawn. I couldn't sleep either."

"Why didn't you use the intercom?" she demanded, plumping up the pillows behind her and glad that he could not see the foolish smile of happiness that was spreading over her features.

"There's no hookup on your phone," he explained. "I was afraid you wouldn't go downstairs to answer it if you knew it was only me."

She laughed. "You're probably right!" But she knew she would have raced to answer it if she had known it was he. "But you're on an extension, how did you ring me? You can't dial your own number!"

"That's a myth," he assured her. "And also my secret. Now that we've covered all the intricacies of modern technology, how are you? Okay?"

Her face softened as she sensed the real seriousness behind his tone, and she replied softly, "Yes, I'm okay."

"I was worried about you," he said quietly.

She sighed and closed her eyes. "Oh, Kyle...I'm sorry I acted like such a fool tonight."

"That's perfectly all right," he replied. She could conjure up his face behind her closed eyes: sensitive and perceptive, and now touched by just a hint of wry humor. "I think indecision is a relatively well-known feminine attribute."

She managed a small laugh. "One you've never been afflicted with, of course!"

"I have many vices," he assured her. "Indecision is not one of them. When I know what I want, I never change my mind. And," he added, "I know I want you."

She caught her breath. She was moved by an urge to tease him out of what was becoming a very serious conversation. "You only want me because I'm convenient," she retorted.

But he refused to play. His voice was deep and musical, and the sound of it, even transformed by such an impersonal device as the telephone, sent a shiver up her spine. "I want you," he told her, "because you're you. Because you're sweet and funny and sad and cute. I want your great big eyes and your perky little nose and your soft, sweet mouth...." She was tingling all over and she wanted more than anything at that moment to touch him, to feel his strong fingers close firmly about hers.... "I want you because you're special, Bobbie. You make me feel good just to be around. I like to see you smile. When you're hurting, I want to make you feel better." She heard his soft, slow intake of breath, and she felt yearning tighten within her at the tender words. Unexpected tears sprang to her eyes. "I just want to be with you, Bobbie," he finished simply.

She had not bargained for this. Her fingers clenched about the receiver as she fought back the wretched tears. The caring and the tenderness in his voice was more than she had planned for, and it touched something deep inside her and stirred it to raw, emotion-ridden life. "Oh, Kyle," she whispered at last. "I—"

"I hope you locked your door," he said suddenly, slowly.

She was startled. "W-why?"

"Because," he answered in a strange, restrained tone, "that's the only thing I can think of that's going to keep me away from you tonight—and I'm not so sure about that."

She found her throat was suddenly so tight she could not answer. *Ask me,* she thought, *and I'll unlock it.* But she was not certain she really wanted to. She was racked with confusion and yearning.

Then he said, his tone abruptly taking on its customary brightness, "Come to the window, then, and let me say good night."

She glanced across the room at the window. Curious, she got out of bed, trailing the telephone cord behind her, and demanded, "Can you see every room in the house from up there?"

"No," he replied. "I've got a good view of the ocean, the living room...and your bedroom." She pushed back the sheers and saw him silhouetted in the light of his own window. He lifted his hand to her. She could almost see his grin as he added, "You should close the draperies when you're dressing."

She gasped and fumbled ineffectually with the sheers, then remembered. "I *did* close them!" She had only pulled them back and opened the window to let in the night air while she was sleeping.

He laughed. "Scared you for a minute, didn't I?" Then he said, more softly, "Good night, Bobbie. Sleep well."

She replied, smiling into the telephone as she watched him across the lawn, "Good night."

She saw him replace the receiver, but he did not move away from the window. Finally she was the one who left, taking the telephone back to its table and turning off the light as she got into bed. She liked to think of him watching her while she slept.

Barbara had disturbing dreams that night, but that was not surprising. The dreams had come, off and on, since Daniel had first been taken ill. A result of stress, the doctor had said. He had prescribed some pills, but she didn't take them. Since being with Michael and Kate, she had slept relatively well, but considering the unsettling events of the day before, she supposed a restless night was only to be expected. She overslept and awoke a little groggy to the bright morning light.

Jojo was no longer at the foot of her bed, but she had left her bedroom door open and she assumed the poor beast had wandered downstairs in search of his breakfast. She dressed quickly in white ducks and a lavender tank top, taking time only to run a brush through her hair and catch it back at either side with combs before descending the stairs two at a time.

At the bottom of the flight she stopped. The first thing she noticed was Jojo's red form streaking by the window, and then she became aware of the aroma of coffee drifting through the house. For a moment she was confused, then she heard sounds from the guest room and she understood. Pausing on her way to the kitchen, she called around the corner, "Good morning, Kyle!"

His muffled voice returned, "Good morning, sleepyhead!"

Feeling absurdly happy, she went to the kitchen and poured herself a cup of coffee.

He was at the desk when she came into the room, apparently deep in concentration on the text he was pecking out with deliberate slowness on the typewriter. She watched him for a moment, surprised at the warm emotions only the sight of him caused to seep through her. The cuffs of his pale beige western-print shirt were rolled up above the elbows, and his slim, competent hands, even when engaged in something so absurd as the hunt-and-peck typing he was doing now, fascinated her. He had stuck a pencil behind his ear, and his face was etched in lines of studied thoughtfulness.

She leaned against the door and sipped her coffee, amusement touching her face as she followed his absorbing struggle with the typewriter. Then she inquired, "Did you feed the dog?"

He did not look up. "Umm-hmm."

Then it occurred to her. She stood up straight. "How did you get in here?" she demanded suspiciously.

"With a key," he responded absently and hit another key.

"But last night you said— You asked me if I had locked the door...." She frowned with confusion.

Now he glanced up, and his eyes were touched by a brief spark of mischief. "I meant your *bedroom* door," he informed her. "The only door in the house to which I do not have a key."

For a moment she was nonplussed, and then she felt like laughing. She came over to the desk. "All right, get up. It will take you the rest of the day to type a paragraph at the rate you're going."

He looked up at her in mock insult. "What do you mean? I'll have you know I've already done a chapter this morning—while *you* were still sleeping."

She brought her brows together in disbelief. "It must have been a short chapter," she returned scornfully.

"Hush now." He turned back to the typewriter. "I'm in the middle of an inspiration."

She could not help shaking her head in amused exasperation as he typed out the last few deliberate letters. Then he rolled the paper out of the machine and presented it to her with a flourish.

At first glance she could tell the white paper was marred by only one line. She gave him a questioning look, but his face remained bland. Then she read the single sentence. It was:

Bobbie—Come live with me and be my love.

She felt a tingle begin in her fingertips and spread in slow, soft waves in her cheeks. She did not know what to say, or do, or even think. The usual quips she found for such occasions simply would not serve. She felt his eyes on her, watching her, waiting for a reaction, but she could not look up from the page. It was only that the simple sentiment, so unexpected and so sweet, had touched her in a way she was totally unprepared to deal with.

After a long time she folded the paper into a neat square and looked up, managing a small smile. "We'd better get to work" was all she said.

Whatever emotion had been on his face was quickly wiped away as he reached across the desk to clasp her wrist. "No," he declared, pulling her around the desk to him. "I've been working all morning. I'd rather show you my house."

He pulled her down on his knee and rested his arm loosely around her waist as he reached for drawing

paper and pencil. Although surprised to find herself
in that position, she made no effort to rise as she inquired, "You mean your cabin in the woods? Do you
have pictures of it?"

"No," he replied and began to sketch. "I haven't
gotten around to it yet. It was just barely finished
when I left for South America." Trees and mountains began to appear on the paper, as if by magic.
"It's built over a stream," he told her, and a bubbling mountain stream appeared by traces beneath
his swiftly moving pencil. "A hot spring, really. Very
handy in the winter for converting heat."

"And in the summer?"

"Well, the summers aren't exactly hot up there, so
I've designed a deflector shield that works quite
well." Sections of the house were sketched in. It
proved to be an A-frame, three stories, with generous
use of glass and railed balconies on the top floor.
"Natural cedar siding," he explained, "with six-inch
foam insulation and a rock foundation, of course,
but that's not the sort of thing that needs to concern
you. You're more interested in things like closet
space and a modern kitchen and washer-dryer hook-
ups, right?"

She laughed. "If I were buying it, I suppose so. I
assume it has all those wonderful things?"

"And more," he assured her.

"It *is* built over a stream," she exclaimed as the
front view was finished. "Just like a bridge! Why,
I've never seen anything like that before!"

"The master bedroom," he said, touching a downstairs window with the point of his pencil, "is situated so that it sounds like you're sleeping right on the
creek bank. I even managed to get a skylight, on this
angle here, so when you're lying in bed, you can look

up to see the stars and you could swear you were camping outside—without all the inconveniences of outdoor life, of course.'' He began to sketch a floor plan. ''The entire west wall of the master bedroom is rock, with a fireplace,'' he explained. ''Two walk-in closets, a twelve-by-twelve dressing room, and an adjoining bath with a garden tub. It really is a garden too; the outer wall is glass and looks out on an enclosed garden.''

''Why, it's enormous,'' she exclaimed, impressed, and he began to draw the adjoining rooms. She pointed to another, slightly smaller room near the master bedroom. ''What is this?''

''Nursery, of course,'' he answered, working on the kitchen. ''Parents don't like to have their children's room too far from their own bedroom, and I never did think it was a good idea to put a child's room upstairs.''

She glanced at him curiously but made no comment. He went through the kitchen, family room, and laundry room, and upstairs to more bedrooms and what he euphemistically called a playroom, and the entire glass-enclosed third floor, which was his study. Barbara exclaimed wonderingly, ''*This* you call a cabin? I'd like to see one of your mansions! What does a bachelor like you need all that space for?''

He frowned a little and admitted, ''I guess maybe I did make it a little too big. That's probably why it seems so empty.''

She supposed that, being accustomed to designing luxurious houses, he had probably borrowed ideas that appealed to him from other plans, thus accounting for the nursery and other rooms for which he could have no possible use. And she was certain the place would have an enormous resale value, which had also probably been in the back of his mind when he designed it. Still, she teased him, "Did the world-famous architect make a mistake?"

He looked at her very seriously. "I hope not," he said. He dropped the pencil to the desk and looped both his arms around her, and his eyes were a very deep green. "What do you say, Bobbie?" he inquired softly. "Would you like to live there?"

For a moment she was stunned. His eyes said he was serious, but the question was so preposterous that her heart actually missed a beat in anticipation and confusion. Finally she managed, flustered, "Kyle, what a question!"

He began to laugh softly, and he buried his face in her breasts with a sigh. "You're right," he admitted, shoulders still shaking with quiet laughter. "I guess you've made me a little crazy. I haven't even gotten to first base with you and already I'm wanting you to move in."

She was relieved to discover that he was not entirely serious. She murmured, bending her face to his hair, "Oh, I think you've gotten to first base, all right, if I remember my high school terminology correctly."

He looked up at her, and though his eyes were still bright with the residue of laughter, she could sense a tensing within him as he lifted his hands to her face. She stiffened quickly and placed her own hands on his chest as though to ward him off. "Kyle," she said a little breathlessly, her voice high and nervous, "you promised...not during business hours...."

He looked at her for a moment, and then agreed, "You're right." He shifted her weight and stood up. Now he was definitely all business. "I think this will go faster if I dictate and you type. Let's try to get another chapter of text done today. We still have a lot of pasting-up and editing to do on this first part.''

She sat down at the typewriter, and there she stayed for another four hours.

Kyle had not been joking when he had warned her he was a slave driver. He worked as hard as he played, and when he was working, he was almost a different person. There was no room for distractions and no time for breaks. This was her first full day working with him and she was amazed by what a stern taskmaster the pseudoplayboy could be. The hands of the clock slipped past twelve, and then one, and Barbara, who had not had any breakfast, complained, ''Don't you ever get hungry?''

He only came over to her with a question about where to insert an illustration, and she did not bring it up again.

The telephone rang, and Barbara leaped for it, glad for an opportunity to get out of the chair. But Kyle pushed her down again, gestured that she should finish typing the sentence, and answered it himself. It was just as well, because it was for him.

From his side of the conversation Barbara gathered that it was not his lawyer, but someone with another problem concerning his work. He groaned once or twice, ran his fingers through his already rumpled hair, and paced back and forth to the length of the telephone cord. At last he said, ''Listen, can't you work around it? I just can't break away right now. The thing is, I just got out of the hospital.... Yeah, yeah, I know. But I'm in the middle of a book.... Not *reading* it, thank you, *writing* it.... No, I can't, and I'm not interested in your opinion of my literary abilities, either.'' Another long pause, and Barbara, who had abandoned typing for the welcome break, listened with interest. "Okay, I'll tell you what I'll do," he offered at last. "No, I know that, but I'll work something out. Don't expect me for six weeks, at least. . . . I told you, I'll work something out. I'll call you back tomorrow morning, I promise."

When he hung up, he looked at Barbara bleakly and explained, "Problems with one of my buildings. In Canada." He turned away from her abruptly, leaning his palms on the desk, and hissed an oath so unpleasant that Barbara looked up, startled. "I'm sorry," he offered in a moment, turning back to her. "It's just that I just got back. Damn!"

"Canada isn't so far away," she offered sympathetically.

"I know, it's just that I could be tied up for weeks." After a moment he shrugged, and some of the misery on his face began to fade. "Oh, well," he said. "At least I put them off for a few weeks."

"I don't understand," she pursued. "I thought when the blueprints were finished, an architect's job was done. Why do you have to keep chasing around the world following up on the work?"

He gave her a wry smile that was mostly self-deprecating. "I make myself too damn available, that's why," he answered. Then, brusquely, "All right, let's get this finished up." And suddenly he looked up at her, puzzled. "Did we have lunch?" he inquired.

She laughed helplessly.

Barbara brought sandwiches and iced tea to the desk and he dictated between bites, sitting on the edge of the desk and sketching out illustrations and diagrams all the while with his free hand. Barbara was amazed and fascinated that anyone could work so hard and so steadily—only another facet of the ever-enlarging personality of Kyle Waters she could not have imagined before. At five o'clock he left her with enough work to keep her busy until midnight, telling her absently that he had to go work out something on the Canadian project before the entire structure caved in. For a time she stared rebelliously at the stack of papers he had left for her to edit, retype, and proof before they began anew in the morning. She wasn't even getting paid for this job! And he hadn't said a word about dinner.

But then she was stricken with remorse. It was Kyle who had worked like a maniac all day, all she had done was type, make a few suggestions, and edit his wording as she went along. He had done all the thinking, arranged the technical data, and drawn minute-detail inserts of graphs, diagrams, and illustrations. And he had done an entire chapter before she had even arrived.

With a sigh she poured herself a cup of coffee and sat down to it. It was, after all, a labor of love.

At seven o'clock she broke down and pushed the intercom, asking Kyle if he would like her to fix dinner. The groan on the other end was of genuine chagrin. "I didn't even realize it was that time," he confessed. "I'm sorry, Bobbie. I've worked you like a hired hand all day, and if anything, *I* should be fixing dinner for you—or take you out at least. But I swear it's the truth, I just don't have time to eat tonight. I've got to get this thing finished up before morning, and even then it doesn't look as though I'll be able to get out of going up there to supervise the whole thing myself."

She felt a strange sort of disappointment tighten her throat. "Oh? When are you leaving?"

"Well, I've got to get this book done, and I think I can put it off until after Kate's party. But I'll probably have to leave that week, maybe the very next day." A pause. "Are you mad at me?"

She laughed. How could she be mad at Kyle? He was so unpredictable, so filled with delightful contradictions and moments of unexpected thoughtfulness that no one could possibly hold a grudge against him.

"No," she told him, "I'm not mad. But you should eat something."

"There's probably something in the refrigerator up here. I'll look into it later."

"Well, I won't keep you. I've got to get back to work myself."

He seemed to be suddenly stricken with an attack of conscience. "Listen, you don't really have to do all that tonight."

She retorted, "Oh, yes, I do, if I expect to be able to keep up with you tomorrow. Besides, it's good for me." She had no doubt she would fall into bed exhausted. No bad dreams tonight.

"We'll slow down in a couple of days," he promised her. "I'll take you out and we'll do the town."

She gave a mock groan. "If I'm still able!"

She heard his soft release of breath. "Bobbie," he said, "I'd really rather be with you tonight."

The smile that came automatically to her face was tender and knowing. "Good night, Kyle," she said softly.

She did stay up to finish the work, but she awoke the next morning refreshed and well rested. She was surprised when she came downstairs to find the house empty, but then she supposed it was Kyle who had overslept this morning. She made coffee and drank a cup, and it was getting near nine. She decided to take the papers to him and invite him for breakfast.

There was no answer to her knock, or even to her call. She tried the door and found it unlocked, but then she hesitated, wondering how Kyle would react to being awakened by her. But then she shrugged and stepped in. After a bad start yesterday morning she was determined to show him that she was as conscientious and as hardworking as he was.

The unmade bed and the sound of the shower told her immediately why he had not answered her knock, but that was not what captured her attention. She caught her breath as she looked about the room.

Of course, the last time she had seen it he had still been unpacking, and now the room looked more like a home with his stereo system in place and his drawing board set up before the huge glass wall. But that was not what stunned her. In the center of the room was an easel, near it a table filled with tubes of paint and brushes and palettes, and on every available surface—the walls, the tables, even stacked up on the floor—were what she at first glance took to be exceptionally well-executed photographs. But as she walked over to one picture of Jojo, she saw that it was actually an oil painting on canvas, so lifelike and so perfect that only the touch of the canvas assured the eye that a human hand had produced the image and not the lens of a camera. There were others: pictures of the house and front lawn at high noon with every shadow and lacy leaf faithfully reproduced, Kate sunbathing on the beach, Michael mowing the lawn, Jojo swimming in the surf. There was a breathtaking seascape at sunset and even a black-and-white reproduction of Michael at the typewriter, which could have credibly been used on the cover of one of his books, except that the artist had captured him in a real moment of concentration, his face in shadow, his mouth grim, his fingers in action. She tried to take them all in at once, then go back and examine each one in detail, but being surrounded by such genius made her feel very small, insignificant, and rather worshipful.

"So." She heard Kyle's voice behind her, and she whirled. "You're here."

He was wearing a short brown velour robe, rubbing a towel through his hair, his legs and his wrists still gleaming with steamy moisture. The expression on his face was tight and not at all pleased, and there was a reserve in his eyes she had never seen before. But she ignored all this as she exclaimed, "Kyle, they're marvelous!" She made a sweeping gesture to include the entire room. "I've never seen anything like them! Did you—"

"Back in a minute," he said suddenly. "Got to dry my hair." He closed the bathroom door and she heard the blow dryer going.

She was still holding the papers she had brought. She placed them on the bar and helped herself to a cup of coffee, still marveling over the portraits as she came back into the living area to sit on the sofa. She thought his reaction was a little strange, but probably he was just shy about his talent—for no good reason, she thought incredulously. Was there no end to the man's genius? Was it possible that such a perfect body could shield a mind of such extraordinary abilities? He was simply too good to be true.

He came back into the room, his hair fluffy and dry. He had pulled on jeans and a blue chambray shirt but had not buttoned it. He went over to the bar and poured himself a cup of coffee, watching her covertly.

"Kyle," she accused, twisting to look at him, "you told me you were an architect, not an artist!"

He shrugged and made a negligent gesture toward the walls, not looking at her. "That's not art."

"Well, I'd like to know what you call it, then!" She jumped up and took the picture of Jojo in her hands. His glossy brown eyes and his lolling tongue were so real she expected him to jump up at any moment and start licking her face; the painting was perfect to the last detail, even the minute lettering of Hartz inscribed on his flea tag.

"Katie liked that one," he commented as he passed. "She wanted to hang it in the living room."

She looked at him, now definitely sensing something strange about his reaction. "Why don't you let her?" she inquired.

He shrugged for an answer and lounged back on the bed, crossing his feet at the ankles and watching her with a strange, almost uneasy expression. She came to stand before him and demanded, "Why didn't you tell me you were so talented?"

He dropped his eyes to study his cooling coffee and replied, "Because I'm not."

She made an impatient sound. "Did you or did you not do these paintings?"

"I did," he admitted, as though it were a crime— or at the very least immoral.

"Then," she demanded again, "why keep it such a secret? You act as though you're ashamed of it!"

"It's just a hobby."

She spread her arms helplessly. "This," she declared, "is the work of a genius! I can't believe you call it 'just a hobby.'"

He gave her a lopsided grin. "Come on, Bobbie, you're embarrassing me." But she thought he was only half joking. He looked at her, and there was still that reserve in his face as his eyes flickered over hers nervously. "You remember that first day we met, you talked about not liking artistic types? I was afraid you would take my little hobby too seriously and pin a label on me—and a handicap."

She stared at him incredulously. "You're always quoting back to me things I've said," she accused.

"I have a photographic memory," he admitted frankly and gestured again vaguely to the paintings. "As you can see. It's a curse."

She laughed suddenly and that seemed to relax him. "Does that mean I'm forgiven for being a 'creative type'?" he inquired. "I'm not really, you know. I'm not moody or self-absorbed or egotistical, at least not to excess. And there's certainly nothing creative about those. That's why it's not really art."

She took up her coffee again and sat down on the sofa, frowning in puzzlement. "I don't understand what you mean."

"Art," he explained, "is creative interpretation. An artist uses all his senses, plus his emotions. I just use one—my eyes. That's why every painting turns out like a photograph. They're flat."

She thought they were anything but flat and she countered, "But that's just what makes them special. They're so real; they let the viewer see exactly what you saw, exactly the way it was. It takes an extraordinary talent to be able to do that."

"There's a technical name for it," he agreed half-heartedly. "I guess there are two or three men around the world who are starting to get some recognition in artistic circles for this kind of work. But it's still considered a bastard art form. Especially when the artist can't paint any other way.''

"Have you ever considered giving a show?'' she said seriously.

He laughed, but she could tell her remark had touched a deep responsive note in him. He stretched his hand out for her, and she came to sit beside him on the bed automatically, gladly, happy just to see him happy. "Oh, Bobbie,'' he said softly, looking into her eyes with undisguised tenderness and welcome. "You *are* good for me." He squeezed her fingers tightly, and she tingled all over with pleasure.

"As a matter of fact,'' he said, sipping from his cup as he still held her hand securely and warmly in his, "I've wanted to paint since I was a kid. My father insisted on mechanical drawing instead of fine arts when I was in high school, and in college I began to see what I've just told you: that what I do is not art. I became an architect to make a living, and it's not that I dislike it. I'll probably never get over the thrill of seeing my blueprints take on life and spring up out of the ground." He sighed. "It's just that lately all the travel has gotten to me, and even the amount of time it takes to get the building on paper from first concept to last detail.... I've been thinking, I'd like nothing more than to retire to my cabin in the woods and paint a little here and there, maybe sell one or two a year. Take time to discover the more important things in life.''

"Why don't you?'' she insisted. "I'll bet there are plenty of galleries all over the country that would be glad to display your work!''

He looked at her. "Don't have the courage, I suppose,'' he replied. ''And maybe—'' now his look became deeper, more meaningful ''—not the motivation. I told you, that cabin is awfully lonely.''

His eyes examined her face slowly, leisurely, resting on her lips, moving to her eyes with the hint of a question. With an imperceptible motion he set his coffee cup aside and she felt his hand caress her shoulder. She began to tremble with wanting and the pure sensation of his touch. There was no way it was going to end with a kiss here, not on this sleepy summer morning on Kyle's rumpled bed. Her chest tightened as his face moved toward hers.

She stood abruptly. ''We'd better get to work,'' she exclaimed brightly. ''The morning is half gone!''

He did not move, only lay there for a time, watching her with gentle scrutiny. Her nervousness mounted.

Then he smiled lazily. ''Slave driver,'' he retorted.

Chapter Seven

The next weeks followed a furious pattern. Kyle kept up a frantic work pace that allowed little time for anything else. Barbara had to force him to eat breakfast and remind him to have lunch—and when she remembered the voracious appetite he had displayed when he had first arrived, that in itself was incredible. Dinner was usually late, both of them pitching in in the kitchen or sometimes going out for pizza or hamburgers. After dinner Kyle crossed the lawn to his own apartment, and although Barbara usually did not stay up much later, his light was always burning when she went to bed. She wondered if he was painting late at night or simply sitting up brooding. She thought of him brooding a lot.

When they were together, he did not do or say anything that might lead her to think he was depressed, but she got that feeling anyway. She rarely saw the flash of humor in his eyes anymore, but then she rarely saw anything except a ruthless determination to finish the job at hand. She knew he was anxious to have the book behind him. He saw it as an unpleasant task, and he tackled unpleasant tasks head-on, with relentlessness and speed. But she suspected something else drove him: a sublimation of energy perhaps, a way to keep himself so busy when he was with her that there was no opportunity to risk the trauma of rejection again. Or perhaps he had decided she was not worth the effort, after all, and was simply anxious to finish the book before she sensed his lack of interest in her. She hoped that last solution was not the case. Somehow it didn't seem Kyle's style at all.

And then one day she picked up the telephone and accidentally stumbled upon another piece of the puzzle that was Kyle Waters's character.

The book was nearing its completion and Kyle was letting up some of the pressure. They had taken the afternoon off because Barbara wanted to prepare the roast for dinner and Kyle said he had some business calls to make. When everything was under control in the kitchen and she started upstairs to take a shower, she happened to glance at the calendar Kate kept by the telephone. The day's date was circled with the note: "Babs, call exterminator to confirm appt. for tomorrow." She snapped her fingers at the reminder and searched through the book for the number. She had almost forgotten.

When she picked up the telephone, there was a moment of confusion as she realized the line was in use. She remembered Kyle's extension just as she heard him say wearily, "God, Stan, what does she expect from me?"

She caught the reply, "Kyle, you've got to understand Roseanne's point of view," before she lowered the receiver guiltily back into place again.

She felt a small flush of shame for the unintentional eavesdropping, but now she thought she understood more about the legal case that had Kyle so upset. Obviously it had something to do with his ex-wife. From what Kate had told her, Barbara could well imagine Roseanne as the type of woman who would bleed Kyle for every penny she could get, but somehow it did not ring quite true that Kyle would be so disturbed about mere money. No, the reaction she had seen from him on the few occasions he had received bad news from his attorney had been raw emotion, not the kind of hurt and anger that was generated from the loss of money. It disturbed her strangely to think that Kyle could still be so upset by dealings with his ex-wife.

Kyle arrived just as she was placing the roast on the table, with a bottle of rich Burgundy and a kiss on the cheek for the cook. "Perfect timing," he announced, eyes twinkling. "Now, if I can plan my departure as well, I might just get out of doing the dishes."

"You try it," she retorted playfully and went back into the kitchen for a basket of rolls, while he poured the wine.

"The table looks beautiful," he complimented her, pulling out her chair. "But to tell you the absolute truth, I prefer eating in the kitchen. It's cozier."

"Serve my gorgeous seven-bone roast at the kitchen table?" she exclaimed in mock horror. "That's sacrilegious!"

"Did you notice I don't have a dining room in my house?" he commented as he was seated across from her. "Anyone who's too good to eat in the kitchen can just stay away." But he lifted his glass and smiled across its rim to her. "It's still a beautiful table," he told her.

She thought how comfortable it was fixing dinner for him, sitting across Kate's candlelit table from him, just being with him, as though they had known each other forever, but they had not yet reached the point where exciting discoveries were not still around every corner. She tried to put the overheard phone conversation and its unsettling implications out of her mind.

Then, as he was carving the roast, he said casually, "Did you pick up the phone this afternoon while I was on it?"

She quickly swallowed the wine she had just sipped, alarmed. Was he angry? She said, "I wasn't eavesdropping. I didn't realize you were using it."

He served her plate and questioned in the same mild tone, "How much did you hear?"

There was no point in disclaiming it. She said gently, "Enough to guess that all your legal trouble seems to somehow center around your divorce. I'm not prying," she added. "Really I'm not. I know it must be awfully . . . messy."

One side of his mouth turned down in a humorless smile. "You could say that." Then he looked at her. There was a trace of pain far in the back of his eyes, and the expression on his face was the need to confide in her, to talk to someone about it. "Bobbie," he began and then hesitated.

She prompted, "Do you want to tell me about it?"

After a moment he smiled. There was still a trace of the aching in his eyes, but his smile was almost natural. "Yes," he admitted, "I do. And I will. But right now you've got your own problems, and you're first priority as far as I'm concerned."

She did not know what he meant by that, but the perfect seriousness of his tone flustered her. He reached across the table to clasp her hand lightly. His eyes were dark; the flickering candlelight reflected within them only a muted glow. He said quietly, "Sometimes I get edgy. A little moody, maybe. I try not to, but I have about six million things on my mind right now, and about eighty percent of them are you.''

She tried to joke him out of the somber mood. ''Only eighty percent?''

At last a smile reached his eyes. It was warm and familiar, and she welcomed it. ''Fighting for one hundred. You're driving me crazy, you know that?''

''You were always crazy,'' she retorted and speared her salad.

He stopped her by stretching his fingers upward to touch her face. She lowered her fork back to her salad bowl, looking at him. ''Brittle,'' he said softly. ''That's what you are.''

She swallowed hard.

''You're always ready with a quick answer, always making jokes.''

''So are you,'' she responded, but it was barely above a whisper. Her eyes were magnetized by the warm light in his.

''I do it because I feel like it,'' he told her. ''You do it because you're scared.''

The moment was becoming entirely too intense. She moved her face fractionally, so that his hand fell away, and lifted her wineglass. ''Let's get drunk,'' she suggested brightly.

The familiar humor was back in his face. She knew she could do it. ''What?'' he mocked. ''And spoil your gorgeous seven-bone roast?''

''I might let you take advantage of me,'' she quipped.

His eyes glittered. ''Promises, promises.''

The meal was off to a more encouraging start.

They left the dishes and took their second glass of wine into the living room. Kyle pulled her down beside him on the sofa and slipped his arm around her. "You're very annoying," he told her, perfectly serious.

Her eyes flew up to him in surprise. "Why?"

"You're perfect," he responded. "Perfect cook, perfect housekeeper, perfect ghostwriter, perfect little body." His eyes intimately glanced over her from head to toe, and she squirmed.

"Look who's talking!" she replied airily. "The man whose work is sought all over the world, who looks and dresses like an ad from a three-dollar magazine, who probably has the I.Q. of a genius and a photographic memory, and who, to top it all, may well be the most promising young artist on the twentieth century!"

His eyes snapped with amusement and pleasure. "More, more," he murmured. "I love it."

"And," she pointed out coquettishly, "who also happens to be just a little bit vain."

He replied, "So, you see, *I'm* not perfect. I'm also a messy housekeeper, an impossible man to work with, and I can't boil an egg without burning it. And, as you've pointed out to me once or twice, I have a terrible reputation with women, which, as I've mentioned, is a sign of insecurity."

The second glass of wine and the intoxication of his nearness, which she had experienced all too scarcely these past days, were making her a little reckless. "Which means," she corrected, "you're either very good or very bad."

"Very good," he assured her, eyes twinkling. A finger wrapped around a strand of her hair and he brought it to his face. His lids dropped sensuously over his eyes as he murmured, "You even smell perfect."

"Strawberry shampoo," she informed him.

He set his glass on the coffee table and brought both hands to her hair, splaying it with his fingers. "You've got to have a flaw," he teased her. "What is it? Do you wear greasy night cream to bed or go to the supermarket with pink and purple curlers in your hair? Do you snore? Do you—"

She snatched up a cushion and threw it at him.

He wrestled her with enthusiasm, disarming her of both cushion and wineglass, and in moments she was pinned beneath him on the sofa, her squealing laughter stopped by the force of his mouth.

The power of his pent-up passion shocked her. He went from playfulness and laughter one moment to violent hunger the next. She was helpless against his demands. Her ribs were crushed against the wild beating of his heart; her arms instinctively wound themselves round his neck, and her fingers tangled in his hair. She couldn't breathe, but she didn't care.

His hand slipped beneath her to arch her body upward against him, then gracefully beneath the folds of her blouson shirt to explore her bare back, his fingers playing delicately over her ribs, the taut flesh near her waist. A series of shudders shook her, and dizziness swept over her in red and silver waves. She felt the change come over him, a tight leash on his emotions. The crushing weight on her chest lightened; his breath was warm and unsteady against her cheek before he sought her lips again, more gently this time. His hands were still.

"I've found your flaw," he whispered against her hair. He lifted his face a little and smiled down at her, one hand seeming all the more powerful for its restraint as it lightly brushed her hair away from her face. "You tremble," he said.

He pulled her to a sitting position, but she buried her face in his shoulder, clinging to him. "Don't," she whispered breathlessly. She couldn't bear it if he left her now, couldn't bear it if he was angry at her. She knew she was being unfair to him, but she didn't seem to be able to help herself, and every fiber of her body ached with longing and misery.

A long, unsteady breath escaped him as he wrapped her in his arms lightly, and his lips found her hair. The tension in his arms and his shoulders and even his voice was rock-hard. "No," he said huskily, and his hands caressed the length of her shoulders and her arms briefly. "You know I don't want it to stop here, and you know you don't want it to go any further. So before we do something we'll both regret...." He took her arms from around his shoulders and pushed her away firmly. His smile was forced and did not reach the emerald-dark screen of his eyes. "Come on," he said. "I'll help you do the dishes."

He stood, but she stayed where she was, curling up in a corner of the sofa and hugging a cushion to her, her eyes wide with abject misery and despair. "Please don't be angry with me," she whispered. "I don't mean to hurt you."

His features softened fractionally. "I'm not angry with you," he said gently. "I know you can't help it."

He reached for her hand, but she dropped her eyes, hugging the cushion to her chest more tightly, as though for protection or reassurance. She was still trembling. "I don't mean to be this way," she tried to explain. Her voice was high and tight. "I don't mean to—to tease you." She looked up at him, her eyes dark with misery. "How can you be so strong?" she whispered.

His hand fell to his side. Tension was evident in every line of his body, and his mouth was grim. "I'm not strong," he said. "I feel as though any minute now I'm going to break into a hundred little pieces, just like one of those cartoon characters who's just run into a brick wall. Because, that's what it's like every time I leave you, you know—like I've just been hit by a brick wall."

She buried her face unhappily in the cushion. Her voice was muffled within its depths. "Why do you bother with me? Why don't you find someone else?"

The hiss of his breath was impatient and exasperated. She heard him take an angry step away from her. "Because I don't *want* anyone else!" he replied shortly. "If I did, do you really think it would be that hard to find someone?"

No, she thought bleakly, *it would not be hard for you at all.* But she did not want him to find anyone else, she realized miserably. She wanted him to be with her and she was torturing them both by putting off a decision that should have come to her as naturally as breathing.

After a moment she heard him cross the room and open the front door. She couldn't even look up to watch him leave.

She was behaving stupidly, she knew. She wanted Kyle and he wanted her, and there was nothing wrong with that. She had almost gotten over the loss of Daniel in every other way, why should she still feel she was betraying him with her body?

The door closed, and she looked up. Kyle was leaning against it, his face drawn and dejected, helplessness in his eyes. He sighed heavily. "I can't leave you like this," he said.

She put the cushions aside and, with an effort,

made herself smile. "I'm okay," she said, standing. "Really."

Slowly his eyes softened. "No, you're not," he answered. "And neither am I. But I guess it will have to do." He reached for the doorknob again.

She took a few uncertain steps toward him. "Are—aren't you going to kiss me good-night?" she invited.

He looked back at her. His eyes rested longingly for a moment on her lips. "No," he said softly. "I don't think so." And he left, locking the door behind him.

She went into the kitchen, ran cold tap water over her wrists, and splashed it on her face with trembling hands to cool the flush and to stop the threat of tears. She was being silly. To fall into a brief romance with Kyle would not be the end of the world, it would not even be a breaking of her marriage vows. There would be only one love in her life, she knew that, but she was too young and at the same time too old to imagine there would not be other lovers. Couldn't she learn to be like Kyle, to take what life offered freely and without guilt?

She dried her face with a paper towel, her hands steadying with the nearness of a decision. Of course she could. She would take it slowly, she would not be afraid. Kyle would not hurt her. She could trust him, because he understood exactly what she needed: a summer of romance and physical fulfillment. He was attractive, he was gentle, he was skilled. Best of all, he would never make any demands on her or ask for a commitment from her. They would both know from the beginning how it must end.

It was very simple, really. She thought she might sleep.

The next morning he came in in his usual brisk, businesslike mood, but she was determined not to let him put it behind them so easily. Ignoring the subtle undercurrents of tension between them would only make the problem worse. She said, looking at him determinedly, "Kyle, about last night—"

"If you're going to apologize," he replied shortly, snatching up a folder of photographs and stretching out in his usual position in the easy chair across from the desk, "I swear I'll walk out and leave you with all this work to finish by yourself."

"I was not going to apologize!" she flared.

He smiled, a spark touching his eyes. "Good for you."

"And besides," she fumed, a nerve touched now, "it's *your* work. You can walk out and not come back till next summer as far as I'm concerned and it will still be here, waiting for you!"

"It might still be waiting anyway," he retorted, "if we don't get busy." He stood and brought the folder to her, all business. "I've marked these photographs with the page numbers to which they correspond. Go through and collate them, will you, and make whatever changes in the text that are needed."

She sat there obstinately, glowering at him, and suddenly he touched her nose lightly. "Don't worry," he assured her, eyes twinkling. "I'm not giving up."

She blushed unexpectedly and turned abruptly back to the typewriter.

At three o'clock the exterminators arrived. "Well, that's it for today," Kyle announced when he returned from talking with them. "Bug spray also kills people. Everybody out."

"Do you realize," Barbara said wonderingly,

gathering up the day's work, "that we're almost finished? I never would have believed it."

He glanced appreciatively at the growing stack of manuscript pages. "So we are," he agreed. "Well, I promised you a night on the town to celebrate, didn't I? This seems like as good a time as any. Go upstairs and change and we'll do it up right."

She laughed. "It's only three o'clock in the afternoon!"

He considered this. "I suppose we should wait until these good people leave. I'll tell you what, get your things together and you can change at my place. I'll hang around down here until they finish, and lock up. It shouldn't take long. Then we'll drive up the coast for an early dinner and a night of drinking, dancing, and loose living."

She laughed again. "Sounds perfect!"

Kyle seemed to be intimately familiar with the coast, all the best restaurants in out-of-the-way places, the nightclubs with the best bands and most interesting atmospheres—as well he should be, she realized suddenly, since he and Michael had grown up here. She wondered aloud if he had also made his home with Roseanne here, and he answered briefly that he had. "If you could call it a home," he added.

"What made you leave?" she inquired curiously.

"New starts," he responded. "And I found a part of the world I liked as well, if not a little better." Now he looked at her thoughtfully. "I think you would like it too," he added.

She changed the subject.

They had some of the best lobster Barbara had ever tasted in a romantic old inn situated on a cliff overlooking the sea. They watched the sunset and lingered at their candlelit table over a second glass of wine. He took her to a nightclub that had recently succumbed to the current craze for country-western ambience; it was crowded and well lit and filled with gaiety. He taught her the Texas two-step and took her into every square dance formation, and for a man who had recently recovered from a serious injury his agility and stamina were remarkable. They laughed and they danced and Barbara could not remember having so much fun in her life.

It was after midnight, as they went back to their table to catch their breath, that she exclaimed, "Don't you ever get tired?"

"I thought you'd never ask," he moaned, laughing. "I'm a little out of practice for all this. *All* my bones ache, not just the broken one!"

"I don't believe it!" she retorted, eyes sparkling. "I'm exhausted, and I wouldn't object if you offered to take me home now."

He slipped his arm around her waist as he picked up the check. "Now, that," he murmured, "sounds like a proposition with promise."

He parked the car in the garage and helped her out. "I'll walk you home," he told her with a gleam in his eye, "but I feel it's only fair to point out that the walk to my place is a lot shorter than to yours."

She felt a tremor go through her, but he simply encircled her hand warmly with his and led her across the lawn. Under the golden glow of the porch light he unlocked the door and bent to kiss her gently. No lingering passion tonight. Perhaps he sensed, more than ever before, that she needed time. And in a way she was glad. After the high pitch of last night her emotions were still in a turmoil.

"Sleep well," he told her, and touching her cheek lightly, he turned to go.

"I had a terrific time," she called after him softly.

He lifted his hand with a smile and started across the lawn.

She went inside and switched on a lamp, feeling pleasantly drowsy and good inside. But almost immediately her senses were assaulted by a sickly sweet, harsh chemical odor. When she took a deep breath, she choked, and nausea churned in her stomach. A faint mist still clung in the air and she realized in alarm that the house had been completely closed up all afternoon. The poison penetrated every corner, worse than paint fumes and twice as toxic. She coughed and squinted her burning eyes, waving at the air. Her stomach weakened and she felt a little dizzy. She turned and stumbled for the door, coughing as she clung to the porch rail and gasping deep breaths of clean night air.

She must have been inside only a few seconds, for it seemed that immediately Kyle was beside her, inquiring, "What—?" But seeing her sickly color, he did not bother with further questions, just pulled her to sit on the steps and forced her head down.

"I'm okay," she gasped in a moment, hugging her arms against a sudden chill as she tried to sit up straight. "The exterminators!"

He groaned and got up, but there was an undertone of laughter to his voice as he pulled the door closed and locked it. "I forgot! They said it wouldn't be safe to go back in until tomorrow. Poor Bobbie." He sat down beside her and slipped his arm around her shoulders, and he was shaking with the effort to hold back chuckles. "You okay?"

She knew she must have made a ridiculous sight, bursting out of the house that way, and she did not mind his laughing at her. She just couldn't find the amusement in the situation yet.

"Lord!" she gasped with a shudder, biting back nausea. "I can't sleep in there tonight. Ugh!"

He pulled her to her feet, an unmistakable twinkle in his eye. "Well," he announced, "it looks like you're coming home with me tonight after all."

She caught her breath, her eyes wide with question. Would it be tonight, then? So soon? She was not certain she was ready for this, although she knew she should be and she could not bear to disappoint him again.

But he simply slipped his arm around her waist as he led her across the lawn and explained mildly, "My sofa can be made into a bed with no trouble at all." He glanced at her, his expression enigmatic. "That is, if the sofa is what you really want."

Another shiver shook her. "The sofa will be fine," she told him.

She felt the need to chatter nervously as they ascended the stairs and he escorted her inside. "I never knew the stuff they used was so lethal. I don't usually have a weak stomach. Why didn't they spray your place too, I wonder?"

He glanced at her patiently as he took extra linen out of the closet. "Possibly," he offered, "because the garage is made of stone."

"Oh," she responded flatly, clasping her hands together and feeling foolish.

"Relax," he told her as he moved the sofa away from the wall and opened it into a generous-size bed. "I promise I won't ravish you in the middle of the night." He glanced up at her with a wink. "Not my style."

She managed to laugh a little. "And I promise you the same thing."

"I can't tell you," he responded gravely, "how secure that makes me feel."

She helped him make the bed, and when it was done, she stood there, hesitant. She was wearing slacks and a ruffled shirt, not very comfortable for sleeping, and the jeans she had left here when she had changed would not be much better.

"I suppose you wear pajamas," he said, as though reading her thoughts. "I don't, myself."

She blushed a little and started toward the door. "I guess I'd better go get a nightgown."

"All your clothes will smell like that stuff for at least another twenty-four hours," he told her, studying her reflectively. Then, "Wait a minute. I might have something."

He went to the closet and pulled out his suitcase, producing after a moment of pair of neatly folded blue men's pajamas. "They make you wear them in a hospital," he explained, perfectly deadpan.

She giggled a little as she accepted them. "I guess they would."

He grinned. "I've always wanted to see a girl wearing my pajama top."

"Don't try to tell me you never have," she retorted. "And I'll take the bottoms too, thank you."

He laughed. "They'll swallow you whole!"

She went into the bathroom. "And no," he called after her, "I never have."

When she returned, he was already in bed, and she hurried past him, trying to keep her eyes away from his naked torso. "Adorable," he grinned as she climbed into her own bed in the overly large pajamas,

and he switched off the light. "Now," he said after a
moment, "isn't this better than sleeping alone?"

She smothered a laugh in her pillow. "Good night,
Kyle."

But sleep did not come easily to Barbara. She would
have been less than human had the proximity of a man
as virile and as attractive as Kyle not affected her. She
would have been less than a woman had not the sound
of his deep breathing in the bed next to hers brought
back memories of nights wrapped in Daniel's arms in
contented lethargy after their lovemaking.... But in
her half-dozing state the memories became confused
and it was in Kyle's arms that she lay, his strong,
naked limbs entwined with hers.... She tossed and
turned restlessly, trying to put the treacherous images
out of her mind, and at last she fell into a troubled
sleep.

She awoke abruptly, shivering violently, her face
wet with tears, and hiccuping with sobs. Kyle was
holding her and she clung to him instinctively.

"It's only a dream," he whispered, stroking her
hair. "Just a bad dream. Hush now."

She tried to stop sobbing, but she couldn't. The
tears came of their own volition, and she could not remember what she was crying about. "I—I'm sorry,"
she gulped at last, curling her fingers around the soft
lapels of his robe. "I w-woke you up. Stupid. I'm
sorry."

"Don't be silly," he responded soothingly, and his
arms around her were warm and comforting. "Everyone has bad dreams."

She looked up at him, trembling helplessly, aware
only that if she could keep him talking, maybe he
would not leave. The nightmare suddenly seemed very
close at hand. "D-do you?"

"Sure, I suppose," he answered easily, as one would to a child. "Not as bad as yours, I imagine." He looked down at her and smiled encouragingly in the dark. "Do you want to tell me about it?" he inquired gently.

She pressed her face against his chest, trying to calm herself to the slow, steady beating of his heart. "S-sometimes," she managed, in a small, weak voice, "I dream I'm being...nailed into a casket." She had never told anyone that before.

His arms tightened about her, his face dropped to her hair. "Poor Bobbie!" he whispered, and his tone was deep with genuine sympathy.

"It's awful," she gulped. "I can't breathe."

"Oh, darling." He drew her closer as another shiver racked her. His voice was soothing and his embrace strong and protective. "Don't think about it. It's over now. It's all right."

He started to move away, and she gasped instinctively and clung to him. But he only lifted the sheet and slipped into bed beside her, drawing her more firmly into the warmth of his embrace. "It's all right," he whispered, holding her tightly. "Nothing can hurt you now. I'm here. I won't leave you."

She fell asleep against his chest sometime later to the soothing sound of those words, repeated over and over again like a charm.

Barbara woke up alone in the sofa bed the next morning. Light from the southern wall flooded the room, and so did memories of the night before. She remembered waking again during the night, stirring faintly and contentedly in his arms and having him inquire softly, "You okay?" She realized vaguely that he had not been asleep at all, but the thought of him standing guard over her throughout the night was so comforting that she only nodded and murmured something unintelligible and snuggled closer into the protective circle of his body.

Now she felt guilty for having kept him awake, and also a little confused for what had passed between them—or, more accurately, what had not happened. But overwhelming both those emotions was a sense of well-being, of happiness, of contentment with the world and everything in it, and she found herself humming softly as she quickly changed into her jeans, made the beds, and put on fresh coffee.

She assumed Kyle had gone down to the house, and she debated whether to make breakfast here or take a chance on the lingering fumes in Kate's kitchen. She rang the intercom to get Kyle's opinion, but he did not answer. She shrugged and walked over to the window to draw the draperies. It was already sultry this morning, and the sunlight pouring in through all the windows would turn the place into an oven by noon.

For a moment she stood at the open window, looking out over the sea. Puffy white clouds outlined in gray were lingering close to the horizon, threatening a storm, and the sea was somewhat duller than its customary blue-green. And then a motion in the breakers caught her eye.

It was Kyle, diving in and out of the surf with the grace of a porpoise, the sun glinting off his skin and glistening in his hair as he turned and swam in strong, graceful strokes away from the shore. She watched until his figure became small and almost indiscernible, then he turned again and began to swim in. As in everything he did, he was a delight to the eyes. She smiled, wishing she were out there with him. He let the surf carry him in, and then stood up and began to walk to shore. He was completely nude.

For a moment she was fascinated by the perfection of his body: the trim, athletic lines; the healthy, but not overdeveloped, muscles; the smooth symmetry and grace of every part. Then shame and embarrassment overcame her and she turned quickly away from the window, closing the draperies as she had intended to do in the first place.

When Kyle came in, she was just taking the bacon up and pouring eggs from a bright yellow bowl into the skillet. "Now, this is what I like to come home to," he declared, tossing his towel onto a chair. "Smells great."

"Scrambled okay?" she called brightly over her shoulder.

"Perfect." He came from behind her and kissed the back of her neck. His skin was still cool from the water. She concentrated on cooking the eggs.

They met as he was taking juice from the refrigerator and she was turning to place the plates on the table. He had pulled on jeans but no shirt, his feet were bare, and his hair, though it had dried quickly in the sun, was still damp about the edges. It was inevitable that a vision of the last time she had seen him should spring to mind, and so was the tingle of a blush that followed it.

His eyes flickered over her with amusement as he went directly to the heart of her thoughts. "Don't knock it," he advised soberly, "if you haven't tried it."

She faced him down coolly, deliberately ignoring the heat in her face. "You'd better hang up that wet towel," she told him.

He made a dry face at her. "Yes, ma'am."

"I went over early and opened up the house," he said as he came from the bathroom, pulling on a shirt. "It's not too bad in there now."

"Well," she replied as they were seated, "thanks for putting me up. You must have been expecting overnight guests when you bought that sofa bed."

"I was expecting overnight guests," he informed her seriously, "when I bought the king-size bed. Which," he added, taking up his juice, "is exactly where I'm going to spend the rest of the day."

She glanced at him curiously as she nibbled at her toast, and he explained, "It might not come as too much of a surprise to you to learn I didn't close my eyes once last night."

"That's odd," she teased him. "I slept quite well."

"Lust," he replied flatly, lifting a forkful of eggs. "It'll ruin a night's sleep every time."

She choked a little on her coffee. "It sounds as though you speak from experience!"

"Oh," he assured her quite seriously, "I've had a few. I remember one night a couple of years ago," he mused, "that was almost—not quite—as bad." Her eyes grew wide with interest as he went on. "I had just quit smoking, and I lay awake all night craving a cigarette like you wouldn't believe. The worst part was, of course, that there was a pack on the night table right next to me. Yes," he agreed thoughtfully, trying to disguise the twinkle in his eyes, "the more I think about it, the more the torture I went through that night seems exactly like what I endured last night."

She suggested, keeping her face very sober, "Why didn't you just get up and throw the cigarettes out the window?"

He contemplated her seriously. "It's an exercise in willpower," he decided.

"Congratulations." She lifted her juice glass to him. "You passed the test."

He grinned. "Don't tempt me. The day is young and the bed is large. Sure you wouldn't care to join me?"

"No, thanks," she replied lightly, turning back to her breakfast. "I'm not sleepy."

He laughed, and she joined him easily. He had rescued what could have been a very awkward morning-after scene with his usual ease and humor, and she was grateful. He had not embarrassed her by reminding her of a childish nightmare, nor made more of the fact of their sleeping together than should have been. He was, she thought, growing more wonderful each day.

Kyle was not joking about being tired, though, and work on the book was called off for the day. It was just as well, because the impending storm was growing closer and Barbara wanted to air out the house before it broke. The afternoon grew thick and heavy, and she changed into a pair of shorts and a halter top as she worked, stringing up a line in the backyard and draping the contents of closets over it. She vacuumed the carpet and scrubbed the floors and covered whatever traces of the unpleasant scent remained with a bright dusting of lemon furniture polish. She was trudging up the stairs with the last armload of linens that had been airing in the backyard when the intercom rang about six o'clock.

"No," Kyle answered her without giving her a chance to ask the question, "I haven't been sleeping all this time, just most of it. Is there any of that roast beef left for sandwiches?"

"Help yourself," she invited. "But I've got to warn you, I'm a mess, and the house isn't much better."

"I'll be a gentleman and pretend not to notice."

"You'd better hurry," she said, glancing at the purplish sky, "or you're going to get wet."

"I'm on my way."

But rain was beginning to spatter as he crossed the lawn, and when he came in, he was brushing droplets off his shoulders and his hair. He took one look at her and said, "You're tired. Go sit down and put your feet up. I'll handle the sandwiches."

She accepted his offer gratefully, pausing only once to glance critically in the mirror. She had pinned her hair up while she worked, and now escaping tendrils clung damply to her face. She pushed them back halfheartedly and decided against changing into something more appropriate for entertaining. Kyle was not exactly a guest in this house, and for once he would have to simply accept her as she was.

He brought roast beef sandwiches and coffee on a tray and they ate in front of the empty fireplace, listening to the rain tinkle on the windows and the metal guard of the chimney with a sort of lazy indolence. The rain became a downpour, its waning and increasing beat hypnotic, sealing them off intimately in a separate world of gentle lamplight. Barbara became aware that neither of them had spoken in a long time and that Kyle was watching her, studying her in a relaxed, contemplative way over his coffee. The atmosphere generated by the cozy room and his steady, easy gaze was both reassuring and close, but at the same time it made her a little nervous. She straightened up a little from her lounging position on the sofa and inquired, "What did you do all day—besides sleep?"

A lazy smile touched his eyes. "I painted a little. I do that a lot when you think I'm busy with transatlantic phone calls or designing the world's first energy-independent skyscraper."

"You still talk like you're ashamed of it!" she exclaimed. "I told you—"

He shrugged. "It's a hard habit to break, I guess. I've been a closet artist for so long I'm not used to other people knowing about it."

She smiled. "At least you're calling yourself an artist now."

"I'm still not sure I believe it, though."

"You don't have to hide your painting from me, Kyle," she told him earnestly. "I think it's wonderful, really. I want you to be proud of it."

His slow smile was tender and touched with something deeper than she had ever seen before. "I know," he said. He placed his coffee cup on the table and came over to the sofa. She started to move over to make room for him, but he surprised her by sweeping her feet onto the sofa, so that she was lying full length upon it, and pushing her back gently against the cushions. Then he sat beside her, simply looking at her.

The rain made whooshing noises against the windowpane as the wind rose, but inside, the yellow lamplight of the room was warm and secure, and there was just the two of them. His fingers gently explored the planes of her face, twisting lightly in her curls, tracing the arc of her eyebrows. His eyes were a very deep green.

His penetrating, unbending gaze made her feel special, wanted, excited—and a little nervous. When he took her coffee cup from her and set it on the table, never once removing his eyes from the study of her face, she had to ask in a high, slightly breathless tone, "What are you doing?"

He looked at her thoughtfully for a moment longer. "I think," he replied softly, "I'm going to take all your clothes off."

She searched his face for some sign that would tell her whether he was serious, and she managed a little laugh. "Why?"

"Because I want to."

She touched his hand as it reached for the string tie at the neck of her halter. Her eyes were wide with a deeper question as she searched his face. "Do you always get exactly what you want?"

A shadow seemed to fall over his face, for just a moment, then it was gone. "No," he answered. "But I always try."

With a gentle tug the bow at her neck gave way. Her fingers tightened about his. "What—what if I don't want you to?" she managed. Her breath was coming with great difficulty now.

"Then," he replied seriously, "you know exactly how to stop me."

Her hand fell away from his and traveled instead to his shoulder, touching his neck, drawing him closer with the light pressure of her fingers. "Kiss me, Kyle," she whispered. "I'll try not to tremble."

He lowered his face and sought her lips gently, almost questioningly, and her response was immediate and welcoming. She let her senses respond to him fully and without inhibition, for with Kyle everything would be right. She loved the exploratory pressure of his mouth as it moved against hers, the faint taste of coffee on his tongue; she loved the delicate motions of his fingers as they traced a titillating pattern across the curves of her body and the feel of his tight muscles beneath the silky fabric of his shirt. It was inevitable that the sensation he aroused as their passion mounted should take her back to nights with Daniel.... But this man was different, she tried to tell herself. He would never replace the love she still held in her heart for her husband, he would never take that away from her, but to share with Kyle one small part of what had been the miracle of married life surely could not be a crime. *Please understand, Daniel,* she thought desperately, trying with all her might to push away the image of him watching her accusingly. *Please don't blame me....* She had been too long without the physical joys of a man-woman relationship, and every movement of Kyle's sensitive, expert fingers and every touch of his lips heightened her awareness of the fact. She knew she did not want to turn back, but Daniel's memory beckoned her. She knew that she wanted Kyle, and when she was in his arms, she would try very, very hard not to pretend he was Daniel.

He moved the material of her halter aside and she yielded to the firm, light pressure of his fingers and then his lips upon her breasts. Somehow the buttons of his shirt were undone and she pressed him against her, his flesh against hers, as the dizzying waves of desire swept her into an embrace so tight they were almost molded as one. Then he moved away slowly, dropped delicate kisses on her breasts and her face, and entwined his fingers in hers. She thought he would suggest they go upstairs. She thought she would say yes.

But for a long, long time he simply looked at her. She was not ashamed to have him look at her, even with a gaze so deep and penetrating. It did not embarrass her or make her nervous. But she found she could not meet his gaze directly; she kept flitting her eyes away, almost as though afraid he might read something there she did not want him to see—some reluctance, perhaps, some denial within her mind of what her body was telling him.

And it seemed her fears were correct. In a moment he released a long, heavy breath. Gradually his fingers loosened from hers. "I'm sorry, Bobbie," he said quietly. "I won't compete with a ghost."

Chapter Eight

Barbara could not even draw a shocked breath. She did not move as he stood up and walked away from her, every line in his body tense with repressed emotion. She could not believe this was happening.

He resumed his seat in the chair opposite, arranging his limbs in a casual, relaxed posture as he unhurriedly refastened the buttons of his shirt. But there was a tautness in his face, in his hands, even in the arrangement of his legs, that belied his negligent demeanor. She struggled to a sitting position, whispering, "I don't understand! I—I—"

One corner of his lips tightened in a mirthless smile. "Don't you?" he replied. "I don't ask much, Bobbie, but I'm afraid I do still subscribe to the old-fashioned principle of two to a bed."

It suddenly seemed very important to get her halter tied, but the stubborn strings kept slipping through her numb fingers. He watched her struggle with absorbing interest. In other circumstances the situation would have been almost absurd.

"That—that's not true!" she cried, at last succeeding in tying a knot. Her color was high and she was miserable all over with a searing heat and an unfilled desire—and with anger because he had read her so clearly, because what he had sensed from her was only what she had tried so carefully to hide. Her nerves felt like fine wires stretched to the breaking point. "I do want you! All this time I've been afraid, but I'm not anymore because I do want you!"

"For what?" he inquired, and there was not a flicker of expression on his face. "You're using me, Bobbie."

She caught her breath, her frustration and her confusion turning swiftly into anger. "That's what people do, isn't it," she retorted, "when they have an affair—use each other?"

His eyes remained blank. "Some people," he answered.

She stood, turning abruptly away from him, hugging her arms to stop the tremors of humiliation and rage. "What is it?" she demanded spitefully. "The chase is more exciting than the conquest? Or maybe you just took on more than you could handle! You never wanted me at all, you—you just wanted to play with me!"

His voice behind her was restrained, and very close. "I want you," he said quietly. "But I'm not an exorcist. That's something you've got to handle on your own."

"You *don't* want me!" she cried, very near to sobbing now.

His fingers closed around her upper arm with a shocking force, whirling her around so that her face was only inches from the dark anger in his. "I *do* want you," he insisted, and his fingers tightened to a painful degree on her arm. "But I want *you*—not just your body responding to mine while you're pretending I'm another man!"

She gasped in shock and hurt, and when he released her abruptly, she stumbled backward and almost fell. He took an angry stride away from her, running his fingers through his hair, and she heard him hiss a single syllable through clenched teeth. Minutes ticked away, and anger was replaced with despair. She clung to the sofa for support and dropped her head. "I don't know what you want from me," she whispered at last.

He turned. Some of the anger was fading from his face too. "I only want to know that you're not comparing me to your husband. If you try to measure us against one another, both Daniel and I will suffer for it. You don't want to do that to Daniel's memory, and I won't let you do it to me."

He came over to her and lifted her chin with one strong finger. "I promise you it will be good between us," he said softly, "but only if you let go—completely. It's up to you."

She could not look at him. "I—I thought I was," she whispered miserably.

The finger moved to caress her face, a sad sort of smile softened his features. "We're good for each other, Bobbie," he said gently. "We could have fun together. We can make each other happy, and it *will* be good. There is room for two men in your life, but Daniel belongs in the past, and I belong in your present." He dropped his hand. "When you find that out for yourself, let me know."

She could not find the strength to call him back, even after the door closed quietly behind him.

The next morning he came down to the house as usual, just as she was finishing her breakfast. She had made a concentrated effort to make certain her sleepless night did not show on her face. A stinging cold shower and the judicious application of makeup did the trick nicely. Her conviction that ignoring a problem only made it worse was conveniently discarded for the occasion. This was one problem no amount of talking could solve. And she was not about to set herself up for another humiliation like the one that had occurred the night before. She was determined to keep her distance—for a while, at least.

"Good morning," Kyle said pleasantly and poured a cup of coffee.

She replied coolly, "Good morning."

He lifted an eyebrow at her reaction and glanced at the evidence of breakfast: a cereal bowl in the sink and a half-finished glass of juice on the table. "No, thanks," he murmured, "I've already eaten."

She poured the remainder of the juice down the drain and returned the box of cereal to the cupboard.

"Would this by any chance be the signs of a feud?" he inquired mildly.

She rinsed off the dishes and dried her hands on a towel. She turned to him. "Shall we get to work?"

He studied her, sipping his coffee. "All right," he agreed. "But—" he quirked an eyebrow at her "—when you feel ready for some good, clean fun, you know where to find me."

She turned and walked toward the guest room. He followed at a discreet distance.

If there was a feud—and Barbara had to admit honestly that she had gone out of her way to start one—he made no further overtures to end it. When he called off work at the end of the day, he said a polite good-night to her and crossed the lawn to his own apartment. Though Barbara watched him jealously, he never left the grounds, though after a couple of days of the drawn-out coolness between them she half-expected him to go out in Michael's car one evening and not return before breakfast, and she didn't know what she would do if that happened. She began to miss him.

Fun. That was all he was asking. It wasn't as though he were talking about forever. Was it so great a price to pay for a start on a new life to put Daniel aside for a time in favor of living in the present? Was it really so impossible to do?

They finished the book in the middle of the morning, almost exactly on his three-week deadline. Michael and Kate were due back either today or tomorrow, and the party was scheduled for the end of the week. Barbara knew that he would be leaving shortly thereafter for Canada, but pride prevented her from asking him for the details. And pride prevented her from dwelling on the fact that their time together was running out.

"Do you know what I'm going to do?" Kyle declared, gathering up the bulky manuscript and neatening the pages. "I'm going to wrap this up and take it into town right now, and mail it before I change my mind. Care to come with me?"

Perhaps if he had looked at her, she might have agreed. But the invitation was offered so much as an afterthought that she declined, replying, "No, thanks. I'm going to go down to the beach and get some sun this afternoon."

He glanced at her. "You could use it," he agreed. "Okay, type me up a cover letter—you know, 'Dear Mr. Editor, enclosed is the manuscript,' et cetera, et cetera—and the rest of the day is yours."

She rolled a fresh sheet into the typewriter. "The rest of the *summer* is mine," she corrected pointedly, but he made no reply.

As she took her blanket down the steps to the beach and stretched out under the warm glow of the sun, she felt a mild depression settle over her. The book was finished, and she would miss working with Kyle. Not by any stretch of the imagination could she say it had been fun, but it had been fascinating, demanding, and a little awe-inspiring to work with a genius. And now there was hardly any reason for them to see one another.

After a time she went inside and fixed herself a light lunch, then rubbed herself with suntan oil and returned to the beach. She would probably suffer for it tonight, but now she did not really care. An unhappy lethargy had settled over her, and sunburn seemed the least of her problems.

She felt, rather than heard, his approach, and she opened her eyes a crack as Kyle's shadow fell over her. He was wearing a pair of red swimming briefs and leather thongs, and he had never looked so attractive, so vitally masculine. He sat down beside her and inquired, "What's your favorite flower?"

She opened her eyes wider in surprise. "Why?"

He looked contentedly out over the ocean. "I want to know what kind to send you in intensive care. You're going to end up with third-degree burns."

She closed her eyes again and muttered, "I haven't been out that long."

But after a while she opened her eyes again, unable to ignore the warm, electric presence of him so near to her again. She studied him for a long time, but he did not notice—or he pretended not to notice—his eyes fixed on the soothing, undulant motions of the sea. His body could have been sculpted from marble, his face modeled after those found on Greek coins. His fingers, long and delicate and strong, were looped around one upraised knee, and only a faint line marked the leg that had been imprisoned in a cast only a few weeks ago. She asked, without meaning to, "How do you keep such a perfect tan?"

"I spend ninety percent of my time in temperatures that would make the devil wish for central air," he replied, and then he glanced at her, a faint upward curve of his lips signaling the inquiry. "Does this mean you're calling a truce?"

A heat that was not from the sun touched her face, and she could not prevent a smile even as she drew her brows together in mock thoughtfulness. "I suppose so," she decided.

The sudden gleam in his eyes should have warned her. "Good," he declared, and suddenly he pounced on her, taking her breath away, and began to cover her with mad, passionate kisses.

She gasped in alarm and then in laughter as she struggled beneath his weight. "Stop it!" she cried, pushing at him and twisting beneath him with no real effort at all to dislodge him. "You're crazy. Stop it!"

"I will not," he replied and began nibbling at her ear. "Wartime truces are notoriously short-lived, and I'm taking advantage of this one while I can."

His lips began to ravish her neck and her ear and her face again, and she moaned with laughter and not a little from the pleasurable sensations his playful, exaggerated lovemaking was creating. "Get up!" she commanded, only half serious. "You're crushing me. I can't breathe!" She grasped his shoulders and demanded in mock severity, "What are you doing?"

He lifted his weight a little and looked down at her, his eyes glittering wickedly. "Guess," he replied and lowered his mouth to hers.

Automatically she responded, slipping her arms around him, her fingers exploring the silky thickness of his hair and the smooth, powerful feel of the muscles along his back and shoulders, loving it, welcoming it. No, it was not impossible at all to put the past behind when Kyle filled all her senses, demanding and receiving a total commitment to the present.

She felt free and joyous, loving the feel of his weight and his warm bare skin, slippery with the oil from her body, against hers. She wound her legs around his and felt his quickened intake of breath as he arched her against him, so that they were touching at all points. The sound of the ocean ebbed far away and then startlingly close in waves of silver dizziness, and above the irregular pounding in her chest she felt the wild thumping of his heart against her breast. In a matter of moments it was no longer possible to ignore the seriousness of his intent or the evidence of his desire, and she welcomed it gladly, knowing that she would make love with him here on the beach beneath the bright warmth of the sun without shame or restraint and that it would be wonderful.

Then he groaned a little and pushed himself away, moving to his side and drawing her into the tight circle of his embrace, as though even a momentary absence from her would cause enormous pain. "On a public beach, already," he moaned softly, his face against her cheek.

She stroked his hair with an unsteady hand. "It's a private beach," she whispered.

She saw his eyes glance away from her, and the expression on his face was pure agony as his arms tightened briefly around her before loosening again. "Not so private as all that," he replied.

In confusion she followed the direction of his gaze, and saw two figures near the steps. It was Kate and Michael.

He sat up, pulling her with him, and his hands caressed her arms and her shoulder lingeringly before releasing her. He made an effort to steady his breathing and compose his face while Barbara smoothed her hair and wondered frantically how much, if anything, her sister had seen. Passion in her died a quick and painful death. But for Kyle it was not so easy.

"I think," he said after a moment, his eyes lingering hungrily on her lips for just a second before he moved them forcefully away, "I'd better take a cold dip in the ocean before I meet our wayfaring hosts. You'll make my apologies, won't you?"

But Barbara was too busy trying to hide her own frustration and guilt to give much thought to Kyle's problems as she saw Kate lift her hand and begin skipping down the steps toward her.

It was a joyous reunion, for despite their inopportune arrival, Barbara was glad to see her sister again, looking so well and happy. Kate followed Barbara upstairs so she could change, chattering all the while about the parties in New York, fishing in Vermont, and a glorious second-honeymoon interval they had spent in a secluded cabin in northern Canada. Kyle was there when they came down, having changed into jeans and a knit pullover shirt, and he came forward and kissed Kate elaborately. "Hey," he accused, "aren't you supposed to be getting fat or something?"

She laughed, pushing him away. "Not for a while yet, with luck!"

They spent the afternoon reliving the details of the trip; Michael fixed cocktails and they made a celebration of it. And then, just as Kate had suggested something be done about dinner, a meaningful glance passed between husband and wife and Michael commented, with assumed casualness, "We saw Roseanne in New York. At a party."

Barbara's eyes went quickly to Kyle's face, but either he was very skilled at hiding his feelings or there was nothing there to hide. He replied, "Is that right? What's she up to?"

"The usual," replied Michael, refilling his drink. He lifted the pitcher and offered, "Anyone else?" At the unanimous negative he crossed the room again and added, "She's got a new boyfriend. He must be ten years younger than she is."

"A daredevil type," added Kate.

"Stunt man," corrected Michael.

Kyle sipped his drink placidly.

"She's all for leaping in to his life-style with both feet," Kate said with only a slight frown as she glanced at the glass of milk Michael had insisted she have instead of alcohol. "She's got this wild little sports car that she drives like a maniac and her new fellow is teaching her to fly—"

Now Kyle's face tightened noticeably and he looked up. "Fly?"

Kate nodded. "Stunt planes. I swear, Kyle, how that woman has lived this long is beyond me. She lives like she's bent on suicide."

"What the hell is she thinking of?" exploded Kyle. He downed his drink in a single gulp and stood abruptly. Furious tension surged through him but was most evident in the tightening of his fingers around the delicate stemmed glass. "She's got no business running around with men half her age and making a fool of herself. Hell, she can't even drive, much less fly!"

A shocked silence followed his outburst, which Michael covered smoothly with, "You know how she is, Kyle. You can only believe about half of what she says, anyway. She was as high as a kite when we talked to her."

"She's always high," snapped Kyle. "That's exactly what I mean." He lifted the pitcher to pour himself another drink, changed his mind, and returned it to the bar.

Barbara said in a small voice, "We'd really better start dinner."

With a glance at Kyle's hard, dark face Kate agreed, and they left the room. In a few moments Barbara heard Michael begin to speak in a low, calming tone, but she could not hear what was said.

In the kitchen Kate turned to her, disturbance in her eyes, and began, "Babs—" But then she clearly remembered Michael's instructions about noninterference, she bit her lips briefly, and then smiled. "Nothing," she said.

It was just as well. Barbara knew she was going to try to explain Kyle's violent reaction to the mention of his ex-wife, and there was really no need. Barbara thought she understood it all too well. And it was only a matter of days before she understood even more.

The four of them were going out to dinner. Kyle had never said a word to Barbara about Roseanne, and by the next morning she could almost believe she had imagined the entire episode. They were talking and laughing and teasing Kate about the tight fit of her dress, which really wasn't very noticeable at all, when the doorbell rang. Kate went to answer it.

She returned rather nervously with one of the most beautiful women Barbara had ever seen. She was almost as tall as Kyle, her perfect figure molded sleekly into a pair of designer jeans and a glittering, daringly low-cut sweater. The ash-blond hair was swept glamorously to a loose bun on the one side of her head, and low over one eye. The color, thought Barbara critically, was certainly not natural. She entered the room with a sweep of Dior perfume and the style of a professional model.

"Roseanne," began Kate uncertainly, "I'd like you to meet my sister."

But Roseanne ignored her, going straight for Kyle with arms outstretched. "Darling!" she cried effusively. "I just couldn't stay away. I heard about your accident and I was simply devastated!"

Not a flicker of expression crossed Kyle's face as he stepped deliberately away from her threatened embrace. "I'm glad to see you survived the shock," he responded coolly, and Barbara's spirits lifted cautiously. Perhaps he had been telling the truth when he insisted he had no more feelings for Roseanne, but Barbara found it hard to believe any man could completely get over a woman as beautiful as Roseanne. She watched them carefully, her apprehension tinged with something unpleasantly like jealousy.

Roseanne did not appear to be in the least affected by the rebuff, but hung on to his arm with a slithering motion, laughing lightly. "Now, sweet, don't be cruel. You know I'm so busy I'm always the last to hear any news, but if I had known, I would have rushed to your side with flowers and candy, you do know that, don't you?"

Kyle gave a noncommittal "Hmm" and disentangled his arm. "I suspect, however, that you've rushed to my side this time for no other reason than a temporary shortage of cash, am I right?"

Roseanne glanced about the room in amusement, and Kate and Michael took a unified stance against her, leaving only Barbara to feel like the intruder. What she really wanted to do was leave the room, but she could not bring herself to miss the exchange, however painful it was to watch, between Kyle and the woman who had broken his heart.

"Darling," Roseanne laughed, "you were always so crude! Do you really think we have to discuss anything as vulgar as money in mixed company?"

"Oh, I don't think anyone minds," replied Kyle casually, and taking out his checkbook, he went over to the desk. "Will twenty-five hundred be enough to make the next payment on your new sports car, or have you wrecked it already?"

Once again Roseanne glanced about the room, looking annoyed at his effective dismissal of her, but greed appeared to get the better of her. Barbara's heart ached for Kyle when she remembered his dry words about his ex-wife: "She found a guy with a bigger checkbook." It must have been miserable for him to be used that way, and she experienced a flare of anger toward the woman, who was so blind she could see nothing more valuable in a man such as Kyle than his bank account.

Roseanne walked over to Kyle and crooned, "I like round figures better, darling." He did not even glance up as he wrote the check, tore it out, and presented it to her. She glanced at it, practically purring with satisfaction, and folded it into her purse. "You're a dear," she said and leaned forward to kiss him.

He caught her wrist. "I also," he told her coldly, "expect some return on my money."

Barbara stared at him as Roseanne drew back, startled, trying to cover it with a laugh. Barbara would never have believed that the gentle face of the man she thought she knew could turn so hard, so frighteningly devoid of human emotion. "Why, love," Roseanne exclaimed, "whatever do you—"

"Come on," he said, giving her wrist a sharp jerk. "We're going to have a little talk."

The other three watched in unanimous surprise as he led her, laughingly protesting, to Michael's study and closed the door behind them.

Barbara felt a slow, wretched color stain her cheeks as Michael and Kate glanced uncomfortably in her direction; she avoided their eyes. Oh, God, she would have given anything not to have witnessed that scene, to have been able to go on imagining Roseanne as a shadowy ghost somewhere in the dim recesses of Kyle's past. Seeing them together, seeing how Roseanne could still manipulate him, and seeing all of the unpleasant facets of Kyle's reaction to her had made "the other woman" a clear and present threat, and it shattered Barbara's secure and untroubled present in an expectedly poignant way.

The moments that passed, punctuated only by the occasional muffled sounds of raised voices behind the closed door, were the longest Barbara had ever spent. She strained her ears to make out the words of the angry conversation, and then forced herself to concentrate on something else. She did not really want to know what was being said. What she had seen was enough, for, whether it was love or hate, it was obvious Roseanne still had a power over Kyle that would not be easy to break. For a while Kate and Michael tried to make conversation, but Barbara was only moderately responsive. Her thoughts were behind that closed door, and her suffering was with Kyle.

They all tensed as the door of the study opened and Roseanne stalked out. Her color was high and her lips tight as she swept through the living room, looking neither right nor left, and out the front door. In a moment a car door slammed and an engine roared to life. She left with a squeal of tires and a flash of headlights on the window.

"What do we have that will get rubber off a driveway?" Michael joked weakly, and then Kyle came in.

Barbara half rose, and then sank back to her chair at his tense, angry stride. His face was ashen under his tan, drawn into grim lines. His eyes were glittering slits of green fire but he did not look at her. Not one breathless moment passed before he was gone, slamming the door behind him with a heavy thud.

Barbara felt a little weak. She had never seen him like that before. Despair tugged at her that Roseanne could do that to him—a woman he claimed to no longer love, but who still had the power to torture him into a blind rage.

Stunned moments passed in awkward silence before Michael stood, touching his wife's arm lightly. "We'd better go," he said, "if we want to keep our reservations."

Kate glanced at him, then at Barbara, and she stood briskly. "You're right. Get your purse, Babs."

Barbara was shaken and still a little befuddled. "Shouldn't—shouldn't we wait for Kyle?" she managed in a moment, in a small voice.

Michael looked at her, and then to the door by which his brother had made his abrupt exit. "No," he said in a moment. Then he offered his arm to her with a smile. "Let's go."

Barbara did not remember what she ate, if anything, nor a word of the banal conversation that must have occupied that evening. She was aware of Kate's occasional sympathetic, anxious glances, but she could not even rouse herself to reassure her sister. In her mind was a constant picture of the two Beautiful People, physically so perfect for one another, and the fairy-tale marriage that had gone bad. She could understand Kyle's attraction to her, and she could understand how deeply and with what cruel ease Roseanne must have hurt him. She wondered if it were possible for him to ever get over a woman like that, when love was all mixed up with pain.

And it was her own understanding of Kyle's pain that hurt Barbara the most. All this time she had been concerned only with her own problems, never thinking that Kyle had a cross to bear as heavy as her own. She wanted to give him the comfort he must have needed from her all along, but which she had been too self-absorbed to see he needed. She had taken so much from him, and he had asked so little from her. He had been through the bad times with her, but until tonight she had been excluded from the unpleasant parts of his life. Having been there and having seen his suffering, she felt closer to him now than she ever had. She wanted to tell him so.

She went to bed early, but lay awake, aching with Kyle's pain. When the telephone rang, she snatched at it, not giving Kate or Michael a chance.

"I'm sorry." It was Kyle's voice, low and heavy.

She sat up, her fingers tightening around the receiver, not bothering to turn on the lamp. "It's all right," she said softly. "I understand."

There was a silence, broken at last by his long sigh. "No, you don't," he replied quietly. "But if you think what you do and can still forgive me, I suppose it's more than I deserve."

Pain bubbled to her throat and she swallowed hard against it. "I—I'm just sorry you're hurt," she said.

Another silence. "Bobbie, will you believe just one thing?"

Silently she nodded.

"It's not that there's still anything between us. I wouldn't lie to you about something like that."

"I know," she said honestly. What was pulling him was something else—broken dreams and betrayed promises, and wishing for a magic wand to make everything different. She had been there all too often, she understood too well. She could see how Kyle might have been infatuated with a woman like Roseanne, even how he had fallen in love, and how bitterly he must have suffered when he discovered what he had built of her was only a dream, shattered by her cruelty and selfishness, leaving him with not even the comfort of a memory or the possibility of hope. No, it was not love that gave her power over him, but something that was almost as strong.

The silence this time was not uncomfortable, but deep with understanding and shared feelings. Then he said, "Happy birthday."

She frowned a little in puzzlement. "What?"

"It's after midnight. Happy birthday."

She laughed a little, pleased and touched that he had remembered. "Is it? Well, thank you!"

"It's going to be a good one, Bobbie," he said softly. "Get some sleep, now. You've got to look gorgeous for the party."

She smiled again into the receiver. "You too."

And, strangely enough, she did manage to sleep.

Chapter Nine

The party was an enormous success. There was much to celebrate, and Michael and Kate's friends were warm, enthusiastic, and easy to get to know. They made Barbara feel welcome immediately; no one was a stranger, and hardly a moment passed that she was not talking to someone, drawn into a group or singled out, laughing and having an honest good time. She felt pretty and feminine in the lavender print crepe, the eyes of other men told her so, and she received extravagant compliments along with congratulations on her birthday. But the highlight of the evening was when she first saw Kyle.

He had stayed so late helping with preparations for the party that he was among the last to arrive. He made his way across the room, greeting old friends, accepting a drink, and all the while his eyes were searching until they found Barbara.

He was wearing a golden-brown jacket and a turtleneck that was startlingly close to the shade of his eyes, and somehow managed to bring it off without the slightest appearance of pretension. Those emerald eyes were bright with an appreciative light as he crossed the room to Barbara, and if she had never felt more beautiful, it was because of what she saw in his eyes. He took her in his arms and kissed her full on the lips, in front of everyone, and murmured "Happy birthday, Bobbie."

She felt her color rise with the thrill of his presence, and she laughed. "Are you trying to make a spectacle of me?"

His eyes crinkled and a smile snapped within them. Then he winked. "Sure you want to stay at this dull old party? It just so happens I know a little place—"

She struck out at him playfully, and he bent to kiss her cheek before they were separated.

It was a long time before they met again. Barbara did not lack for company, but she kept looking for Kyle. The house was so crowded, even spilling out onto the lawn, that he was not easy to find. Occasionally she caught glimpses of him, laughing and talking with other people, and more often than not the other people were female. She was aware of a jealous scrutiny on her part on these occasions, but to all appearances Kyle's relationship with these other women was strictly casual. Although there was naturally a lot of playful touching and kissing in the festive atmosphere among good friends, Kyle's behavior was beyond reproach. And she never saw him with the same woman twice.

As the hour grew late and some who had driven great distances for the occasion began to leave, the atmosphere grew more intimate. A few couples were dancing to slow ballads in the living room, others were sitting on the terrace or walking along the shore. Kyle was not among them. Barbara went into the dining room where the bar and canapés were set up, but he was not there, either. Roger Daily, a plump, bald little man to whom Michael had introduced her earlier, came over to her.

"Michael tells me you're an editor," he said.

She laughed and corrected, "Was."

His eyes twinkled in a friendly, open way. "You wouldn't be looking for a job, would you?"

She was caught off guard. "Well, I—I hadn't thought much about it. . . ."

"I have a little outfit in Portland," he explained. "Advertising and market research. I could sure use an assistant right now. The reason I thought of you is because most of our advertising consists of a technical publication we put together six times a year. Naturally I need someone with a strong journalism background and an ability to understand and interpret technical data. I also understand you helped Kyle with his book."

"Well, yes. . . ." she floundered, completely overwhelmed. Portland! It could be the chance she had been looking for, to stay here and start a new life.

"We're a small operation," he continued, "and very exclusive. We handle products that never get to the mass market, of course, dealing mostly with big industry and a few government projects. I'll tell you what, Barbara," he offered, pulling out his card. "If you're interested, I think this could work out quite well for you. The salary wouldn't be much to start, but then I wouldn't expect you to work full-time. You could take on whatever assignments you felt you could handle and set your own schedule. You wouldn't even have to come into the office every day. But eventually, if it works out. . . ." He smiled. "Well, we're a growing business, and I'm looking for a right-hand man— or woman. Will you think about it?"

She took his card hesitantly. "I—I will," she said. "Thank you!"

He nodded and left her examining his card in wonder. It was all so sudden, she just wasn't certain. She supposed Portland was as good a place to settle down as any, and she did want to be near Kate and the baby, but she wondered if she was really ready to make an important decision like that. She put his card safely away in a drawer of the buffet and turned at a tap on her shoulder.

"Do you know," Kyle whispered, "I've been trying to catch you alone all evening? You're a pretty popular lady."

She stepped very naturally into his embrace, her hands against his chest, as his arms encircled her waist lightly. She tipped her face up to him coquettishly and inquired, "And what did you want to catch me alone for?"

His fingers were restless on her waist and his eyes darkened with a leap of flame. "Let's not go into that," he said huskily. He turned to lead her out of the room. "A dance is safer."

"Kyle," she said excitedly as he drew her into his arms in the midst of the other couples dancing in the living room, "do you know what that man did?"

His brows drew together as he looked down at her cautiously. "What man?"

She hardly even noticed his tensing. "Roger Daily," she explained breathlessly. "He offered me a job!"

He relaxed and laughed softly as he drew her closer. "Is that right? And I was getting ready to tear into some poor fellow for making a pass at you!"

She giggled and snuggled against him, and for a moment everything else faded away as she surrendered herself to the slow, sensuous movements of the dance and his body against hers. And then he stepped back a little, looking down at her with an unreadable expression in his eyes. "So?" he inquired.

She looked up at him in confusion. "So what?"

"The job. Are you going to take it?"

She frowned a little before resting her face against

his shoulder again. "I'm not really sure. It sounds perfect. But I'm just not sure."

She thought he released a slight breath before drawing her close again. "You think about it," he advised her gently. "But don't make any sudden decisions."

But right then she did not want to think of anything at all. She wanted only to be with Kyle and hold him and move around the room with him to the soft rhythm of the music and to feel the swelling of contentment within her as she knew this was the happiest night of her life. Could it have been only a few months ago that she had come here, almost reluctantly, never dreaming that happiness would find her here and present her with a new life? She tightened her arms around Kyle and released a sigh of quiet joy. He bent to kiss her hair.

"Kate looks tired," she murmured, noticing her dancing with her husband in the thinning crowd.

"I know. I suggested to Michael a few minutes ago it might be time to wind this whole thing up. It's getting late, anyway. And speaking of which—" He suddenly stepped out of her embrace and caught her hand. His eyes were veiled with mystery. "Come along."

"But what—?" she began in confusion, but he silenced her, leading between the dancing couples with a gentle tug on her hand.

"You'll find out."

He took her to the guest room and closed the door behind them.

"Kyle," she laughed a little nervously, glancing at he closed door, "what is this? What will Kate think?"

"She'll think," he assured her solemnly, "that I want to be alone with her sister."

He walked over to the desk and drew from behind it

what was unmistakably a framed portrait. He came
over to her, turned it face up, and presented it to her.
"Happy birthday, Bobbie," he said.

She took it in her hands wonderingly, moved to
speechlessness. It was a portrait of herself playing
with Jojo on the beach. Her head was thrown back in
laughter as sea spray glistened in the air; the wind
whipped her hair away from her face and her violet-
blue eyes were a shade brighter than the sea. His eye
for detail and photographic precision had never been
more evident: the damp spots on her jeans and her
red-checked blouse where water had splashed, grains
of sand sticking to her arms and to Jojo's fur, the
ships on the horizon, every glistening shell fragment
and drift of seaweed on the beach. She knew immediately it was a masterpiece, but it was more, because it
was of her. With his brush he had explored her body
intimately and gone beyond to discover her character
and capture one moment of it forever on canvas.
This was Barbara Ellis as seen and remembered by
Kyle Waters. Her hand shook slightly as she caressed
the portrait. "Oh, Kyle," she whispered.

"You know," he confessed, "I thought it would
be hard to give it to you. It wasn't."

Because he trusted her. He trusted her with something he had been unsure of with other people, and
that was special. Very special indeed. "It's beautiful," she said softly, worshipfully. "Kyle, it's
just...beautiful." Then she glanced at him shyly.
"You flatter me."

"You know I don't do that," he told her simply.
"I can't."

She stepped forward and caressed his neck with her
hand, the other lovingly shielding the portrait. His
kissed her tenderly, with a depth of feeling that

transported her beyond passion, and she returned it fully. She had never felt closer to him, more a part of him, more complete and whole in her own right and anxious to share every part of herself with him. She had never wanted him as badly as she did that night.

He moved away, but the wanting was as deep in his eyes as it was in hers, probing to the depths of her very soul. He stroked her face gently with his hand, and in a moment he said, somewhat huskily, "I think I'd better leave now."

She touched his hand as he stepped away, closing her fingers lightly around his. Her eyes were wide and dark with the promise within her message. "Kyle," she whispered, "I don't want you to."

He looked at her for a moment, a cautious question in his eyes. She answered it softly, a hint of shyness tinging her cheeks. "Tonight," she whispered, her eyes wide and luminous as they searched his, "it's just you and I. The past is really over, Kyle, you've made me see that. Tonight I only want to be with you."

For a long moment their eyes interlocked, exploring the silent secrets within, and his face altered with tenderness and wanting as he brought her fingers slowly to his lips. "I never lock my door," he said softly, and in another moment he turned reluctantly and left.

She knew he was only giving her time to make sure of her feelings, and she smiled to herself because she knew her feelings would not change.

She took the portrait secretly up to her room and stayed there a long time, looking at it. Tomorrow she would share it with Kate and Michael, but for tonight it was hers—a very special something between her and Kyle that transported her into a world of discoveries about herself, and about him, and each discovery she made was a new experience of wonder and delight. In the moment he had chosen to capture on canvas she had been free, unfettered by care or memories of the past, open to the joy of the world around her, simple and honest. And in giving it to her he had somehow set her free again, and the experience was rich with promise and delight.

When she came downstairs, the last guests were departing. Kate was leaning against Michael, smiling with contentment, but her eyes were half closed and she was pale with fatigue. "You," Barbara told her sister, "had better get straight to bed. I'll straighten up down here."

"Oh, leave it till tomorrow, Barbara," Michael replied, sounding happily weary himself. "We'll make a day of it. Either that or call in a cleaning crew."

"I'm too excited to sleep," Barbara told him. "I'll just empty a few ashtrays and gather up the glasses." She walked over to them and kissed Michael on the cheek, and then her sister. "Thanks for the best birthday I can ever remember," she said, smiling.

He returned her smile as Kate hugged her. "I'm glad you had a good time, Barbara," he said.

"But the guest of honor doesn't have to clean up afterward," Kate reminded her as they started up the stairs. "Leave it."

"Go to bed," Barbara told them.

Meticulously she emptied every ashtray and stacked the glasses in the dishwasher to capacity, just as she had said she would. Then she left the house quietly and climbed the steps to Kyle's apartment. The door was open.

Bright moonlight flooded the room, softer and more muted than the day, but just as clear. It bounced off the white stripes of his cocoa-brown sheets, caressed his smooth brown chest, and turned the streaks in his hair to glowing silver. He was propped up on his elbows in bed, as though waiting for her, and his smile was warm and welcoming. "Hi," he said softly. "What are you doing here?"

She closed the door and stepped inside. "I have come," she replied, her voice softened with anticipation and warmth despite the light tone, "in answer to your advertisement. 'Good clean fun, no strings attached, satisfaction guaranteed or your money cheerfully refunded.'"

His smile deepened with hers as she reached behind her and the zipper of her dress opened with a whispering sound. She let it fall to her feet and stood before him for a moment in a pale lavender teddy, its wide lace edging forming delicate shadows against her breasts and her thighs in the moonlight. Then she stepped out of the dress and walked over to the bed.

He drew her into his arms, gently, wonderingly, his breath soft and warm against the sensitive areas of her skin. Light, lingering kisses played over her face and her neck, as though she were a gift too precious to be explored in haste. She felt herself drowning in the warmth of those kisses.

In a silken graceful movement he released the straps of her teddy from her shoulders and drew the garment down over her hips, then discarded it. Then they were together, flesh against flesh, his naked limbs entwined around hers just as she had yearned for so many times, and the warmth of their bodies flamed to fire as the urgency of a need too long contained swelled within them.

His hands cupped the roundness of her shoulders and trailed gently down to the curves of her hips, while his mouth sought the softness of her breasts. She wound her fingers in the silky length of his hair with a little moan as his tongue sent shivers of electricity on fine wires from the sensitive tips of her nipples to the core of her abdomen. He followed that path with his mouth, placing gentle kisses along her ribs, the soft flesh of her stomach, at last resting with maddening deliberation on her navel. Her own hands moved restlessly over his body, exploring the strong cords of his neck, the muscles of his back finely sheathed in smooth skin, the hardness of his buttocks, and she wanted him, she wanted to know every part of him, to make him a part of her as it should always have been. His strong thighs gently separated hers and she did not know why she had fought it so long, for it was right, what was happening between them. She should have known all along that with Kyle it would be right....

He brought his face to hers, his hands cupping her face on either side and his fingers separating her hair with a fine, worshipful delicacy. In the dim moonlight she could see her own joy and wanting reflected in his eyes, and he whispered, "Bobbie...." But she stopped his words with her lips, drawing him to her.

Their union was easy and natural, the way it can be only when two beings are in perfect harmony with one another. She had known making love with Kyle would be perfect, she had imagined it would be extraordinary, just as everything else about this man was extraordinary, but the emotions that moved her in his embrace took her completely by surprise. She was transported beyond the sensual experience into realms she had not imagined to explore ever again, where minds and spirits, as well as bodies, were in perfect unison. The sweetness of the experience was so intense she felt tears of pure joy bathe her eyes and she drew him closer, and closer, wanting it never to end.

When at last the peaks of starbursting joy had faded into the shimmering stillness of the night, they lay wrapped tightly in one another's arms, contentment enfolding them like a feather blanket, unwilling to move away from one another by even a few inches or for only a moment. At length he stirred to bring his lips to her neck, his breath warm and gentle on the curve of her jaw. She stroked his hair with an unsteady hand as he placed a kiss on her throat, another on her ear, another on her hairline. "Oh, Bobbie," he murmured with a sigh, his arm tightening once again around her as his head rested against the pillow. "There's no more truth in advertising."

She smiled languorously in the dark as she ran her fingers through the softness of his hair at the temple. "Whatever can you mean?" she challenged him softly, her voice husky with contentment and the residue of passion, which even now was beginning to build again.

His embrace loosened somewhat, so that he could look down at her. His face was very sober, and a deep light of tenderness burned in his eyes. "I love you," he said quietly. "I want to marry you."

Chapter Ten

For an endless moment Barbara could not move, or think, or even breathe. Waves of shock began to wash over her, sending pinpricks of ice to her lips and her fingertips. And then, slowly, she pulled away.

Confusion began to cloud the smile on Kyle's face as she got up and stumbled across the room, groping for her dress. Her breath was coming raggedly. "Hey," he joked weakly, although there was a sharp undertone of fear in his voice. "What is this? You're running away just because I decided to make an honest woman of you?"

She stepped into the dress blindly, hearing a small ripping sound above the thundering of her heart as she jerked it over her hips. Kyle flung back the covers and pulled on his robe, all pretense of humor gone now. "Bobbie, did you hear me?" he demanded. "I said I love you! What are you doing?"

"I—I'm leaving." She tried to zip her dress with shaking hands, but the zipper caught and she tore at it, almost sobbing with frustration. She searched for her shoes.

He caught her arm. His face was drawn, his eyes dark with bewilderment and fear. "What did I do? What the hell is this?"

She broke away with a cry and covered her face with her hands to smother the sobs. "Stop it!" she managed to gasp at last, and then only in a whisper. Her lips were numb, and she could only repeat what was racing through her mind, over and over again, "I can't handle this.... I...can't...handle this...."

She broke away from him and ran out the door. She made it halfway down the steps before she tripped and almost fell, but she caught herself against the rail and then sank to the step, clutching the wood rail and shaking. She was not sobbing, but her uneven gasps for breath made it sound so. It wasn't fair, it simply wasn't fair. She had not bargained for this!

She heard the door close behind her, and Kyle sat beside her. He did not touch her. "Bobbie, I don't understand," he demanded desperately. "What is it? What did I do?"

She made a concentrated effort to steady her breathing. "No," she whispered. "Don't say that. You don't have to say that. Why did you say it?" She turned to him, pleading.

"Because it's true," he insisted, clutching her hands tightly, and deep down inside she knew that it was. Despair gripped her. "I love you and I want you—not just for a night, or a few weeks, but *forever*."

"It's...not supposed to be that way!" she gulped, trying to withdraw her hands. He held them firm. "That's not the way I wanted it! No promises, no commitments.... I didn't bargain for this!"

"Dammit, Bobbie, I want you to be my wife. I want to—"

"It could have been so good!" she cried, jerking her hands away. "Why did you have to spoil it? I never asked anything from you, I never—"

"What are you afraid of?" he demanded, rising as she struggled to her feet. His face was very white now, and angry. "Why are you acting this way?"

She jerked away from his touch, propelling herself down the steps with her hands on the rail.

"Damn it all, Bobbie," he cried desperately. "I love you! Don't you understand that?"

She reached the bottom step, and somehow she managed to turn around. "Don't follow me," she said. Her voice was high and tight between gulping breaths. "And don't...say that anymore!" She turned and ran across the lawn.

"I will!" He called after her, and there was despair in his voice. "I will because it's true, and you know it!"

BY TEN O'CLOCK in the morning, she had cleaned the house thoroughly, except for the vacuuming, which would disturb the still-sleeping Michael and Kate. She went through the motions numbly, trying not to think, trying not to feel. It wasn't her fault Kyle had fallen in love with her. It wasn't her fault she could not give him what he wanted. Hadn't she made it clear to him her heart belonged to another man, and would forever? Hadn't she made it clear? Wasn't it enough that he should ask her to share her body with him...and wasn't it enough that she had learned to give it freely and without constraint? What did she expect from her?

She couldn't think about it. She couldn't keep dwelling on it. It was over and it hurt her to hurt him, but she had to go on. She had to get her life together before she managed to shatter it irrevocably, belaboring things she couldn't help.

She slowly took the business card from the buffet drawer and dialed the number.

Roger Daily sounded pleased when she identified herself. "Barbara! Does this mean you've come to a decision in my favor?"

She managed a weak laugh. "I'm not sure whether it's entirely in your favor or not, but I do appreciate the offer of the job and I'd like to try it."

"Wonderful!" he exclaimed. "I don't think you'll regret it. Michael explained to me that it's been a while since you've done this type of work, and this will be the perfect opportunity for you to get back into it slowly, to take it at your own pace. There was one thing I didn't mention to you last night. There will be some occasional travel involved. Is that going to be a problem?"

"No," she answered. Travel would be perfect. It would be exactly what she needed. "In fact, I'll enjoy it."

"Excellent."

They made an appointment at his office for the next day, discussed a few more details of the job, and he mentioned a salary that Barbara thought was very reasonable considering the fact that she would only be working part-time. Of course, it would mean she wouldn't be able to afford a place of her own for a while, but maybe Michael and Kate wouldn't mind putting her up for a few more months, and if she worked really hard, she was certain she could convince Mr. Daily to take her on full-time sooner than he had planned. She hung up feeling vaguely satisfied with the first real step she had taken toward a new life. When she turned around, Kyle was standing there.

He was still wearing the same green turtleneck and slacks from the night before. His face was haggard and unshaved, and his eyes puffy and red rimmed, as though from drunkenness, or sleeplessness. For a moment she was actually afraid he was drunk—she had never seen him like that. But when he moved past her to pour a cup of coffee, not the faintest scent of alcohol clung to him, and she released a cautious, tight breath of relief. To face him at all this morning would be difficult, but she had known it was inevitable, and at least he was sober.

"You took the job," he said expressionlessly, filling his cup.

"Y-yes." She could not look at him without remembering the ecstasy she had experienced in his arms the night before, she could not remember it without experiencing a twist of agony and yearning.... She had to move away, so she walked as casually as she could back to the breakfast nook, where her own coffee waited. Her hands were twisted tightly before her and she forced herself to release them, lest she betray her awful nervousness to him. "It was really too good to turn down."

"I see," he said heavily. After a moment he sat across from her. His eyes were a careful mask concealing a depth of pain too close to the surface, and for a moment he concentrated on his coffee, saying nothing.

She watched him bring the cup to his lips, and her eyes fell upon those strong brown fingers encircling the mug. A wash of pain so acute it was almost physical struck her as she remembered the delight those hands had created within her last night. Oh, God, she still wanted him, with every fiber of her body she wanted him, and surely he could sense what it was costing her to face him this morning, so calm and rational, knowing that it must never be again.

Then he said, "I imagine the job looked a lot better to you after you left me last night."

She dropped her eyes. She knew she had to find a way to explain it to him. They were both rational adults; they had to discuss it. But just then she was saved by Michael.

He came in yawning, in jeans and a T-shirt and bare feet. He said, "Barbara, you're unbelievable. I wouldn't know it's the same house. What did you do, stay up all night? Where do you get your energy?"

"I wanted to save the vacuuming until Kate gets up," she said, glad for the distraction. "I was afraid it would wake her."

"That may be awhile yet," he answered, stirring sugar into his coffee. "As a matter of fact, I'd like to see her stay in bed the rest of the day." He glanced at his brother, an expression of mild distaste crossing his face as he reached the same mistaken conclusion Barbara had. "Sorry I can't offer you anything stronger than coffee, old man," he commented, "but I've found the best cure for a hangover is not to drink yourself under the table in the first place. And I always thought we gave very sedate parties," he mused and wandered off, presumably in search of the morning paper.

Kyle stared down into his coffee cup. "I imagine you'll be staying here, then—now that you have a job."

"In Maine, yes," she answered, glad he had chosen a neutral subject. "I'll get a place of my own as soon as I can, but Kate and Michael might have to put me up a little while longer. It doesn't pay that much to start."

"It will probably be good for you," he agreed, "to stay busy." Then he looked up. "Bobbie, I have to leave."

She could not answer, surprised at the confusing onslaught of emotions that statement caused, not one of them definable in words. She had known it was coming, but it was still a shock.

He went on, toying with the handle of his coffee cup. "I've put it off too long. Ontario. I know this is not the best time—"

"No," she corrected, proud of the steadiness in her tone. "It's probably the best time in the world. You'll stay busy, just like I'll stay busy, and we'll forget all about last night."

"No," he said sharply and looked up. The muscles of his jaw tightened and his eyes were determined as he said firmly, "I'm not going to forget it and neither are you." Suddenly his eyes shifted to the door by which Michael had left, and then, with resolve, back to her. "Bobbie, we've got to talk."

Her own courage was beginning to falter beneath the forcefulness in his tone. "We—we are talking."

He shook his head impatiently, and before she could move them, he grasped her fingers tightly, pulling her up. Even his touch sent weakening tremors of yearning through her, and she did not know how she could go on much longer, looking at him, being with him, talking to him, trying to pretend that her world had not been turned upside down in the past twenty-four hours and that she was not being torn apart inside bit by bit with every movement he made, every word he spoke.... "Michael will be back any minute for a refill," he insisted, "or Kate will come down, and we're going to talk this thing through. Let's go outside."

She knew it had to be done, and when he had closed the patio doors behind them and they stood on the terrace, she decided to take the initiative. "Kyle," she said gently, "I've thought about it a lot, and I don't want to hurt you."

"Then why do you have to?" he demanded.

She shook her head and continued, with as much calm as she could, "I don't think you really realize what is happening here. You—"

"Is it that you don't love me back?" he interrupted.

"It's that you don't love me!" she cried, for a moment losing the calm, rational tone with which she had promised herself she would see this thing through. Then, more steadily, she explained, "You told me yourself you were in love with the idea of being married." It all sounded very rational and plausible, but she was aware she was trying to convince herself as much as she was trying to convince him— and that even she could not really believe it. "That's all it is, Kyle," she insisted rather desperately, seeing the rejection beginning to form in his eyes. "You want a wife to fill your dream house and children for your nursery and a place to call home." He hissed impatiently and jerked his head to the side, staring out at the sea, but she continued, undeterred, "It's not a bad thing, Kyle. In fact, it's kind of wonderful, for some other girl, but not me. You know—"

"Do you think I'm a complete fool?" he demanded, anger flashing in his eyes. "Don't you think I've thought of that, examined it, tried to tell myself over and over again that's what it is? I've been burned once, and badly, do you really think I'm idiot enough to leap right in and do it all over again?" He turned back to the sea, leaning on the rail, and released a long breath. He shook his head sadly and finished, more quietly, "It just won't wash, Bobbie. Because it's not true. Because I really do love you."

He turned to look at her, the anger fading from his eyes. His words were quiet and deliberate, no more pleading, no more demanding, simply stating facts. And each one of them drove another spike into her heart. "I don't know when I first started to love you," he said. "That first time on the plane I was attracted to you. You were cute, I thought, and different. Sometime the next day I knew I wanted you, and before the week was out, I liked you a lot. I think I began to love you the first time I held you trembling in my arms and I knew the most important thing in the world to me was to stop whatever was hurting you from hurting you anymore.... Bobbie, can you honestly say you didn't know it? Did you really think all I wanted from you was your company in bed?"

She looked down at her hands, one of which was locked about the finger that bore her wedding band in an instinctive protective gesture. "That," she whispered tightly, "was all I was prepared to give you."

"I'm in love with you, Bobbie," he said quietly. "I'm not in love with the idea of marriage or trying to live out a fantasy. I don't even care if you love me back. I just want to be with you the rest of my life and love you. That's all."

That's all. It *was* all, it was too much....

There was a long, long silence. Then he said, "I've got a plane to catch at one o'clock." She looked up, startled. So soon! He was leaving so soon, and this was how it must end...? Seeing the brief alarm in her eyes, he said quickly, "You know that I've had this planned for a long time, don't you? You wouldn't get it in your head that just because of last night I've got what I wanted and I'm dropping you?" She shook her head in silent protest, but he seemed unconvinced. He took a step toward her. "Because I'll stay. Say the word and the Ontario project can rot as far as I'm concerned because—"

"No." Her voice came out in a croak, and she had to clear her throat. She did not know how she made herself say the words at all, but to ask him to stay would be disastrous, and she had to protect herself. She managed an almost convincing smile. "I know, I really do. And it's best."

He dropped his eyes, but not before she caught a glimpse of disappointment there. "I wish you'd stay at my place while I'm gone," he added in a moment, unexpectedly. "I know how you feel about imposing on Kate and Michael and it will make you feel a little more independent. Besides, I don't want to put my things back in storage so soon, and I'd like to think of you living there."

She looked up at him with an effort. The wedding band was digging into her finger. "How—how long will you be gone?" she had to ask.

His eyes were dark with determination, the lines of his face set. "I'll be back," he told her grimly. "I'm not giving up."

She went into the house and fixed breakfast for Michael as Kyle went up to his apartment to pack. She told Michael about her job and he seemed thrilled, and while she was talking to him, she was able to keep her thoughts away from Kyle, away from the hurt that was gnawing at the core of her stomach, away from the desperate determination that had last been in his eyes.

An hour later Michael announced that Kate was awake, but that he had decreed she should stay in bed the rest of the day to recover from the party. Barbara fixed a tray for her and sent it up with Michael, then did her vacuuming, keeping busy.

The tray was returned with a note from Kate: "Help! I'm being held a prisoner of love!" Barbara smiled as she read it, and the smile turned unexpectedly to tears. She blinked them back angrily, and then she heard the back door open. Kyle came in.

He had changed into a dark suit and pin-striped shirt and a tie; he was shaved and neatly groomed. But his eyes still looked awful. She managed a bright smile as she looked at him. She would not have tearful good-byes. "Nice," she said, indicating his outfit.

He smiled weakly and made a deprecating gesture toward the suit. "My Canadian counterparts are very conservative, British to the core. I have a meeting as soon as I get there."

She appreciated his effort to make everything seem normal, but she could not maintain the pretense, or the eye contact, much longer. She turned away quickly and began clearing off Kate's tray. "Is Michael driving you to the airport?"

"I suppose." Then he noticed the tray. Concern tightened his voice. "Is Katie sick? There's nothing wrong with the baby, is there?"

She managed a reassuring laugh. "No, she's just tired. Michael's acting like a protective husband and father-to-be. He's making her stay in bed."

He stepped forward and touched her arm. "That's what I want to be for you, Bobbie," he said softly. "A protective husband, a loving husband, and—" Something flickered across his eyes; she knew what he said next was not what he had originally intended. He changed the subject in midsentence. "Will you walk with me on the beach one more time?"

She hesitated, not wanting to, but not wanting even more to have him walk out of her life like this. She let him take her hand.

"I mean it," he said as they went down the steps, "about moving into my place. I think you'll find it's important to you, once you start getting out on your own, to have that feeling of independence. And,'' he added pointedly, glancing at her, ''if you don't have Kate and Michael around all the time, you won't have any excuse not to think. And I want you to think a lot while I'm gone.''

She swallowed hard. She did not want to have to say this to him, she didn't want to see the look in his eyes, she did not want him to leave. They were on the beach, the sand firm and cool beneath her feet, the wind lifting her hair off her neck. Unconsciously she began to twist her wedding band. ''Kyle,'' she said softly, ''I don't want to hurt you....''

''You keep saying that.''

She looked at him, her eyes filled with sorrow, pleading with him to understand. ''I never intend to marry again,'' she said simply. ''I've had my chance. What Daniel and I had was wonderful, it was magic, it was the kind of love that comes only once in a lifetime. Don't you see nothing can ever compare with that? Nothing can ever take its place.'' She dropped her eyes miserably. ''If—if I told you differently, I would be lying, and—and it would never work, don't you see? Because I could never forget... I could never forget.''

He did not answer for a time, and she was afraid to look at him. Her hand, resting so securely and firmly in his, seemed like a betrayal but he stroked it gently and she did not protest. ''I'm not asking you to forget,'' he said quietly at last. ''The past is something we carry with us always, for better or for worse, and Daniel's memory is something I hope you never put aside, because it's too precious to you...it's part of what makes you you. I'm not competing for Daniel's love, Bobbie,'' he said and stopped, so that she had to look at him. His eyes were the color of the sea at great depths, placid on the surface but hiding unfathomable secrets. "I'm not trying to take his place in your heart...I know it's already occupied. But there is room for both of us, separate and different, to walk side by side, if only you'll let it be."

She withdrew her hand from his, bringing it once again to cover her wedding band in a nervous, absent gesture. "I can't, Kyle," she whispered. "I just can't." She was being pulled in two directions, and the agony was almost crippling. Part of her could not bear to be separated from him, but the other part knew only tragedy would ensue if he stayed. Still, he was asking more than she could give. He wanted all of her, and she was not ready to make this commitment—she did not think she ever would be. But she did not want him to leave.

"You learned to stop comparing us, didn't you?" he reminded her. "You learned to let go enough to let me into one part of your life. The next step is a small one—just to believe that I'm not threatening what the two of you had together or trying to erase his memory."

She could not answer. Tears were choking her throat. She only wanted it to be the way it was before; she wanted his friendship, his companionship, his *presence* in her life. She only wanted this never to have happened. She could not bear to lose him, but she couldn't, she just couldn't, give him what he asked. For he asked for the type of love that lasts a lifetime, and Barbara had already had hers.

He glanced after a moment at his watch. "I have to start for the airport," he said.

She managed, "Will you...be gone long?"

His face was dark with regret. "I'm not sure. At

least three weeks. Maybe longer." He lifted her chin gently with his finger. Sincerity and wanting was in every line of his face. "Say the word and I'll stay," he said softly. "Tell me you need me, and the rest of the world can go to hell, I'll stay as long as you want me to."

Afraid he would read the answer in her eyes, she lowered them. She could not do that to him, for in the end it would only be good-bye again. The tears were burning painfully in her throat and any moment now she would start sobbing. *Please don't let me cry,* she pleaded to herself over and over again. *Don't let him see me cry. . . .*

He brought up his hands to grip her shoulders hard. Fierce determination was in his face, raw pain was in his eyes. "This is not good-bye," he said hoarsely. "I'll be back again and again and I'm not going to let you go. Dammit, Bobbie, I'm not going to lose twice in one lifetime!"

And without warning he drew her into his arms. His kiss was hard and possessive and tasted of salt— her own tears, she realized in a moment. When he released her, he walked quickly away, and she held back the sobs until he was out of sight.

Chapter Eleven

Kate offered Barbara unlimited use of her car for the trip back and forth to Portland, and for the first week Barbara hardly had a moment to herself. She returned each night with a briefcase loaded with papers and a sense of satisfaction and importance. The second week passed and she established a routine of going into the office only three times a week, although she stayed long hours observing and learning about the operation. She soon discovered the necessity of setting up her office space at home, and she asked Kate if it would hurt her feelings if she moved into the guest house.

Naturally Kate took it personally. She was afraid she and Michael had done something to offend Barbara or were taking up too much of her time or getting in her way. It was Michael who proved to be her ally. "Don't mind Kate," he told Barbara, laughing, "she's just afraid she'll have to start cooking again. Of course you need your privacy, we understand that."

"It's not that," Barbara tried to explain, already feeling guilty. "I love staying here with you two, but it can't be easy on you, having someone else in the house when you're used to just the two of you. Now that I'm working, I feel like I should pay my own way. I've been freeloading on you for long enough."

"Well, we can't charge rent for the guest house," Michael reminded her. "It belongs to Kyle. But if buying your own groceries and keeping your own hours will make you feel more self-sufficient, then by all means, I think you should do it.''

"Kyle said it would be all right," Barbara put in, not wanting him to think she was moving in without permission.

Michael laughed at his wife, who, as Kyle had predicted, was sometimes a little moody. "Don't look so glum! She's only moving across the lawn.''

If she had not really needed the extra space for all the work she was bringing home, Barbara was not certain she would actually have gone through with it. Being in Kyle's apartment for the first few hours was an exercise in torturous memories. Every inch of it spoke of him. Even the scent of him, elusive traces of cologne and lingering masculinity, clung to every corner. His paintings were everywhere, taking on life of their own and reflecting the humorous, tender, pragmatic man who had created them. It was very much like coming home to the apartment she and Daniel had shared after the funeral and finding the signs of his life everywhere she turned. The temptation to keep Kyle's apartment as a sort of shrine, moving carefully around his possessions, not touching or displacing anything, was great. Even his easel still stood in place, paints and brushes in readiness for his return. The difference, of course, was that Kyle would be coming back. That realization filled her with a tenuous sort of joy.

And when she got cautiously into his bed at night, remembering the last time she had been here so clearly she could almost touch him, a great, yearning ache filled her. It was a long time before sleep came.

Then one afternoon Kate came up to the guest house with a letter for Barbara. Even before she told her it was from Kyle, Barbara's heart had already missed a beat. Who else would be writing her?

She took it cautiously, joking weakly, "He probably just wants to know how his new tenant is maintaining the property!"

She was aware of Kate's curious scrutiny even as she joked back, "All we got was a postcard!"

Kate lingered, and Barbara did not open the envelope. She put it on the bar as casually as she could and offered her sister coffee.

Kate waved her hand negatively and replied, "Off my list." She looked around the room. "It's really incredible, isn't it? All these marvelous paintings, and he keeps them locked up."

"What he lacks in self-confidence he makes up in talent," agreed Barbara, pouring a cup of coffee for herself. More than anything, she wanted to discuss Kyle with her sister, but what would Kate say if she knew the depths to which their relationship had progressed? She would worry, first of all, that Barbara was unhappy, and then, she might try to push Barbara into something she was not ready for.

Then Kate made a comment that caused Barbara to suspect she knew more about Kyle's relationship with her sister than she had previously revealed. "What did you think of Roseanne?" she asked innocuously.

Barbara grimaced as she sipped her coffee. "About the same as everyone else, I suppose. There's no mistaking that type of woman."

"She sure played a neat game to trap Kyle though," remembered Kate. "As sweet and demure as you please till she left the altar. Then she let her true colors show. It's a shame," she added sadly.

"She's done everything she can to ruin Kyle's life."

"I don't suppose," ventured Barbara, "that he'll ever really be rid of her."

Kate glanced at her cautiously. "Financially, I suppose," she agreed, "she could cause him problems for a long time. Not that he can't afford it. But emotionally—" she shook her head "—all she can do is make him mad. He got over his infatuation with her, or whatever it was, quickly and completely. Of course," suggested Kate, and her face now was suspiciously innocent, "if Kyle was to marry again and have a family to invest his money in, I'm sure he would cut her off pretty quick."

Barbara avoided the lead-in, wondering if Kate was trying to pry a confession from her. It would be only natural for Kyle to have discussed his problems and his feelings with his brother, and perhaps Michael had relayed some of the conversations to Kate...or perhaps it simply would have taken a blind person to ignore what had been going on between Kyle and Barbara over the summer. The temptation to pour her heart out to her sister was great. But Michael's policy had been best: noninterference. She couldn't involve Kate in something that was tearing her apart, not while she was still so confused herself.

After a while Kate wandered off, joking, "If you write Kyle back, ask him if he's coming home for Christmas!"

But even that mild joke caused a shaft of alarm to go through Barbara, for it wasn't so much of a joke at all. It could very well be Christmas, or beyond, before she saw him again. She tore open the letter with shaking fingers.

Dear Bobbie,

I think about you all day long and at night I dream about you. I've been trying to write this letter ever since I got here but every time I started it, it came out all wrong, and I know you don't need any more pressure from me. I just wanted you to know I never stop thinking about you and I miss you so much it hurts.

She had to stop and close her eyes before she could read further. *I miss you too, Kyle,* she thought desperately, *more than I ever thought possible.*

Do you remember you asked me once if I ever had bad dreams? I do now. I dream sometimes that you're calling me and I can't reach you, or that I come home and you're not there. I hope you're not planning to make that particular dream come true because you know I would follow you all over the world if necessary, and I wouldn't stop until I found you. I told you before I'm not giving up, and if you don't believe anything else I've told you, believe that.

The bold, artistically curved and looped letters of his handwriting began to blur into black smudges on the white paper. She blinked rapidly and tried to focus.

I know what you're going through, Bobbie. I know what you're thinking. Of course it's hard for you. Maybe that's one reason I forced myself to make this trip even though I didn't want to, because I knew you had to have time alone, to work it through by yourself. There are going to be problems, Bobbie, more than you know, and I won't try to tell you otherwise. But we can work them out. Because I know nothing is going to stand in the way of my loving you—not even you.

I know you were hoping this would be a "cooling off" period for me, you were hoping that when I came back I would be ready to admit I had been impulsive and unnecessarily romantic and everything could go back to the way it was before I spoiled it all by telling you I loved you. It's simply not true. I knew it would frighten you, I knew the chance I was taking when I told you how I felt, but it simply couldn't be any other way. Bobbie, what I have for you is the once-in-a-lifetime magic you were talking about. It's changed my life and made everything that happened before this point seem like a waste. I didn't ask for you to come into my life, Bobbie, I'll be the first to admit I wasn't ready for it when it happened, but there you were and nothing has been the same for me since. You make me laugh when I'm low, you share the good times when I'm not, you're smart and you're tender and you're vulnerable and you're strong...you're everything that makes up the other half of me and when I try to imagine life without you I can't.

I wish it hadn't happened now—now, before you've completely adjusted to the loss of Daniel, now, when it's so easy for you to think I'm simply on the rebound from a bad marriage. But you're lucky, you've known love before. I've had my share of empty relationships—my marriage ranking high among them—but I've never known love before. And I would rather it had come now than not at all, because whatever happens, Bobbie, you can't take that away from me. My love for you is for a lifetime, no strings attached, absolutely guaranteed.

Darling, it's three in the morning and I have to be on the job site at six. I'm going to try to get some sleep but I don't think I will: The bed is too empty and my mind is too full. I don't know when I'll be back. Every day it drags out a little longer and I don't suppose I'm helping matters much—my mind is not exactly on my job. Maybe they'll fire me and I can come back to you. That's not entirely a joke, Bobbie, some strange thoughts have been going through my head lately and I want to talk to you when I get back. You're the only one I've ever been able to talk to about things that are really important to me, and right now there's so much I want to say.

Think of me, Bobbie, and know that I love you—

                                        Kyle

She folded the letter with trembling hands and whispered at last, "Oh, Kyle!"

Those two words seemed to encompass all she was feeling, or capable of feeling. Think about him? It was impossible to do anything else. Day and night he surrounded her, penetrated every corner of her mind, was an unshakable part of her. It was so easy to allow herself to be drawn into his fantasy, especially late at night when she was lying in his bed and wishing with all her might that he was beside her. She could allow herself tentative explorations into his world, imagining what it would be like, seeing only the good parts.

But she was too pragmatic to allow herself that escape for long. It simply wouldn't work. Everything was against them, and how could Kyle, not usually a dreamer, ignore that? There were too many ghosts lined up ready to march against their happiness. Roseanne was still a very real part of Kyle's life, a constant reminder to Barbara that Kyle had been mistaken in his feelings once, and always there to make her wonder how much Kyle still felt for his ex-wife. Marriage would be hard enough without those unspoken suspicions lurking in the shadows. Marriage. How could she consider such a thing, even in daydreams, when she was already married to Daniel? His memory would ever be with her, reminding her of her betrayal if she took another man's name. No, happiness, true happiness, only came along once in this life, and Barbara had had hers.

But she couldn't stop herself from wanting Kyle, from missing him, from lying awake at night torturing herself with reasons why it wouldn't work.

She was kept busy the next few weeks, and for that she was grateful. Most of what she was doing now was observing and learning the business, but she carefully supervised the production of the latest issue of the technical journal, made a few suggestions, and was gratified by the promise that the next issue would be entirely her responsibility. A whole new world opened up for her in the form of inventors, engineers, and those ingenius people behind the designs that make huge corporations work and modern-day life the technological miracle that it is. One of Mr. Daily's first priorities was that she take every opportunity she could to meet their clients; clearly he was grooming her for that right-hand position. Accordingly he sent her on a two-day trip to Washington, then later accompanied her on an afternoon visit to a convention in New York. She was growing in awareness of herself and her capabilities, and the only flaw in her new life was that she had no one to share it with.

Gradually her confidence in her work began to extend to other parts of her life. At first she had felt awkward and shy coming home every afternoon to Kyle's apartment; she saw herself as an intruder and was not really comfortable there. She was overzealous in her housekeeping, always making certain that nothing that belonged to him was ever even a fraction of an inch out of place and that all evidence of her occupancy was well hidden. And then one day she looked around and saw that some changes had been made, almost without her being aware of it.

Her clothes hung boldly in the closet next to the few articles he had left behind. His drawing board had been rearranged slightly to make room for her desk and worktable. She no longer carefully hid her files and paperwork at the end of the day, but left them arranged comfortably on her work space, where she could pick up at the point she had left off when next she returned. She had placed her portrait on his easel, because she liked to look at it and think about him when she was lying in bed. A few paperbacks she had bought and some other books borrowed from Michael's library were intermingled with his own collection, and she was listening to one of his record albums with as much ease as if it had been her own, for their taste in music was another thing they had in common. She actually felt as though she belonged here, and part of it was seeing their possessions interspersed and side by side. Separate but together.

She had even brought up a television set from the house, a small portable model that had once been in the downstairs guest room, and she was watching the end of a not-very-enthralling movie when the telephone rang one night. She knew Kate and Michael were in, and it was answered on the third ring. She divided her attention between the movie and the remnants of a crocheted baby sweater Kate had started and made a mess of and had begged Barbara to try to fix. Then the intercom rang.

She sighed, thinking it was probably Mr. Daily wanting her to come in tomorrow, and she had already promised Kate she would go shopping for nursery furniture with her. She picked up the extension. "Who is it?" she asked her sister.

"Surprise," responded Kate and disconnected.

Barbara's heart was pounding as she pushed the other button and said an uncertain "Hello?" and she told herself she was being foolish. It was probably just her mother, who had gotten into the habit of calling once a week to check on Kate's progress. But their mother usually called on Saturday nights. . . .

"God," Kyle said softly, from almost a thousand miles away, "it's good to hear your voice."

For one moment everything was suspended, frozen in time, even her breathing. Then the happiness and the yearning flooded over her, choking off words and filming everything over with a shimmer of unexpected tears, and more precious seconds were lost. At last she managed to whisper, "Kyle!"

He said, "It was beginning to look like just getting a call through to you was an impossible dream. There's only one telephone in this place and it doesn't work half the time. . . . Bobbie, how are you?"

It was not the kind of question that was meant to be answered with a simple "I'm fine." It was deep and full of concern, and nothing less than complete honesty would serve. "I—I miss you," she said softly. "I really do."

"I know," he responded with a sigh. "It seems like a year, doesn't it?"

She nodded silently.

"How do you like your new living quarters?"

She laughed a little. "I'm making myself right at home."

"Good. I was hoping you would."

"Kyle, I love my job." She wanted to share it all with him, every detail she had saved up over these past weeks, but she knew that was impossible on long distance. It was frustrating and only served to make her more eager for his return. "I was afraid I couldn't do it at first, but I've learned so much! And it's all so exciting. I've been to Washington and New York—"

He laughed. "Whoa there, you're not turning into a jet-setter behind my back, are you?"

She laughed with him. "Hardly! But it feels so good to be working again, doing something responsible, something that I enjoy."

"I told you, didn't I?" he reminded her. "A new job was exactly what you needed."

She hesitated. "I got the feeling you didn't want me to take it, though, when it came right down to it."

"That," he replied quietly, "was for personal reasons."

She quickly changed the subject. "And so, how is Canada?"

"Having a rotten time," he returned. "Wish you

were here. Bobbie, you're not going to believe this—"
his tone fell "—I have to fly to Mexico tomorrow."

"Mexico!" She was stunned. "But. . . how long
will you be there?"

"Not long," he assured her. "It's just that I was
packed and ready to go home. This time tomorrow I
would have been holding you in my arms. And then
the call came. Well, I can't put it off. A couple of
weeks at the most, and then—well, I'll tell you all
about that when I see you. We have so much to talk
about, Bobbie," he finished quietly.

"Yes," she agreed, but her tone was bleak. Another two weeks, and already he had been gone too
long. What was it, that she couldn't live without him
and she couldn't live with him. . . or was it that she
wouldn't *let* herself live with him?

"Have you been thinking?" he insisted, reading
her thoughts.

"Oh, Kyle," she replied miserably. Even hearing
his voice had weakened her reserve and wiped out the
careful fortifications she had built against him. What
would it be like when she was in his arms again,
which was, above all places, exactly where she wanted to be right now? "I'm so confused. I miss you so.
And I do want to be with you, only—"

"Only you won't take a chance on committing
yourself forever," he returned flatly.

"Don't sound that way," she pleaded. "Kyle, you
know it wouldn't work! What we had was good, the
way it was, why—"

"You still don't trust me, do you?" he interrupted
quietly. "You still think I'm just trying to live out
a fantasy with you. Good God, Bobbie, I'm almost
thirty-five years old. Don't you think I know my own
mind by now? I've made mistakes, plenty of them,

just like everyone else, but this is not one of them. I know it won't be easy, and I know the reasons why. I know we've got a long way to go, and we have more things working against us than the average couple. We can handle all of that, one step at a time. The important thing right now, the only thing that matters right now, is for you to learn to let go and maybe admit that you care for me a little.''

"No," she whispered, for now was the time for perfect honesty. She squeezed her eyes closed against the tears. "M-more than a little." He was her confidant, her adviser, her protector. He was the one who had given her a whole new life. He was more than a lover. He was her very best friend. And she wanted him so badly it hurt, deep within the core of her, like a heart that was preparing to break.

She heard the whisper of his sigh across the miles that separated them. "Bobbie," he said softly, "I love you."

She fought a valiant battle with the tears that were trying to choke off her voice. "If you ask me," she managed at last thickly, "I'll fly to Mexico with you. We could be together. . . ."

"We're going to be together," he assured her, "for a lot longer than two weeks in Mexico. I won't settle for less."

"Oh, Kyle," she whispered, her voice breaking, "don't do this to me."

"You're doing it to yourself," he said sadly. "But I'm not going to let you do it for very much longer. I'll be with you as soon as I can, Bobbie, and you'd better be prepared for a fight if you want to get rid of me, because I'm not letting you go. Is that perfectly clear?"

She smiled weakly through her tears. "Yes, sir."

"I love you darling," he said softly. "It won't be long."

"Good night," she whispered.

"I HOPE you don't have any plans for the weekend," Mr. Daily said.

Barbara looked up suspiciously. It was Friday afternoon, two weeks later, and she was packing her briefcase for a four-day absence from the office. Actually, the only thing she had planned was to help Michael and Kate paint the nursery, but she had looked forward to having the weekend to herself. There was enough paperwork in her briefcase to keep her busy at her home office all day Monday and Tuesday, and she had learned to value her free time whenever she could schedule it.

"Nothing definite," she had to admit reluctantly. "Why?"

"There's a client I'd like you to meet," said Mr. Daily, benignly ignoring Barbara's reluctance to give up her weekend. "He's a very busy man, but he's managed to schedule us this weekend to go over a promotional campaign for his latest invention. It will be a nice chance for you to get away too."

"Oh," she replied, enthusiasm for the project waning with each word he spoke. "Out of town?"

"Oregon," he answered. "I thought we would book an early-morning flight tomorrow, spend Sunday and Monday working on the campaign, and fly back sometime Tuesday." He gave her a sheepish grin. "My wife worries if I'm away for very long."

She frowned. "Oregon! But that's quite a trip for just two days of work. Wouldn't it be better to wait until he's in town?"

He shook his head. "I told you, we have to work

around his schedule. Besides, the client always pick up the bill for expenses, you know that.''

''Yes, but—'' She was still trying to think of some way to get out of the trip, which sounded strenuous and unexciting. ''For both of us to go—''

''Obviously it's important for you to meet a client who does so much business with us, and I'll have to be there to guide you through the first time. I know I don't always accompany you on these trips, but—'' he winked ''—this is a good-looking, single guy, and my wife would never forgive me if I let you go un-chaperoned.''

Barbara managed a conceding laugh but inwardly she groaned, *That's all I need. A weekend fighting off a good-looking, single wolf-client.*

Their flight was so early that Barbara slept through most of it. She apologized to her boss when they reached their hotel, knowing he would want to brief her on some of the particulars before they arrived, but he waved it aside. ''You just be fresh and alert for the meeting tomorrow,'' he told her, ''and every-thing will be self-explanatory. We don't expect a lot of input from you this time, but next time I expect you to be able to handle something like this on your own.''

Barbara did not press him for details, and they spent that afternoon ironing out the details of a few other projects Mr. Daily particularly wanted to have out of the way before the midmorning conference he had scheduled with the client they had traveled across the country to meet.

The automobile ride the next day was over an hour through mountainous Oregon countryside, beyond the cities and the suburbs, through national forests, and Barbara complained, ''This is really ridiculous, you know. Couldn't your very important client have at least made an effort to meet us at our hotel? There are conference rooms for that sort of thing, you know.''

''He's a little eccentric,'' admitted Mr. Daily. ''Doesn't like to travel.''

Barbara thought, Oh, brother. A weekend in a mountain lodge with an eccentric inventor could mean anything from three-martini lunches and wild parties all through the night to garbled ramblings and mad-scientist-type inspirations, none of which forecasted a very productive working weekend. She wished she had stayed at home and painted the nursery.

She tried to enjoy the passing scenery, which, on the first of September, was already tinged red and gold and orange against the blue and shadowy background of white-capped mountains. She had to grudgingly admit that the view was almost worth the trip, but she couldn't shake the feeling that this was going to be a wasted weekend.

They turned off the main road onto a short, tree-lined drive, and Barbara drew in her breath as they got out of the car. ''What a beautiful house!'' she exclaimed as her employer reached inside for their briefcases.

Set against the background of snowcapped mountains and surrounded by brilliantly colored deciduous trees, it was a three-story cedar A-frame that blended effortlessly into the environment of natural beauty. A suspension footbridge led to the front door across a musical, rushing stream, and she stepped onto it, charmed and at the same time struck by something almost familiar about the place. . . .

The front door opened and he came out.

He was wearing a low-necked casual tweed sweater, jeans, and sneakers. His tan was striking and brilliant in the noonday sun and so were the streaks in his ruffled hair. For a moment nothing moved at all, even the wind seemed to still and the birds stopped singing, and then she was running.

He caught her against him in the middle of the bridge, her joyous cry was muffled in his neck, and the suspension bridge rocked crazily in the violence of their embrace. She whispered, in a half-choked gasp, "Kyle!" and he held her tighter, his face rough and warm against her neck, threatening to crush her ribs, and for a moment he seemed incapable of saying anything.

They both became aware of the amused spectatorship of Roger Daily at the same time, and Kyle set her on her feet again, looking down at her with eyes sparkling madly. Electricity coursed through the firm grip of his hands on hers and set every fiber of her body to tingling as he demanded, "Surprised?"

She turned to Mr. Daily, trying unsuccessfully to disguise the radiant joy in her face with severity as she accused, "This was all a trick!"

"I certainly hope not," replied her boss, although his eyes too were sparkling with pleasure. "I don't mind doing a little something to further the cause of romance now and again, but I do expect to get a little work done this weekend!"

"And so you shall," declared Kyle expansively, pulling Barbara's arm protectively through his. "We're going to get that out of the way first thing."

"You mean you really are a client?" questioned Barbara, amazed.

"Well, certainly," replied Kyle, leading the way across the bridge and then around the house. "How do you think Roger got to know Mike in the first place? He's marketed all my designs for energy-saving gadgets. I told you about them, remember?" Barbara could only shake her head in helpless wonder that there seemed to be nothing Kyle could not do. He simply shrugged and went on, "Well, this one is a new type of heat pump that I plan to be using for commercial buildings, and I'm really anxious to see it on the market, but we'll get into all that later. If it's not too chilly for you two," he suggested, glancing over his shoulder at Roger, "we'll work on the deck. It gets the afternoon sun and it's better than being cooped up in the house all day. I have everything set up and we can get right to work."

Mr. Daily enthusiastically agreed, and Barbara felt like Alice in Wonderland. "But," she managed in a moment, looking questioningly at Kyle, "I thought you were in Mexico!"

"I was," he replied. They came around the back of the house and to a set of steps that led to a large red-wood deck overlooking the stream and the panorama of fall colors spreading below them as far as the eye could see. "I just got in last night."

"But," she insisted, still confused, "why didn't you just come home?"

"This *is* home," he reminded her gently and pulled up a padded deck chair for her. "Now," he said brusquely, "to work. I don't want to spend all day on this thing."

Kyle brought a platter of sandwiches and soft drinks, and Barbara knew from experience that when he said work he meant just that. But she was in a daze. The interchange between the two men went over her head and several times she had to ask them to repeat questions that were directed at her. At first she found herself repeatedly looking for an excuse to touch him—his hand, his shoulder, his jeaned knee under the table—just to assure herself he was really there. But every time she did she could see his face soften, his concentration falter, and his body tense with the effort to maintain his thought, and she had to force herself to find a position less close to him. She tried to make herself focus on the present purpose of the meeting, and she was even able to insert one or two suggestions. And as the late afternoon sun began to glitter on the treetops, Roger Daily gathered up his papers and announced, "That should do it, then. Kyle, you're amazing. It would have taken twice as long to get this mapped out with any other man."

Kyle grinned and his eyes wandered to Barbara with a promise that made her start to tingle all over again. "I was in a hurry," he said. He stood as the other man did and added, "Make me a million on this one; I'm going to need it."

Mr. Daily glanced at him curiously. "Oh? Problems?"

"I'll explain it all to you another time," Kyle assured him and shook his head. "Roger, thanks—for everything."

"No problem at all," he replied, and then glanced at Barbara, his eyes twinkling. "If you have no objections, young lady, I believe I'll go on back to the hotel. Since we finished up so much sooner than I planned, I might even see if I can get an earlier flight home. Do you think you can trust this renegade to get you on a flight to Maine sometime within the next week or so?"

Barbara laughed happily and teased, "But you're

supposed to be chaperoning me! What will your wife say?''

He winked and assured her, ''I think she'll say I left you in very good hands.''

They walked around to the front to see him off, holding hands, and hardly had the black tail of the car disappeared from sight before Kyle turned and drew her into his arms. ''Now,'' he whispered huskily, his eyes searching her face eagerly and hungrily, ''let's get this reunion off to a proper start.''

Their kiss was a melding of spirits, a wild explosion of joy that met passion and surpassed it, a deep contentment, an end to a yearning, a beginning of an adventure. It was like coming home. They each emerged weakened and strangely fortified, and stood for endless moments more on the swaying footbridge beneath the slanting sun, holding each other, their hearts and their breaths in unison. Time stood still when they were in one another's arms.

Then Barbara looked up, caressing his face, loving every line and plane of it and expressing it in the gentle touch of her fingers. She said softly, ''I still don't understand. Why did you bring me here?''

''I wanted you to see my house,'' he explained simply.

She smiled. ''We still haven't been inside.''

''That,'' he assured her, slipping his arm about her waist, ''is an oversight I was just about to correct.''

He led her inside, and the multiple windows illuminated a vast and empty room covered in dark gray carpeting and paneled in a lighter gray driftwood. ''But,'' she exclaimed, standing still, ''it's not furnished! No wonder it seemed so empty to you!''

''Furnishings,'' he told her simply, ''are something

that should be chosen by *both* the people who live here. Naturally I wouldn't do anything without consulting you first." A small warm thrill went through her, but he did not give her a chance to speak. "Of course, I had to have a bedroom suite," he went on, "and I've put a few things in my study." He opened the door first on a large unfurnished room, which, she remembered, he had designated as a nursery. "I'd like to do a mural on these walls," he suggested. "What do you think?"

She took a step inside. It was bright and airy with many high windows and sunshine-yellow carpeting on the floor. "It certainly is big," she commented.

"I expect to have a large family," he told her, and again she felt that alien little thrill go through her.

He took her on a whirlwind tour, the kitchen, second-floor rooms, his upstairs glass study, ending at last in the master bedroom, which was furnished simply with a king-size bed and matching teakwood bureaus, crying out for the finishing decorative touches that would make it look permanent and lived in. She looked at him, a small smile tightening the corners of her mouth. "Kyle," she said, "you didn't even know me when you built this house. You should have furnished it to your own taste."

"After I met you," he answered her seriously, "I didn't want to."

He kissed her, and this time passion had full rein. Heat coursed through her body as his restless hands roamed delicately over her thighs and hips and back, teasing the zipper of her dress, and the bed was only a few steps away. Suddenly he pushed her away, his eyes dark with passion and unreadable, and in the same motion he caught her hand. "Let's take a walk," he said abruptly.

She could not help laughing as she allowed him to pull her rapidly out of the bedroom. Her happiness was bubbling over, and there was time, plenty of time. For the moment just being with him was more than she had dared dream of.

They walked along the silent mountain trail by which the car had come, and Kyle said, "I jog along this road every morning and don't see a soul for miles. When the sun comes up, it's like being on another planet. The colors are so rich and pure, and even the quality of the air is different from anywhere else I've ever been. I love it up here, Bobbie."

"It is beautiful," she agreed softly.

He turned to her, the hint of a question in his eyes, but then he carefully subdued it and said instead, "I want to do it, Bobbie. Get out of the business, try to paint for a living." His hand tightened around hers as he looked at her, his eyes dark with intensity. "You know it's what I've always wanted to do, but until you I didn't have the courage to just chuck it all and start a new life. Now I know it's the only thing in the world I want to do."

"Oh, Kyle," she cried, her eyes shining with enthusiasm as she turned to him. "I think that's wonderful!" She could not restrain herself from throwing her arms around his neck. "You know that's what I've always thought you should do! I'm so glad!"

He caught her arms, looking down at her with a cautious excitement as he questioned, "Are you? Do you really think it's best?"

She nodded enthusiastically and this time he returned her hug. After a moment they began walking again, and he went on. "It won't be easy, at first. I'm not exactly a millionaire," he told her seriously, "but

I'm not a pauper, either. I have a few investments, and my patents, and the house and this property are mine.''

She laughed. ''You sound like a prospective suitor trying to prove his worth to a Victorian father!''

''That's exactly,'' he told her, only the faintest hint of a smile in his eyes, ''what I am—a suitor.''

Her laughter died into sudden nervousness.

''Of course,'' he went on quickly, ''I'll probably still do a little designing now and then—houses, not buildings. It will take me a couple of months to wind up everything I'm working on now, but after that—'' He stopped and turned to her. ''The important thing,'' he said, searching her eyes deeply, ''is that I will have time, time with my family.''

She dropped her eyes, her throat suddenly dry with speechlessness.

She felt his hands on her shoulders and he said quietly, ''I only want to be with you, Bobbie. Could you live here and share my life?''

She raised her eyes to his, deep and shining with the simplicity of the need that was filling every part of her, and she whispered, ''I—I want to be with you too, Kyle.''

He pulled her to him, and his lips were desperate upon hers with a quiet demand, a forceful possessiveness, a deep yearning. She yielded to him, for the first time completely, for the first time with all of herself. And when he drew away gently, she knew her life would never be the same.

''Bobbie,'' he whispered, his fingers tight upon her shoulders and his eyes burning their intensity into hers, ''listen to me. We can't have this thing between us any longer. People die, Bobbie, people cheat on each other and leave each other and hurt each other every day, and leave a string of innocent victims behind. If I had the power over life and death," he told her lowly, his fingers tightening, "I could promise you you would never be hurt again. But I *can* promise you that nothing that is in my power to control will ever hurt you, not ever. Oh, Bobbie, is that enough?"

She looked at him, and the rosy-golden shades of the sunset played in her hair and across her face, illuminating eyes that no longer had anything to hide. She whispered, "I love you, Kyle."

He drew her slowly into his embrace, tender and warm, simply holding her. And after a long time he said softly, "It's enough."

They turned and started walking back to the house, their arms around one another, and time stretched out benignly before them. On the bridge he stopped and, taking her left hand, slowly slipped the wedding band off her finger. She caught her breath, her eyes searching his anxiously, and then he took her right hand and placed the ring on its third finger. He smiled. "All right?"

She smiled and nodded, dropping her eyes to the bare finger of her left hand. She knew it would not be bare for long. And there was room in her life for both a memory and a love, side by side, separate and different.

In the house she felt the need to break the spell that had fallen over them with simple, sensible, and mundane matters. She declared, making her way to the kitchen, "You have that hungry look on your face. What shall I make you for dinner?"

His smile was lazy and provocative as he leaned against the bar, watching her. "That hungry look," he replied, "doesn't necessarily have anything at all to do with food."

She opened the refrigerator door to hide a blush that was mostly from anticipation. "Eggs, cheese, milk..." she inventoried out loud. "Not much of a selection."

"I told you I just got in last night," he apologized. "I didn't have time to buy much."

She heard his steps behind her and felt his shadow fall over her as he reached around her and pushed the refrigerator door closed. When she turned, his face was very close, the meaning in his eyes unmistakable. "We'll eat later," he said and swept her off her feet.

He carried her across the echoing emptiness of the house and into the bedroom; she pressed her face against his chest and tightened her arms around his neck as he kicked the bedroom door closed. Her heart was thudding so loudly it seemed to reverberate throughout her body, and it was difficult to distinguish the rhythm of her own heart from his. He lowered her gently to the bed, and then she felt his weight beside her, the fan of his breath on her cheek, the light touch of his lips on her hair. "I love you," he whispered and took her face in his hands, his eyes dark with tenderness and sincerity. "Forever." His lips came down upon hers and she wound her arms around his neck, welcoming him with a promise that was just as deep, just as unshakable, as his.

The slatted wooden blinds on the window cast dusky patterns of light and shadow on their bodies, and their lovemaking was slow and exquisite. Time seemed to stretch out forever in their reverent and unhurried exploration of one another, as they tasted, touched, felt, every nuance of pleasure and memorized to the finest detail the magic of the sensual and richly emotional experience of their union. Forever took on a new meaning to Barbara, filling the empty places of her life with the promise of his presence even as his body reminded her she was only half complete when separate from him. She wrapped herself around him, fully a part of him, and joy like none she had ever known swept her away in waves of shimmering ecstasy. Forever, with Kyle, was more than she had ever dared hope for from life and all she wanted, and she loved him with all her heart.

She must have dozed, for the shrilling of the telephone caused her to open her eyes to a blue-gray twilit room and Kyle smiling lazily down at her. His arms were warm around her and his skin was pleasantly fragrant with the scent of his cologne and the aftermath of their lovemaking. She stirred and smiled and reached to brush away a lock of hair from his forehead. The telephone continued to ring. "Aren't you going to answer it?" she murmured.

"I'd rather make love to you," he replied and did not take his eyes away from the tender appraisal of her face.

"Later," she promised, and he dropped a light, lingering kiss on her lips before swinging his legs to the floor and reaching for the telephone.

After his first rather curt "Hello" Barbara knew something was wrong. His color faded beneath the tan, his lips grew white, his eyes darkened. Something was terribly wrong, and Barbara's first panic-stricken thought was *Kate. Something's happened to the baby.* She sat up, touching his arm anxiously.

She heard him say in an odd, unsteady tone, "I'll be on the next flight." Then he slowly replaced the receiver.

"Kyle," she insisted, fear mounting. "What is it? What's wrong?"

He looked at her for a moment as though he did

not know who she was. Then, abruptly, he seemed to recover himself. He stood and pulled on his jeans, then crossed quickly to the closet to drag out a suitcase. "It's Roseanne," he said, without looking at her. "There's been an accident. I have to leave."

Chapter Twelve

From that second on, everything blurred together in Barbara's mind and she would remember little of it. She did not know whether she questioned further or simply sat there in stunned, agonizing silence, watching him fling an assortment of clothes into a suitcase. She did know that she got no answers. There was the frantic ride to the airport and the flashes of light and shadow streaking across Kyle's white face and she kept thinking that Roseanne was in trouble and he would run to her, as he would the rest of his life, and whatever doubts she had about his feelings for his ex-wife vanished sometime during that terrible night.

If he said anything else to her during that trip, she did not know it. Arrangements were hurriedly made at the airport and he found a flight that was leaving for New York almost immediately. She followed him, as in a daze, to the boarding gate, and she remembered his turning to her, a look of purest torture on his face, and he said, "I'm sorry.... There's so much I should explain to you...but I can't. Bobbie, please understand."

She thought she nodded.

She also thought she understood.

Her own flight to Maine did not arrive until sometime late the next morning, and, in a daze of shock and sleeplessness, she let hours go by while she sat in the coffee shop and stirred cup after cup of cooling coffee, before she called Michael to come pick her up. He looked at her as though he immediately understood, and he too was silent on the trip home.

She went to the guest house. She did not unpack. She did not even undress as she lay down on the bed and slept for twenty-two hours.

It was Kate who woke her. "I was worried about you," she said, and concern was etched on every line of her face. "I checked on you all yesterday afternoon and several times during the night. It isn't like you to sleep so much."

"I was tired," answered Barbara flatly. After her long slumber there was no confusion about the events that had led her to that retreat. It was all just as clear and painful as it had been the moment she had looked into Kyle's white face and known he was leaving her for his ex-wife.

The anxiety on Kate's face deepened into reluctance, and she said, "Kyle called."

Barbara sat up but was totally unprepared for the next words.

"Roseanne is dead, Babs," Kate said quietly. "A small-plane crash. Everyone on board was killed on impact. In the Catskills."

Something sharp went through her. Part of it was shock, part of it was pain for Kyle, part of it was just a horror of death when it came so suddenly to someone as young and beautiful as Roseanne. But she managed to ask, "Did he say when he would be back? Was there a message for me?"

Kate said sadly, "No. He was pretty upset."

It was a long time after Kate left that she began to cry. She cried for the death of a vital young woman whose time had been too short, she cried for Kyle's pain, she sobbed her rage and her grief out loud because Kyle had loved Roseanne, and there was no power on earth stronger than the love for a ghost, and it wasn't fair.... It wasn't fair that she should lose twice in one lifetime.

The dark lethargy that possessed her during the next week took her back to the blackest period of her life over a year earlier. She didn't go to work, she didn't eat much, and she hardly ever got out of bed. She spent many long hours staring sightlessly out the window, feeling nothing, thinking nothing, completely unaware that she was reliving the same depression that had seized her after Daniel's death. As it had been then, nothing seemed to matter anymore. She insulated herself against hope just as she did against pain; the world went on about her and she knew nothing of it. She only knew that Kyle was gone. Love had passed her way twice, and twice it had left her behind. There hardly seemed any point in going on.

It was Kate, with alarm on her face, who forced her back into the world of the living. "Look what you're doing to yourself!" she cried, indicating the unkempt apartment, the unmade bed, and Barbara's bedraggled appearance in a worn terry housecoat. "This is the same thing that happened to you after Daniel died and it's *not* the same, Babs! Kyle loves you," she pleaded with her. "It's no secret—we've known it for a long time. He told Michael so, way back, after we got back from our trip." She took Barbara's hands and sat down beside her, trying to force her sincerity into her sister's mind. "And do you know something else, honey? He never said he loved Roseanne. He would say things like, 'She's beautiful,' or 'We'll have fun together,' but he always avoided the word *love*. He *loves* you, Barbara. It will be an adjustment for him, but he'll be back. And when he does come back, he can't find you like this. You've got to be strong, because he'll need all the support you can give him.''

Barbara did not understand everything Kate was saying about "adjustment" and "support," but she had to come to realize that she was dramatizing her situation. Of course Kyle would be back, eventually. He would come back aged and worn with the wisdom only a close experience with death can bring, and in his eyes would be grief and regret for all the time he had let slip by without Roseanne, and the shadow of those lost years would stand between them for the rest of their lives.

She went back to work mostly because she saw what worry over her silent grief was doing to her sister. But eventually, mostly through the day-by-day routine, she started living again. If her actions were automatic, her lack of interest did not reflect in her work. In fact, she was doing a better job than ever, and she worked long hours to prove herself capable and to keep herself busy. The New England autumn blossomed bright and clear in multicolors, Kate grew plumper and more contented, and one morning she awoke without the dread of facing another day, ready to face whatever came along.

It was not a matter of forgiving Kyle. How could he ask forgiveness for something he could not help? Roseanne had needed him, he had shared his life and his bed with that woman, and even if he had hated her, he would have gone to her side at the moment of her death. Barbara could understand that. She loved him too much not to understand, and although it did not mitigate her sorrow at losing him, the very least she owed him was understanding and compassion.

She had managed to save some money over the summer, and as her hours and responsibility increased, so did her salary. She began looking for an apartment in Portland. Mr. Daily was very generous with her wages, and he promised a full-time managerial position by the first of the year if all continued to go well. She thought she should be able to manage on her own financially if she lived frugally until then, and it was important that she get on with her life. She had started a new life once with Kyle's help; she could do so again because he had taught her.

She came home late one Friday afternoon with an armload of groceries Kate had asked her to pick up, and there was no sign of her sister downstairs. Michael's study door was closed so she did not bother him but took the groceries to the kitchen and started to put them away. It was then that she heard the sounds from upstairs, strange sounds. Kate's voice was among them, and splashing water, and high, childish laughter. Curiously she started up the stairs. And then one sound distinguished itself above the others, familiar masculine laughter. . . .

Her heart was in her throat and she clung to the banister to steady her steps as she slowly reached the top of the stairs. There was Kate, on her hands and knees before the bathroom door, laughingly wrestling a naked blond-haired little girl of about two. Water had splashed all over the hall carpet and the front of Kate's maternity smock and she was trying unsuccessfully to gather the child into a towel, enjoying the playful battle thoroughly. And, as Barbara watched in incredulity, Kyle emerged from behind his sister-in-law, another naked child, a boy, wiggling in his arms.

He was as wet as Kate, and laughing as he tried to dry the baby's hair with a towel held in one hand and attempt to prevent the slippery little body from sliding to the floor with the other.

It seemed they both saw her at the same time, and the only sound was the echoing, inappropriate sounds of childish laughter. Everything froze as Kyle's eyes locked on Barbara's and a thousand emotions and unspoken phrases flashed between them.

Barbara broke the unbearable moment with a laugh that made her proud of its normalcy, and she exclaimed, indicating the foray before her, "What in the world is going on up here? It sounds like an orgy!"

Kate managed to wrap the little girl in a towel and busied herself with briskly drying the child's fine blond hair. Kyle smiled weakly. "Bobbie," he said, "I'd like you to meet Jason and Jennifer. My children."

Chapter Thirteen

There was no time for amazement, shock, or adjustment, as the children began to noisily demand attention from the two adults who were supposed to be caring for them. Jason pulled at Kyle's hair and began to shriek to be let down; Jennifer lifted her arms to Kate and begged to be picked up. "We were trying to make a good first impression," Kyle said with a grimace, disentangling the small fingers from his hair, "thus the bath. I guess we blew it."

Barbara only stared.

"They're twins," Kyle added unnecessarily as Kate bundled Jennifer back into the bathroom, and then returned for Jason. Kyle shifted him into her arms, inquiring, "Can you manage?"

"I need the practice," Kate assured him and closed the bathroom door on the high, querulous voices.

Kyle came toward her slowly, wiping his hands nervously on his water-splotched jeans, and offered, "They're two years old. They're supposed to be that way."

Barbara's face softened with wonder and incredulity as she reached out one hand to touch him. "Kyle—"

"Can we walk?" he interrupted suddenly. "Will you give me a chance. . . to try to explain?"

Her mind was whirling with confusion and she could only nod. Children, she kept thinking over and over again. Twins. Blond-haired, green-eyed two-year-olds who belonged to Kyle. She could not get out of her mind the picture of him, standing at the top of the stairs with a naked baby in his arms, and all she could think or feel then was that he had never looked more beautiful to her eyes, she had never loved him more. . . . But children.

He did not speak until they were on the steps leading down to the beach. "I just couldn't tell you over the phone or in a letter, Bobbie," he said quietly, without looking at her. Then he lifted his face to the cool breeze and repeated, almost in a whisper, "I just. . . couldn't tell you."

But explanations could wait, for the moment. She reached for him automatically through the fog of her confusion, and immediately she was in his arms, the place where she had always belonged. His kiss was like that of a starving man presented with a feast, greedy and tenuous, as though afraid to believe his good fortune, expecting it to dissolve into a mirage at any moment. But her open, honest, and sure response calmed him, and gradually the kiss began to reveal more—pent-up longing and desperate desire, possessive dominance and the steady assurance that he loved her still. It told her all she wanted to know.

Somehow they were sitting on the steps, possibly because Barbara's legs would not support her any longer; they were wrapped in each other's arms in a tight and steady embrace that would weather all storms. He whispered against her hair, "Bobbie, tell me you love me. Tell me you still love me and that I didn't just dream it."

She held his face in both her hands, looking up at him. Her eyes were steady and tender. "I do love you," she said softly. "I never had a choice. I can't stop loving you."

Joy illuminated his face before it came down upon hers again, and this time the kiss was full of wonder and promise that swept aside all else. Eventually, however, they had to come back to the present, but it was with a new courage and a cautious confidence to face the problems of the future.

He took her hand and led her down to the beach. "I've been fighting for custody ever since the divorce," he began simply. "Roseanne was not a fit mother, and I tried everything I could to prove it."

"That was the legal case that had you so upset!" Barbara exclaimed, looking at him. Then, in wonder, "It was the children all along."

He nodded grimly. "I love my babies, and she held it over my head to get everything she could out of me. They would have been much better off with me from the beginning—they didn't see their mother enough to even know who she was. But she played a little dirtier than I did, and she blocked my every move. The finale was when she got an international custody ruling that kept me from even seeing them. She kept them in a penthouse apartment in London with a nanny. I can't say they were physically abused or mistreated in any way, and they had every material comfort, but they had no parents. Bobbie, you can't imagine what it did to me, thinking I would never see my kids again."

She nodded and tightened her arm around him sympathetically, understanding so much now. What she had mistaken as a morbid attachment to his ex-wife had really been no more than concern for the welfare of his children, and that night it had been to their side he had rushed, not to hers. "But, Kyle," she questioned in confusion. "You never mentioned them. Why didn't you tell me?"

He sighed, holding her hand tightly through their linked arms as though he were afraid she might try to escape. "I never wanted to keep it a secret from you. At first, well—" he gave her an abashed look "—my interest in you was not exactly of a permanent nature, and I didn't think it mattered. You made it pretty clear that first night you weren't interested in children, and I didn't think bringing out the old wallet stuffed with baby pictures would exactly turn you on."

"But, Kyle," she objected, "that's not—"

He silenced her. "I know that now. I realized pretty quick that the things you said that night were just your way of building up defenses against the family you never had." She dropped her eyes, moved almost to tears at the depth of his perception.

"Later," he went on and sighed, tightening his fingers around her hand. "Bobbie, this is complicated, so please try to understand. I knew that I loved you and that I wanted to spend the rest of my life with you, and I knew it a long time before I told you so. I knew that the twins would always be a part of my life and that I would never stop trying to get custody and that would affect your life too. But you were skittish, always looking for a chance to bolt. I knew when I asked you to marry me I was taking a chance on losing you. A ready-made family would have given you all the excuse you needed." He turned to her, holding her shoulders, his eyes deep with sincerity and need. "Bobbie, please understand. I knew you needed time to adjust to loving me, to letting *me* into your life. Until you were able to do that, there was no point in going any further. And I thought we would have the time, time for me to convince you of my love and time for you to get used to sharing yourself with me, before we had to face the other problems our life together would bring. Your needs were very special, love. I couldn't pile it all on you before you were ready.''

But she had to ask, ''And when would you have told me?''

Again he sighed, and they started walking again. ''I started to tell you several times. Maybe I should have. I knew I wasn't being fair. But I was doing the best thing I knew, under the circumstances. I would have told you that night,'' he answered, ''that night we were together. I knew you were ready to accept my love, and I had to believe you were ready to accept whatever came with it. And I couldn't have kept it from you any longer. It wouldn't have been fair— to either of us.''

''And then fate intervened,'' she said dully, and there was a silence.

''I went directly to London from New York,'' he went on after a time. ''I had to stay there, going through all the legal channels. I couldn't call you. I couldn't explain it to you over the phone. I had to take the chance. . . that you would still be here.''

She simply nodded. They walked for a long time in silence, the salt breeze cool against her face and Kyle's arm warm against hers. Barbara knew the silent turmoil he was undergoing, and her heart reached out to him in shared grief and understanding, but she allowed him the time to put his feelings into words. ''I think,'' he said at last, very low, ''I must have been afraid all along it would end like this. The way she lived. . . I should have been prepared. But I wasn't.''

She tightened her arm around him, wanting to draw him close to her and ease his pain, understanding as no one else could what he was going through. "No one," she assured him softly, "could be prepared for something like that."

He shook his head a little, throwing his face back to the breeze, as though to seek cleansing from the clinging nightmare of the past few weeks. "I don't know, Bobbie," he said after a breath. "She was a stranger to me. I realize now I never knew her, yet she bore my children, and a big part of my life was tangled up with hers. I still find it hard to believe that all this has happened. Shock, I guess. It doesn't seem fair—no matter what she was or what she has done—that it should end this way."

"Oh, Kyle," she whispered and, turning, drew him into her arms. "I know. I really know. . . ."

They clung together, his face against her neck and the wind tangling their hair with one another's, for an endless moment, in which mutual need and shared sorrow imparted strength, a strength that would buffer them against present problems and weather all storms to come. Then he lifted his face to look into her eyes and said a little desperately, "Bobbie, if you hadn't been here—thinking about you was all that held me together these past few weeks, and if you hadn't been here, if I had come back and you—"

But the remaining words were drowned as their lips met in a kiss that was fierce with longing and determined possessiveness, and Barbara was lost as the familiar passion swept her. She pressed her fingers against the hard muscles of his neck and felt the strands of his hair brushing against the backs of her hands and the eager hunger of his lips on hers and she did not know how she could have ever imagined her life without him. His hands pressed against her slim waist, powerful in their strength yet gentle in their restraint. Her thighs were crushed against the hard length of his, and his hands roamed urgently upward to brush the curves of her breasts. Shivers of desire shook her as she knew again the ecstasy of being in his arms, and then he broke suddenly away.

"Oh, Bobbie," he whispered, his breath hot and unsteady against her cheek. "How can I bear to leave you again?"

For a moment shock precluded speech. Still trembling with the heat of the emotions he had aroused, she could not even think, for surely she must not have heard him correctly. Then, as he slowly pushed away, brushing back his hair and taking a few slow breaths to regain control of his own thoughts, the tragedy of the present and the problems of the future came creeping slowly back.

"It's true," he admitted heavily. "I have to leave again right away." Still she could not speak, and he explained, "It's more important now than ever that I go on with my original plan, and I've got to wind up what I have on the drawing board now so that I can settle down as a full-time father. I hate to do this to the kids, they've just gotten to know me and at this age they forget so fast."

He said suddenly, urgently, "They're good kids, Bobbie. I was expecting all sorts of psychological problems, but if they have any, I can't tell. They're open and they're happy and I guess shuffling them around from one place to another, one nanny to another, has made them adaptable, because they get along with anybody." He closed his eyes briefly and released another heavy breath. "I know what this is asking of you, Bobbie. You didn't bargain for a pair of noisy two-year-olds when you let yourself love me. Being a wife is a job in itself, much less a mother on such short notice, and a mother to someone else's children. I wouldn't think less of you if—''

She opened her mouth to speak, but he silenced her with a finger laid lightly across her lips. "Please," he entreated. "Don't give me your answer now. Kate has agreed to baby-sit for me while I'm gone, and if you will, take the time to get to know them, to think about it...and tell me when I get back. Will you do that for me? Please?"

She dropped her eyes, her brow marred with confusion and a slight hint of desperation. "Kyle, I—"

Again he silenced her, this time with a gentle touch of his lips. "Please," he insisted. Then he looked at her, his eyes deep with sincerity. "I just want you to know that whatever your decision I'll understand. Don't think I'll think less of you if—if you decide what I'm offering is not for you. Because I'll always love you."

She looked at him, wanting only to be held again in his strong embrace and to feel his body warming hers and to imagine it would be that way forever, pushing aside all sorrow and unpleasantness and the problems that threatened their happiness. But the decisions that hung over her could not be ignored so easily, and she did not speak again as they started slowly back to the house.

IT WAS one of those rare, bright November days with temperatures in the fifties, probably the last one of the season. Michael had gotten a little ahead of himself, inspired by the presence of the twins, and erected a play yard on the front lawn, complete with sandbox, climbing dome, slide, and tunnel. His niece and nephew were doing a fine job of breaking it in for the new arrival, and Barbara and Kate sat in lawn chairs nearby, laughing at their antics, while they waited for Michael to return from the airport.

Kate, adjusting the afghan that covered the bulge of her abdomen, commented, "They look just like Kyle, don't they? It's unusual, at their age."

Barbara agreed, but there was a lot unusual about those children. They had their father's stunning good looks, his effervescent personality, his quick intelligence. Already they were stringing together sentences that were actually intelligible. They were energetic and inquisitive and had to be watched constantly, but when scolded they could melt the heart with a look and they knew no adult could resist a quick hug and a beaming smile and the simple words "I love you." They still occasionally called Michael Daddy, although they made a concentrated effort to repeat the phrase "Uncle Mike" when he reminded them. Auntie Kate" was easier, and although they addressed both Kate and Barbara as Mama, Barbara thought they called her Mama more often than Kate.

Barbara turned to her sister. "Why didn't you tell me about the children?" she asked for the first time.

Kate shook her head wonderingly. "I thought you knew. I really did. Michael and I had agreed to stay out of it, but I thought all along that was what was keeping you and Kyle apart. I thought," she confessed, "that you were afraid Kyle was just looking for a mother for his children. There was many a time when I caught Kyle looking at you with that hurt and wanting in his eyes, and it was all I could do to keep from pounding some sense into your head."

Jason became stuck on the slide just then, and Barbara got up to help him. She took him on two squealing rides down the slide, then had to repeat the same for Jennifer, and when she left them happily playing again and returned to her seat, Michael's car was pulling into the driveway.

She was aware of taking several calming breaths, automatically smoothing her hair beneath the woolly hat that protected it from the wind, and forcing herself to relax before she saw Kyle get out of the passenger seat. Their eyes met for just a second; he gave her a cautious, questioning smile, and then he went over to the children.

It was probably true that they did not remember him, but the twins, like their father, had never met a stranger. They greeted him enthusiastically, especially when they saw the large, multistriped ball he had brought them, and they spared him a quick hug each before noisily demanding his attention with the ball.

Michael and Kate watched them fondly for a moment, dreaming of their own future, and then Michael scolded, "You shouldn't be sitting out in this wind. Come on inside."

Kate groaned as he helped her struggle to her feet. "He's going to kill me with kindness," she complained. Then, "I'll make some hot chocolate. You'd better not keep them out too much longer."

"I won't," Barbara responded. "It's almost time for their naps, anyway."

Kyle left the children absorbed in the fascination of the new toy as Michael and Kate went inside. Barbara gave him a cautious smile as he approached. "Rough trip?"

"The usual," he replied, and his smile too was a little reserved.

"Did you get everything accomplished you set out to?"

"Sure did."

He sat on the ground at her feet and linked his

fingers lightly through hers. For a moment he simply studied their entwined fingers, and then he looked up at her. His smile was brave and encouraging, his eyes were filled with both dread and hope. "Well, friend," he said softly, "there's no time like the present. Tell me what you've been thinking."

But even as she looked at him, she knew he had prepared himself for the worst. She took another deep breath, dropping her eyes. "Kyle," she began, "you were right—it's not a decision to leap into hastily, and I've given it a lot of thought." She had to look at him. "They're beautiful children, Kyle," she said softly. "They're sweet and they're smart and they're so like their father it breaks my heart." She felt his fingers tighten on hers with a leap of hope, and she went on quickly. "But you wanted to know what I've been thinking, and it's this: There's so much to consider, Kyle. I've just now gotten my life back together again, I love my job, and I have a chance at a really rewarding career in a position of responsibility."

She felt the despair seep through him, heard his catch of breath, but she had to go on. Anything less than perfect honesty would be unfair. "You were right when you warned me we would have more problems than the average couple, and, well, I'm not very good at adjusting, I'm afraid. I don't know anything about children, about being a mother." She felt him slowly retreating from her. His head was bowed. "It's not that the twins aren't easy to love," she insisted, "it's just that I'm wondering if it would really be fair to them for you to take on an underconfident, inexperienced wife. They are going to need all your attention and all your love for a while, and it won't be easy—"

"It's all right," he interrupted quietly, quickly. "I understand." He looked up at her, and the pain in his eyes was almost unbearable. "I told you," he said, "that whatever you decided I would understand." He stood, letting her hand drop. He could no longer look at her, and he turned to the children. "Jason, Jenny," he called. "Come along. Time to go inside."

He glanced back at her. "I, uh, guess it would be better—" he shoved his hands miserably into his jacket pockets, dropping his eyes again "—if we left right away. As soon as I get the kids packed and cleaned up." He looked at her for one brief, agonizing moment. "I do still love you, Bobbie," he said softly and turned back to the children.

She gaped at him in astonishment.

"Come on, kids," he called, forcing brightness in his tone. "We're going on an airplane ride!" The children, involved, ignored him.

Barbara stood and swept passed him into the play yard. "You didn't let me finish," she accused.

She knelt and opened her arms to the twins. "Didn't you hear your daddy!" she exclaimed. "We're going on an airplane ride! Come on!"

She heard Kyle's surprised breath and his cautious step behind her as the children ran happily to her. A slight flush of anger colored her cheeks as she looked defiantly up at him, an arm around each child. "You wanted to know what I thought," she told him, "and now you know. Are you interested in what I've decided?"

He looked bewildered, cautiously hopeful, thoroughly confused. "I—I thought—"

"You're always thinking for me," she returned in annoyance. "You *thought* I wouldn't like your paintings, you *thought* I didn't like children." And then her face softened. "One of the things I love most about you, I suppose, is that you almost always know what I'm thinking, but in this case you were wrong." She smiled at him. "I hope you made reservations for four, because we go as a set."

For a moment a joy so intense it transfigured his face swept over him, then he knelt beside them and included all three in his embrace. The children thought it was a marvelous new game, and they laughed and squealed and finally escaped, until only the two adults remained, their arms linked loosely around one another, cheek against cheek. "Idiot," Barbara whispered, stroking his hair. "I didn't need all this time to think about it. I know life doesn't come with a money-back guarantee. I know there will be problems. But I love you. We can handle them."

Kyle's arms tightened around her waist, his lips brushed her hair, and joy surged through Barbara in slow, pulsating waves. The children played happily in the background and for a moment both adults turned to watch them, experiencing the same emotion, sharing a single dream of a home ringing with laughter, dozens of children, and love filling every corner of their lives.

Then Barbara turned to him. Her lips met his in a flood of contentment and happiness too great to be expressed in words, her back against the past and her arms around a future filled with the promise of a lifetime.

It was enough. It was more than enough.

For more than 30 years,
Harlequin has been
publishing the very best
in romantic fiction.

Today, Harlequin books
are the world's best-
selling paperback
romances.

Enter a uniquely exciting new world with

Harlequin American Romance T.M.

Harlequin American Romances are the first romances to explore today's new love relationships. These compelling romance novels reach into the hearts and minds of women across North America...probing the most intimate moments of romance, love and desire.

You'll follow romantic heroines and irresistible men as they boldly face confusing choices. Career first, love later? Love without marriage? Long-distance relationships? All the experiences that make love real are captured in the tender, loving pages of the new **Harlequin American Romances.**

What makes North American women so different when it comes to love? Find out in the new **Harlequin American Romance!**